# RECIPE *for* DEATH

ALSO BY JANET LAURENCE

*Hotel Morgue*
*A Tasty Way to Die*
*A Deepe Coffyn*

# RECIPE *for* DEATH

by

*Janet Laurence*

A Perfect Crime Book

DOUBLEDAY

New York London Toronto Sydney Auckland

A Perfect Crime Book
PUBLISHED BY DOUBLEDAY

a division of Bantam Doubleday Dell Publishing Group, Inc.

666 Fifth Avenue, New York, New York 10103
Doubleday is a trademark of Doubleday, a division of
Bantam Doubleday Dell Publishing Group, Inc.



Library of Congress Cataloging-in-Publication Data

Laurence, Janet.
Recipe for death / by Janet Laurence.
p. cm.
"A Perfect crime book."
I. Title.
PR6062.A795R43 1993
823'.914—dc20 92-32068
CIP

ISBN 0-385-46796-6

PRINTED IN THE UNITED STATES OF AMERICA
MARCH 1993
FIRST EDITION IN THE UNITED STATES OF AMERICA

*To my sister, Ingrid, with love*

## ACKNOWLEDGEMENTS

*There are a number of people I would like to thank for helping me with information for this book. Charlotte and Bill Reynolds spent precious time showing me their organic farm and talking to me. Any resemblance between Swaddles Green Farm, near Chard, Somerset, and the fictional Fry's Farm in these pages, lies in the deliciousness of their meat and charcuterie, plus some details of equipment and routine. The Reynolds themselves, however, do not appear in any guise. I owe thanks also to various members of the Avon and Somerset CID but especially to Detective Sergeant Jim Mallen for putting me straight on a number of points of police procedure. Also thanks to Anna Best, who has over the years given me much valuable insight into cookery competitions. But the one in which Darina Lisle is a judge at the beginning of this book has only the most fleeting of resemblances to Sainsbury's FutureCooks Competition. The young cooks who take part in that, though their food is comparable, do so with a sangfroid which no adult could emulate. Michael Vearncombe helped with some farming background. Finally, as always, deep thanks to my husband, Keith, for putting up with the continual intrusion of word processor or typewriter into his life and for his help and support at all times. If, despite all endeavours, there are errors in the following pages, the above are in no way to blame. A few actual places are mentioned; other than these the locations do not exist and all the characters and their actions are imaginary. Their names and experiences have no relation to those of actual people, living or dead, except by coincidence.*

# Chapter One

The tension was rising higher than a skilfully made soufflé. Knives flashed, flesh was severed, ingredients chopped, mixtures mixed and dishes assembled with a verve and innovation that bordered on desperation. The cookery competition final was well under way.

Darina Lisle watched a contestant chopping parsley, handling the heavy knife with swift, sure competence. In no time the crisp green frills were reduced to fragments. A garlic clove was peeled and similarly dealt with then the two ingredients magically mixed together with a few passes of the broad blade. She was a slight girl, her head crowned with a floor mop of straight fair hair cropped close into the nape of her neck. A large white apron covered most of her body, the strings brought round a slender waist and tied into a neat bow over her board-flat stomach.

Darina made a note on her judge's marking sheet and passed on to the next contestant.

The competition had been sponsored by a noted importer and merchant of specialist oils eager to raise the profile of its products with the British cook. Each contestant was required to cook a three-course menu using not less than four different single-variety oils. Regional finals had seen two dishes prepared. Now, under the cerulean and cream porcelain prettiness of the Savoy Hotel's Lancaster Room, the eight finalists were hard at work on a different menu. Ingenuity of choice faced the challenge of the time factor.

Darina's heart went out to a young man struggling with home-made pasta. Every time he passed it through the stainless-steel rollers of the little machine, the pasta stuck to itself or in some mysterious way frayed into sticky lace. 'Let it rest for twenty minutes or so,' she whispered to him but he appeared deaf to her advice. *Crab Ravioli with a hazelnut oil sauce, pasta made with olive oil* said his menu standing on an elegantly laid table awaiting the completed meal. She checked his other courses: a mousseline of fish with pistachio oil, served with Potatoes Rosti with olive oil accompanied by a tossed salad with walnut oil dressing, to be followed by profiteroles made with arachide oil instead of butter. She checked her watch, noted they were halfway through the competition and that neither the choux pastry nor the mousseline of fish had been started, sighed inwardly and made a notation in her column for working method.

She found she had come to the end of the row of temporary kitchens, set up in the ornate ball-room with all the élan of cavalry tents erected in a royal park, and made her way to the central table where her fellow judges were sipping mineral water and making notes.

'Not much doubt who will be the winner,' said a television presenter whose combination of hectoring charm and ability to set sleepy celebrities at their ease currently enabled millions to greet the day with something less than outright animosity. With no pretence to culinary expertise, his role was to represent the taste of the general public. He wielded his pencil in a series of rapid flourishes, making heavy marks on his judging form. It was divided into columns for choice of menu, choice of ingredients, working method, presentation and, finally, bearing the most marks, taste of the dishes.

Darina followed his gaze to where a contestant was preparing chicken liver and bacon for her salade tiède with hazelnut oil.

'Appears to know her stuff,' agreed the third judge, a chef noted as much for his personal appearances as for his food, 'but that salad's such a cliché.'

'I noticed at the regional finals that the winner often seems obvious until you actually start tasting the dishes,' said the elegant young managing director of the oil merchants sponsoring the competition. He'd been a judge at all stages. 'Then suddenly you have to revise all your ideas.'

'At least she has her tagliatelle prepared,' said the television personality leaning back in his chair and looking first at the little piles of curled pasta on one side of the working area and then at the generous bosom poured into a plunge-necked cotton dress. Dark curls framed a round face, ordinary but blessed with large brown eyes and a soft mouth. He caught her glance, dropped one eyelid in a wink of encouragement, then looked towards the end of the line to where the young man had now abandoned his pasta and was heating the water and oil for the choux pastry, panic in his eyes, spiky hair standing on end.

The contestants were a mixed bunch. There was a middle-aged lady, looking as though her natural place was in front of an Aga with a pile of freshly dug garden vegetables, efficiently mixing a dressing requiring an amazing number of recherché items.

An elderly cleric, totally oblivious to all the activity around him, carefully peeled the burnt skins off peppers. A girl with an air of fierce determination lavishly sprinkled estate-bottled olive oil over ratatouille. And a woman who looked like everyone's favourite grandmother assembled a sesame dressing containing both oil and seeds.

Darina looked again at the various menus. She was interested in how the contestants had solved the problem of using speciality oils for a pudding. The elderly cleric had ducked it completely by coming up with a final course of salad with a goat's cheese marinated in olive oil, the whole dressed with walnut oil. The most common solution was mousse set in a mould lined with almond oil. But a quiet woman in her mid-thirties, hair scraped back from a plain face not flattered by her choice of heavy tortoise-shell spectacles, had prepared a walnut and honey baclava. It stood now next to her oven, golden and glistening with walnut and arachide oil instead of butter, making Darina's mouth water. Then she gave a little sigh as she wondered how many calories the tasting was going to represent. Even a mouthful of each of eight starters, eight main dishes and eight puds was going to add up to a treacherous total. Working with food provided a constant battle between temptation and weight.

It had come as a surprise to Darina to be asked to join the judging panel. She had not realised what a name she was making for herself in the food world. With the success of her first book had come a regular column in a national newspaper, one that had already printed a number of her articles. She had been accepted into the Guild of Food Writers and now a steady stream of invitations to functions of all sorts, from sausage breakfasts on the Thames to salmon teach-ins in Scotland landed on her doormat. Not to mention news of restaurants that seemed unable to exist without her patronage.

And it had all come by happenstance. She had been asked to update a classic cookery book written some twenty-five years earlier by her cousin. Always a steady seller, his publishers were eager to cash in on the renewed interest stimulated by his murder. Having solved the mystery of his death, the invitation to bring it up to date seemed to Darina an interesting challenge. And the timing was apposite. She had given up a successful catering business to try and achieve her ambition to run a hotel. But more involvement in murder had deflected that aim and left her not at all sure in which direction her career should go. The book provided a useful nudge and she had discovered a new and compelling interest. The time between the completion of her editing and the book's publication had been filled by writing articles, a surprising number of which had been accepted and Darina found herself launched on a new career.

She completed another section of her judging sheet. Now there was nothing to do until the contestants produced their meal except watch the final frantic preparations and survey the audience.

Behind a flimsy barrier of silk rope were lined up several television cameras, a battery of flash-cameras and an assortment of press and guests.

The public relations side of the firm had obviously been busy, the media representation looked more than respectable and Darina recognised a number of faces she knew. But she was more interested in the contestants' guests. Anxious relatives and friends sat at a series of large round tables laid for lunch, many drinking the excellent wine on offer, or wandered around with small cameras, leaning over the restraining rope, trying to catch their particular cook in action.

A male face caught her eye, its combination of intelligence and fun immediately arresting. Early thirties, she estimated. Coal-black eyes sparkled in the bright television lights and dark wiry hair was cropped close to a bullet-shaped head. He was snapping the girl in the large white apron. As the young cook threw him a quick glance, he grinned and gave a thumbs-up sign.

The chef beside Darina waved a welcoming hand. 'Simon, good to see you,' he called. 'Talk to you later.'

The young man acknowledged the wave then worked his way back to sit at one of the guest tables. Two women sat at the other side, isolated from him by more than the chairs between. Glad to have at least one contestant's family identified for her, Darina looked at them more closely.

The older, in a sludge-coloured shirt dress that matched her weather-beaten complexion, was taut with tension. White hair cut short wisped round an anxious face. As Darina watched, the younger woman bent close to whisper some comment, and the juxtaposition of faces underlined the strong similarity of cheek-bones and jaw line. There was no discernible resemblance, though, between either of them and the girl cooking. Neither woman paid any attention to the young man.

There was an announcement that the competitors had ten more minutes to finish their dishes.

The young man with spiky hair abandoned his attempts to stuff his ravioli, took some sorry-looking choux puffs out of the oven, threw the baking tray on the working surface in disgust, pulled off his apron and walked out through the banqueting room's double doors, pushing his way past cameramen and press, ignoring an approach from the competition organiser. A young man from the back of the ball-room hurried after him.

At the other stations, food was being dished up with amazing speed, contestants desperately providing finishing touches, their faces agonised.

Darina watched with horrified sympathy. Used as she was to providing food under pressure, the challenge of the competition seemed unbearable to her. Why did they do it? What was it that made the tension, the risk of public humiliation, worth while? But she knew the answer. Winning could open a whole new career. There would be opportunities for books, articles, media appearances. For a creative cook struggling to break into the highly competitive food world, winning a major competition such as this could provide a priceless opportunity. But what determination was needed to reach the winner's rostrum!

A bell announced the end of serving-up time. Darina and her fellow adjudicators picked up their little sets of cutlery and, flourishing them like weapons of war, advanced towards the kitchens flexing their taste buds.

After a gargantuan grazing session, they finally retired to a room behind the scenes. There their marking sheets were gathered up by the competition's organiser and a bottle of champagne was opened.

'Amazing,' said the television personality, drinking deeply and offering his glass for a refill, 'the tasting played havoc with my order of merit.'

'There can't be any doubt over the winner,' said the chef, tasting his champagne with a rather more professional appreciation. 'Exceptional food, full-bodied flavours, simple style, yet authoritative and technically perfect.'

'Quite, no déjà vu nouvelle cuisine, yet it all looked as good as it tasted. What did you think?' The oil merchant turned to Darina.

She added her praises, said she was particularly pleased the food had left pretension behind with the dairy fats and asked if he was happy with the result.

'It's given us everything we hoped for. Thank heavens! We've invested a packet in the competition, double our usual advertising budget. But the publicity has already been worth it and there's more to come. I'm sure we're on the verge of a breakthrough in oil use. And I'm very pleased with the winner's recipes, they are just right for the booklet, interesting, unusual but not off-puttingly complicated.' Part of the prize was for the winner's dishes to be featured in a brochure the oil company was producing to encourage the use of their products.

'I'd check where they came from,' warned the chef. 'I'm sure I remember those fillets of John Dory in hazelnut sauce from somewhere.'

'Not quite the same, I hope? I'd hate there to be a copyright problem.'

The chef pursed his lips disapprovingly. 'Almost impossible to prove plagiarism if the ingredients and wording aren't exactly the same but it's always happening. Some chef spends hours refining his ideas for a successful dish then it's lifted and published by someone else without a word of acknowledgement.'

The managing director hastily promised any proper attributions would be given then started to detail lovingly the various oils that had been used by the competition's winner.

'Hazelnut for the fish, sesame for those marinated strips of beef, of course, and wasn't that lemon grass and fresh ginger marvellous? But what was used with those little slices of stir-fried parsnip with pine nuts?'

'A mixture of pumpkin seed and arachide,' said Darina, checking her set of recipe sheets. 'Unusual but very effective. And

I loved the pudding.' It had been peach halves caramelised in almond oil and golden sugar and served with a peach sorbet, its clean freshness offsetting the richness of the other fruit perfectly.

There was a little silence as the judges paid tribute to the food offered by the competition's winner.

The organiser came up beaming. 'Nice clear-cut decision. I hate it when only the odd mark separates first and second but we've no trouble here. Pity number eight never finished.'

'Hopelessly ambitious,' said the chef. 'Can't have timed anything beforehand and the balance of his menu was diabolic.'

A little later they straggled back into the ball-room where cameras, television and still, professional and amateur, were catching the remains of the dishes, tantalisingly appetising even though plundered by the tasting.

Darina stood with the other judges; well over six foot in her heels, she was taller than all but the oil merchant. She had at last come to terms with her height and stopped trying to wear effacing clothes. Today she had on a bright green linen suit with a white sleeveless top, her long fair hair caught in green clips either side of her head.

The oil merchant took over the microphone, thanked everyone concerned and detailed the prizes: cases of specialist oils for all, a meal for two in a top restaurant for the third place, two days' training in a three-star kitchen for the cook coming second, a week's training for the overall winner, plus a trip to a Tuscan oil estate and inclusion of the winning recipes in the forthcoming brochure.

The contestants stood beside their kitchens, fixed smiles on their faces, hands betrayingly fiddling with knives or spoons, or thrust deep into pockets. The plain woman in glasses blinked her eyelids ever more rapidly. The girl with dark curly hair and the sensational bosom flicked a red tongue over her lips. The fair girl in the large white apron seemed to have reached a state bordering on the catatonic with her gaze fixed unwaveringly on the floor. Only the young man who had abandoned his cooking appeared at all relaxed. He lolled against his oven, what looked like a stiff whisky in his hand, exhaustion on his face.

Everybody's favourite grandmother came third. Total astonishment and pleasure on her face, she was clapped heartily as she received her prize. Second place went to the plain girl in glasses, who looked equally overcome.

There were five cooks left. The girl of fierce determination had a mixture of apprehension and exultation on her face, a state echoed by the girl with dark curls. The middle-aged woman looked resigned, the aged cleric as though he was reciting some private prayer and the girl in the white apron now had a face to match.

The oil merchant hesitated for a moment, building the tension to greater heights. Darina silently willed him to get on with it.

'And the winner, who produced some of the most scintillating food we judges can remember tasting, is . . .' another pause, 'Verity Fry.'

For a moment nothing happened, then the girl in the white apron gave a small, bemused shake to her mop of fair hair, her face broke into a smile and she clasped her hands above her head in a triumphant boxer's salute. As she came forward, the cameramen elbowed their way into the scene.

Darina spared a glance for the losers left by their stoves. The determined girl stood stock-still, as if unable to believe she was going away with nothing, apart, that is, from the cases of specialist oils. Then she was lost to view as her family swept consolingly around her. The cleric gave a deep sigh and was enveloped in a warm embrace by his wife. The middle-aged woman shrugged her shoulders, retrieved a couple of cardboard boxes from behind her kitchen and started packing away equipment. The girl with dark curls fought back tears, clearing away her debris with trembling hands, oblivious to the presence of the television personality now trying to console her.

The chef greeted the dark-haired young man who had been snapping the winner.

'Simon, my boy, good to see you again. How goes it down in darkest Somerset? Lamington, isn't it? I hear great reports of your restaurant.'

'It's an uphill struggle, chef, but I may be winning. At least the guides seem to be on my side. Did you have a hard job of it today?'

'Clear-cut winner, no doubt at all. Friend of yours?'

The young man gave his engaging grin. 'Worked for me at one time. Not as a cook, front of house, but she helped behind the scenes as well. Great girl.' He glanced towards Verity Fry, now surrounded by press trying to persuade her to stand this way or that, sit with her food, take a mouthful, give an interview, give another interview. She seemed to be taking it all in her stride, in fact appeared to be enjoying herself hugely.

The chef turned to Darina. 'Let me introduce Simon Chapman, once worked for me as a trainee, now in the forefront of today's up and coming young chefs. Meet another of the judges, my boy, Darina Lisle, one of our up and coming new food writers.'

Darina shook Simon Chapman's outstretched hand. 'I spend a lot of my time in Somerset and I've eaten in your restaurant; we had a marvellous meal.' Immediately he wanted to know when she had been and what she had eaten and the three of them talked food for a while.

'Did I hear,' asked the chef after a little, 'that you are producing a book, Simon?'

'For my sins. A publisher pressured me after I won that Restaurant of the Year award at the end of last year. I was mad enough to take an advance and suppose I must now produce the goods. But writing down recipes is a dozen times more difficult than creating them.'

'What you need is some experienced help, that's what I found with my first book. So many problems with listing ingredients, spelling out method, let alone what you say about the recipes to introduce them. Why not ask Darina here for some advice?' The chef threw the comment into the air between them as he disappeared to talk to another colleague.

Simon Chapman looked speculatively at Darina. 'That sounds like a positive recommendation. How about it? I can offer free meals. Or am I railroading you?' His smile was spiced with mischief.

'One of your meals is an offer almost impossible to refuse. But I'm writing a book of my own at the moment and I'm not sure how much time I shall be spending in Somerset in the future.'

'You must come for a meal on the house if you are around,' he urged. 'Then maybe you'll let me have a go at making you change your mind.'

Darina laughed and said she would try to drop in next time she was down in Somerset, having no difficulty in sounding interested.

'Simon, darling! We did it!' Verity Fry flung her arms round the chef's neck, pulled his head down and gave him a smacking kiss. 'Oh, it's wonderful, I can't believe it, and I'd never have done it without you.' She disentangled herself from his embrace and turned to Darina. 'Thank you so much, I'm just so thrilled, I don't know what to say.'

Her small face was alight with excitement. She had removed her white apron, revealing a lithe body as vibrant as the colourful T-shirt and pedal pants it inhabited. The fact that her nose was too large for her other features only became apparent at a second glance. Perhaps it was her vivacity, the blaze of her blue eyes, or her hair, so thick and fair, cut so expertly, its bevelled mop flopping over a broad forehead, but somehow she gave an impression of beauty that even the nose, when you noticed it, couldn't wipe away.

'Darina spends lots of time in Somerset, she's going to help me with my book.' Simon smiled at the girl.

'You do? Fantastic! Come and meet my mother and sister.' Verity Fry dragged at Darina's hand, leading her through the throngs of people trying to congratulate her to where the two women Darina had noticed earlier were packing up her kitchen.

'Mother darling, Pru, meet Darina Lisle, you must have read her cookery column in the *Recorder*, it's great.'

The older woman put a collection of wooden spoons into the bottom of a square wicker basket, automatically wiped her hand down the side of her skirt, then held it out and introduced herself as Constance Fry. Before the winning announcement her strong face had looked stern with a stoicism straight from ancient Rome. Now it was warm with pride. She reached out and smoothed her daughter's cap of fair hair. 'Congratulations, girl, you've done well.' Her voice had a comfortable Somerset burr.

'And this is my sister, Pru.' Verity introduced the younger woman silently packing bowls into the basket.

Pru's face was as strong as her mother's. With weathered olive skin and short dark hair, she looked something of a gypsy. She curtly acknowledged the introduction without warmth. She too had the stamp of Somerset in her vowels but her sister's voice was crisper, spoke of London not the country.

Verity's attention was whipped away by a journalist and Darina found herself alone with the two women. She chatted easily about Verity's food, the recipes and the superb quality of the ingredients. With mention of the beef, Pru became animated for the first time.

'Verity insisted the animal was specially killed and hung a month ago so it would be just right for today.'

'You raise beef?'

'Lamb, pork and poultry as well. All organic. Fry's Farm, just outside Lamington.'

'Why haven't I heard about you? Lamington isn't far from where I've been living. I should have known about a source of organic meat that close.'

'We can't afford advertising and, anyway, we do very well without it. Why don't you come over?' Pru looked at Darina properly for the first time. 'I'll show you around the farm if you like. You don't have to write about us but we can always do with a bit of publicity.'

'We're going to give a party to celebrate Verity's success,' said Constance Fry. 'You must come. I'll send you an invitation.'

Touched by the gesture, Darina handed over one of her cards and scribbled her Chelsea address beside the Somerset one. 'Send it to London,' she suggested, 'I'm spending most of my time here at the moment but I'd love to come to Verity's party if I can.'

'That's wonderful!' Verity was back with them. 'Isn't it all exciting! Oh, why isn't Oliver here? He promised to arrive in time for the announcement.' The full lower lip pouted slightly, then her face lit up with the force of a nuclear power station as a tall man strolled up to them. She rushed at him. 'Darling, I won, I won!'

Darina watched as the newcomer steadied and gently kissed her then stood looking down at her flushed face with the same quiet pride her mother had shown.

'At last we meet the great Oliver Knatchbull. She calls him her fiancé,' said Pru drily, packing up the herbs and spices from the little kitchen. 'She says they are engaged.' She laced a leather strap through the creaking wicker to secure the lid over well-packed contents. 'But I haven't heard any marriage plans; he seems happy enough just to have her living in his penthouse.'

'I'm sure it'll be official soon,' put in her mother. 'Particularly now this competition is over.'

'Hmm, I wonder how Mr Big-Man-in-the-City is going to like having an ambitious wife.' There was cynicism and even a touch of bitterness in Pru's voice.

He was considerably older than her. Forty at least, Darina estimated, while the competition winner looked to be in her early twenties. He was the very picture of a successful businessman; a hint of fleshiness around his jaw spoke of a steady diet of rich meals, though his weight seemed under firm control in a well-shaped body. Everything about him spoke of expensive restraint, his clothes, his cuff-links, his haircut, his manner. But there was nothing restrained about his smile as his fiancée told him about all her interviews.

'And I think I may even be on television this evening!'

'All evening or will we have time for our celebration dinner? I've booked a table at Tante Claire.'

'Oh, darling, how wonderful. But you couldn't have known I'd win, I was sure I wouldn't, everyone else looked so confident and so expert.'

He ruffled her hair lightly. 'Well, if you hadn't won, it would have been a consolation meal. But I was sure you would. Now we must get down to planning the next stage in your career.' Contrary to the suggestion behind Pru's barbed query, he seemed to welcome his fiancée's success. Darina was aware of a fierce stab of envy. Then wondered if he realised yet exactly what winning the competition could mean for his fiancée.

Simon Chapman had been standing slightly apart from the group. As he came up to Darina, his face broke into another of his wide grins. 'I'm off back to the sticks,' he said. 'Back to the engine-room, just snatched a few hours away to offer Verity moral support. I can't offer you a lift to Somerset by any chance?'

Darina thanked him but said that apart from the fact she had promised to stay for the lunch, Somerset wasn't on her current schedule. 'But I'll take you up on that offer of a meal before too long,' she added at his look of disappointment.

He gave another quick grin and walked out of the ball-room, turning at the door to look back for a last time at Verity standing with her family and fiancé, Oliver Knatchbull's arm holding her close against him, his face transformed as he laughed at something she'd said. Simon's face suddenly lost its insouciant smile and acquired a dark look, the way a country scene can when bright sunlight is replaced by threatening clouds. The next moment he had gone.

# Chapter Two

The invitation to the Verity Fry celebration party arrived a few days later but by then Darina had almost forgotten both the competition and its winner. Nor had she given thought to visiting Chapman's or its chef-patron.

Her time had been taken up with organising the repainting of her Chelsea house, badly battered after occupation by a family of Americans whose children seemed to have combined the destructive powers of a small army with the free expression of budding Picassos. And with trying to fit in her cookery writing commitments around appointments with decorators, visits to wallpaper and fabric showrooms and answering the telephone.

She stood in the hallway checking her post, the front door open, painters bringing in their ladders and dust-sheets, and looked at the white card. The party was for ten days hence, a Sunday lunch-time. With the invitation was a brochure for Fry's Fine Meats bearing at its top a pen and ink sketch of a traditional Somerset farmhouse, cattle and sheep grazing in an orchard to one side. Darina glanced through a lyrical description of the organic raising of meat then looked around her.

Summer sunshine had followed the painters through the open door and lay in a golden rectangle on the dirty parquet floor. Dust danced in its light and the sullen roar of traffic drifted down from the King's Road. Quantities of paint pots began to progress through the entrance to be lined up in the hall. Beyond lay rooms stripped for redecoration.

Darina made a swift decision, went to her office and started packing up papers, some reference books and the first draft of her new book. A couple of hours later they, her word processor, a few clothes and herself were packed in the car and she left the house to the mercies of the painters. After all, it could hardly suffer worse with them than it had with the tenants. She silenced the little voice that reminded her she was paying the decorators, not they her.

What was impossible to stifle once she approached Stonehenge, the point where she always felt the West Country began, was the knowledge that she could no longer call her destination home, as she had done for nearly eighteen months. For a short while ago she had left that hearth, home and lover – intending never to return.

But William Pigram had turned up on her Chelsea doormat and thrust the keys at her.

'Keep it warm for me,' he'd said. 'I'd like to think of you in Spring Cottage.' Then, without waiting for a refusal, he'd left for the airport.

Quite suddenly Darina felt she couldn't go on driving. She turned off the dual carriageway, drove into a small village and stopped at a pub. She ordered a spritzer and took the glass of white wine and soda water outside to sit sipping her drink and staring at the little garden.

The scene had started after William had told her he had to go to New York. The credit card case he was involved in had revealed itself as part of a much larger American operation and the New York police wanted him to work with them to smash a ring responsible for the loss of so much money that the credit card company was prepared to underwrite the expenses of the trip. The Avon and Somerset police force where William was a detective sergeant in the CID had been unable to afford to send him themselves but willingly released him for the investigation, which would take anything from several weeks to months. 'Come with me,' he'd urged. 'You can write your book anywhere. Why don't you stop playing around and marry me.'

'Playing around?' She had stared at him. He stood in the kitchen of the little cottage, fiddling with a piece of the string she had been using for sewing up a boned chicken, his height suddenly crowding the small room. There was an appeal in his eyes that hadn't found a way into his voice. She ignored it.

'Playing around?' she repeated. 'Playing around?' The unfortunate phrase sparked off a row that had been brewing for some time.

He seemed unable to comprehend the depths of her frustration, to acknowledge the seriousness of her aims.

When she had insisted that becoming a wife, even his wife, was not part of her plans, he said it need not make any difference to her ambitions, that she could continue her career quite easily after marriage.

'You mean I can easily write the odd little article and create a few nice recipes around looking after you. You don't mean I can write books that demand all my energies or disappear up to London for meetings or around the country on demonstrations. You're a high-flier and in your world chief superintendents need clean underpants in the airing cupboard and nicely polished furniture, not a wife who could do a bit of flying herself if she was given the chance.'

He protested that he wanted to give her the chance but she knew he had no conception of the sort of equality she required from marriage.

'I don't mean to be selfish,' she had cried at last, 'but you don't seem to realise that I have to be me. I have to have room to develop my own interests, I can't just follow you everywhere.'

He asked if she couldn't learn to compromise a little.

'And what about you?' she'd cried. 'How about you compromising a little?'

But he did, he said wearily, looking at the messy kitchen.

The unspoken slight on her housekeeping was the last straw. She really did dislike disorder as much as he. When in catering she had managed to keep at least the kitchen of the flat she'd occupied at that time immaculate but the acquisition of deadlines had had a disastrous effect, pushing small details such as floor cleaning and dusting to the bottom of the priority pile. Darina knew it was all a recipe for disaster. Just as she knew how certain ingredients in cookery would never combine well, so she knew that the sort of marriage William expected would never work for her.

He'd said, bitterly, that she didn't love him after all.

'Love! For you it always comes down to that, doesn't it? What about mutual respect, understanding, a willingness to allow the other person their point of view?'

'But surely that's just what you refuse to allow me!' He'd turned away from her, gazed out of the window at the daffodils dancing under the apple trees. He looked, she thought, like a schoolboy battling with the enormity of being told his beloved dog had died. Almost she weakened.

'Can't you think about my point of view while you're away?' she said after a few minutes. 'Perhaps when you come back . . . '

'No!' he said violently. He turned back to her, his face set in rigid lines. 'Let's end it here and now. There's no future for us, at least you've made me understand *that*. I prefer to go without ties of any sort and I think it will be better for you as well.'

Typical, she'd thought later, that he should manage to infuse a totally selfish statement with a tiny hint of thoughtfulness for her, like adding a twist of lemon peel to a dry martini. It contributed flavour without changing the basic nature of the drink.

She had moved out then and there, thankful her house in Chelsea had just lost its tenants.

And then came the offer of the cottage keys, made on his way to the airport. Almost, she knew, he had asked her to wait for him but not quite. Almost she had said she would be there when he got back. But not quite. That had been several weeks ago and she had not heard from him since.

Now she had the choice of going to the cottage or to her mother, who lived not far from there. But having endured one session already of the Hon. Ann Lisle's laments and recriminations over the failed relationship, it was not really a choice.

Darina finished her spritzer, returned to her car and continued on her way.

William's letter followed her down from London a couple of days later, forwarded by the friend who had volunteered to look after her mail and check on the decorators' progress.

Darina propped the unopened envelope against a vase of lilac set on a kitchen table crowded with papers and the morning's shopping and looked at it as she ate her lunch of mustardy pork chops, a test recipe for her new book on cooking for two. Her taste buds were on automatic pilot, her mind considering the flimsy envelope in front of her. She had resisted her immediate urge to tear the letter open. It needed a more careful approach. Why was he writing to her? Was it to tell her he still loved her, was missing her, wanted her to write to him?

If so, what should she do?

She had missed him. Oh, how she had missed him. The moment

she had walked into the unnaturally tidy cottage and registered just what a spring clean he had organised – she had forgotten the kitchen floor was that colour – she had wanted him there, even if it was only to hear him complain he couldn't find any clean socks. At night she had lain in the double bed they had shared together and ached, physically ached, finding no relief from her need to feel his touch. In the mornings she had missed his tuneless humming as he shaved while she snatched another five minutes in bed; in the evenings she found herself waiting for his return, for the kiss he always gave her before serving them both a drink and selecting a choice anecdote from his day's doings to start the winding-down process. She missed his sense of fun, his intelligent appreciation of what was happening in the world around them and she missed him.

On the other hand – yes, there was always an 'on the other hand'. On the other hand she had been able to work on her book and her next monthly article without worrying about the need to get a meal ready for William. She could suit herself exactly when and what she ate. There were no shirts to iron and she could ignore the dust. But if she was to be truthful, none of that stood for anything beside the emptiness of the cottage and her life.

She reached for the letter, slit it open and carefully drew out the single page within.

A few minutes later she folded the page, returned it to its envelope with the same care and got up to make herself a cup of coffee.

It was, she supposed, the act of a gentleman to let her know he had found someone else. Or thought he might have.

We seem to enjoy each other's company, he had written. She's got a lively mind and is showing me a different New York from the one I am discovering through the precinct station. And she's introduced me to her family in Pennsylvania. Curiously enough, her father knows my uncle through business and they feel like family friends. Which is good when you are far from home. Elaine is a lawyer, even does some criminal work, so we have a lot in common. And I think you would like her. She asked me if I had anyone in England, wouldn't accept my 'no ties' statement. How punctilious some Americans can be! So I told her about you and she suggested I write and let you know we are becoming close.

'Thank you, Elaine,' Darina said out loud, savagely. 'And what makes you, my dear William, think I would like her? Because you've always said you admired *my* lively mind? And thank you for hoping I find happiness myself. Even though you obviously think it's unlikely, being, as I am, unable to put someone else's needs before my own.'

She moved jerkily with her coffee into the garden. Just outside the kitchen door was a paved area with a wooden table, a bench and some chairs. Sheltered from the prevailing winds, as long as the sun shone at all, it was a warm haven from spring into late autumn.

Darina settled herself. Beside her sat the ghost of past times, times she and William had shared meals, alone or with friends, laughed together, discussed life, dismissed cares.

How could he have forgotten it all so soon? How could he have fallen for someone else in the few short weeks he had been away?

Short weeks? Hadn't they been the longest of her life as she tried to fill the vacuum his going had created?

So maybe he had felt the same. Maybe this was a rush to get some other meaning in his life.

Slowly Darina drew out William's letter from her apron pocket and read it again. There slid into her mind a picture of Oliver Knatchbull with his arm round Verity Fry.

Then with a quick scrunch Darina crumpled the flimsy paper, pushed it into her empty coffee cup and went back into the kitchen.

She found the local telephone directory and looked up the number she wanted.

The phone was answered by Simon Chapman himself.

'I thought you'd forgotten me,' he said. 'I was just about to turn detective and hunt you down. If you're not doing anything else, come along tonight; it doesn't look as though the restaurant will be very busy and we can have a good chat after dinner.'

# Chapter Three

Darina put down her glass of red wine with a sigh of satisfaction. Chapman's offered food of exceptional quality, she decided. And if its chef was prepared to divulge exactly how he achieved the depth of flavour offered by his Oxtail *Ragoût*, she would not grudge the price of his book. She picked up the dessert menu, determined not to miss any aspect of this gastronomic experience. Then found it plucked from her hand.

'Only one dish you're allowed tonight, my Apple and Armagnac Tart.' Simon Chapman placed a plate with an individual round of the pastry before her. He drew out the other chair at the table. 'May I join you?'

Darina welcomed him enthusiastically. The chef was still in his whites, name neatly embroidered across his breast pocket, his air of energy seemingly undiminished by the evening's efforts. When Darina congratulated him on the meal and asked if he wasn't exhausted, he laughed.

'You saw how many covers we had tonight, seven, including you, hardly the most demanding of evenings. Friday and Saturday are our best nights. Ah, would you excuse me for a moment? The Bradleys are leaving.'

He bounded over to a couple who had just risen from the only other table still occupied. In a moment he was shaking them warmly by the hand and they were laughing at some quip he'd made.

There were ten tables of various sizes in the restaurant; Darina estimated that maximum capacity would be around forty. Ancient beams and an ingle-nook fireplace, filled now with an arrangement of dried flowers, gave old-fashioned charm, nicely set off by the severe simplicity of plain white linen and framed coloured illustrations from old cookery books. On each table was a small vase of spring flowers.

'How long have you been open?' she asked when Simon returned to her table.

'About three and a half years.'

'As long as that! I only heard about you recently. We came here in the New Year on a friend's recommendation.' Oh, that betraying 'we'.

Simon said wryly, 'I didn't want a big advertising campaign – no money for one thing – but also I thought it important to play myself in, as you might say. Build up a reputation gradually. And my partner agreed.'

'Who's your partner?'

'Local businessman. Well, Bristol-based actually. He was a regular client at the hotel where I was Head Chef. He said if I ever wanted to set up on my own, he'd back me. So one day I took him at his word.'

'Is he an active or a sleeping partner?'

'Very active when we first opened, too active actually, always wanting to change the food, jazz up the decor. Finally I had to tell him, the finances were his part of the operation, the running of the restaurant was mine. We almost bust up there and then but he eventually saw things my way. Only drops in occasionally now. In fact . . . ' he hesitated and Darina waited, but Simon said nothing else.

Finally she prompted him. 'He's happy with the financial side?'

The chef gave a small grimace. 'We do extremely well on weekends and struggle during the week. Winning that Restaurant of the Year award has helped. The publicity is filling a number of tables. Getting the locals to come to a restaurant like this on anything like a regular basis is quite impossible.' Simon twirled a glass of the chilled Barsac he had provided for both Darina and himself and grinned at her. 'Food's too fancy, prices too expensive.'

She objected. 'From what I've seen you're producing gutsy food with fantastic flavour; not over-refined, tweaked dishes that look three times prettier than they taste. And as for your prices, I think they are incredibly reasonable.'

'Can I hire you as my press agent? But, seriously, don't you know how conservative the locals round here are? And they are considered sophisticated by general Somerset standards. If we didn't also have the plain steaks and chops on the menu we'd hardly see a native, and if it wasn't for the tourist trade I would have to close tomorrow. Take yourself, for instance. You came in the New Year. Five months ago! How often have you been back since?'

His smile was challenging.

Darina felt guilty. 'We wanted to but my boyfriend got involved in a time-consuming investigation, he was a policeman.'

'*Was* a policeman? Is that past tense because he's left the force or because you've left him?'

Darina hesitated. 'He's in the States at the moment, but our relationship is at an end anyway.'

Simon Chapman grinned at her again. 'He must be the idiot of all time not to have handcuffed you to some solid piece of furniture before leaving. I shall take advantage of his stupidity.' He laughed. 'So,' he continued, 'do you think you could have time to give me some advice on this book-writing lark?'

'Do you really need it?'

'Does a mayonnaise need eggs?' He reached into a back pocket and brought out a thin sheaf of paper. 'If you really want to sing for your supper, cast an eye over this.'

Darina studied the scruffy pages, squinting in the low light at a scrawl that looked like markings made by a demented spider who had stepped in something nasty.

At last she asked despairingly, 'Haven't you ever read a recipe book?'

Simon Chapman appeared unabashed. 'Of course! Not many, I admit. Mostly those written by chefs but also Elizabeth David when I first began to cook, some of Jane Grigson when I started being interested in our English tradition and Natalie Duke widened my appreciation of Mediterranean food. Her *Grecian Pots* sent me out to sample the food first hand.'

Darina agreed that Miss Duke was indeed a compelling cookery writer then asked him if he hadn't noticed such details as ingredients set out in order of use and methods properly described, not noted down in terms only someone trained in a professional kitchen would understand?

Simon shifted uneasily in his seat, caught the eye of the waitress relaying the used tables and asked her for coffee.

'That bad, eh?' he said finally.

Darina felt that she had been less than tactful. 'Look, the recipes themselves sound marvellous, I can't wait to try them. But if I was someone who'd learned my cooking from watching mother or reading a couple of books, I wouldn't have a clue how to start. But don't worry, it's quite simple to put right.'

Simon sighed deeply. 'That's the bit I find so boring. It takes such time spelling everything out. After all, what matters is the result.'

'But if your reader doesn't understand how to achieve the result, all your effort has been wasted. You might just as well abandon any idea of writing a book and concentrate on your restaurant. Which would be a pity because what's here,' she tapped the paper in front of her, 'could be the beginnings of a very successful book.'

The chef looked sceptical. 'You really think so? Don't most people want books that are produced with the amateur cook in mind? That don't call for difficult techniques and hard to get ingredients?'

'There are people who enjoy the challenge, want to have their cooking horizons stretched, learn something from a top-class, well-trained creative talent and find something different. Exclusivity is what they get from a chef's book. Anyway, I can't see many hard to get ingredients in these.' Darina picked up the pages again.

Simon took them from her and spread them out on the table. 'Oh, you can get all of them all too easily if you aren't fussy about quality. But the finished dishes won't be anything like those my clients have here. Take that ragoût of oxtail you had.' Darina leaned forward eagerly. 'The meat was organically raised and, apart from the flavour itself, long cooking releases nothing but goodness. A whole oxtail was used for the stock as well as for the dish itself and without that it would be nothing. Try it with the usual stuff ninety per cent of people buy from their supermarket and the result couldn't compete with what you tasted tonight.'

'Do you get your meat from the Frys?'

'Too right! What Constance and Pru have built up there is outstanding. But you must have bought meat from them yourself, their reputation is fantastic.'

Darina shook her head sorrowfully. 'I'm afraid that's another bit of local news that didn't reach me soon enough, the first I heard of them was at the Savoy.'

Simon beamed. 'What a fantastic day! Dead chuffed they all were. Even Constance had a smile on her face.'

'Did you say that Verity worked here at one time?'

'Did the front of house for a bit. She was wonderful, everyone loved her, never had such good mid-week business as when Verity was here.'

The coffee arrived. The waitress pushed down the plunger of the cafétière, poured out two cups of coffee, then left it on the table with a plate of petits fours. As she turned to go, Simon Chapman told her not to wait – he would clear the table himself.

'Where did Verity learn her cooking?' Darina asked.

'In London somewhere, but she was always in the kitchen wanting to know how I'd done this or that; said it helped to explain the food to the clients, but that was just a flam.' Simon grinned. 'She was always making suggestions for new dishes, sometimes I'd even take one up. Then she'd insist on being in on the testing, I'd tell her she just wanted a free meal.'

The chef lay back in his chair, hand idly toying with his glass of wine, refilled twice during their chat. Darina could see the pretty, enthusiastic girl and the energetic, darkly attractive young man working together. How closely had their relationship developed and why had Verity left the district?

'When did she get back to cooking herself?'

Simon hunched forward over the glass as though studying the light shining through the wine's golden depths. 'About two and a half years ago. She went back to London, started cooking directors' lunches. That's where she met Oliver.'

'He seems very interested in her career.'

'It was he who suggested she enter the competition. Under all that sweetness and light, she's really very ambitious.'

Had a dash of bitterness been added to his voice?

'And he doesn't seem to mind that?'

'Encourages her. Just as well, he'd never hold her otherwise.'

Perceptive Simon, wise Oliver.

'But she asked you to help with the recipes?'

'Most of the ideas were her own but, yes, we did work on them together.'

'No wonder you were so delighted.'

Simon gave Darina another of his engaging grins. 'Could you resist being pleased she'd won?'

Darina confessed that, yes, she had been personally delighted to find it was Verity Fry who had emerged a clear winner.

'Do you think she would like to open a restaurant?'

Simon shook his head. 'Nah, never. She saw enough here to cure her of any ambitions in that direction.'

'What do you mean?'

'Too long hours, too exhausting for too little return.'

'You don't believe that, surely?'

Simon sighed. For a moment, as at the Savoy looking at the Fry family group with Oliver Knatchbull, the lightheartedness that was so attractive disappeared. The black eyes contained a disturbing light. 'There are times when running a restaurant seems the craziest way to make a living anyone ever invented. But, you are right, I wouldn't want to do anything else.' His mood did not lighten.

After a moment, Darina said, 'There's something wrong, isn't there? Do you want to tell me about it?'

He gave her an opaque look. 'I swore I wasn't going to breathe a word to anyone but you have a knack of making one talk.' There was a curt laugh. 'Soon I may not have a restaurant.'

'Business that bad?'

'Not the restaurant business, my partner's. He says he's on the verge of bankruptcy. He's in import/export of some sort, the details have never seemed important, but the recession hasn't been kind and he says that the last few years' interest rates have crippled him and he has to have his money out of the restaurant. I can't afford to buy him out, the bank won't help and if I can't find the money from somewhere else the place will have to go on the market.'

There was a small silence.

'Well,' said Darina bracingly, 'I'm sure there are any number of top kitchens who would be overjoyed to take you on as Head Chef.'

Then she jumped nervously as Simon's hand crashed down on to the table. 'I do not want to join one of "any number of top kitchens". My whole soul has gone into this restaurant. It's mine, I've sacrificed everything, everything,' he repeated with emphasis. 'I would do anything to keep it from closing.' He flung himself back in his chair, moody and depressed, the effervescent charm vanished as completely as if it had never existed.

'Then you will have to find the finance to keep it open,' Darina contributed calmly. 'There must be someone, somewhere, who could help. This place is too good to disappear.'

Simon finished his wine in one swift gulp. He replaced the empty glass on the table and smiled at Darina with a sweetness quite different from his previous good humour.

'Do you know, I think I almost believe you? Will you join me in a brandy?' Darina shook her head and he refilled her coffee cup. 'Do say you'll help with these recipes, I can't afford to return that advance I so rashly accepted and, anyway, publication might help keep this place alive.'

The talk turned back to his book and naturally progressed on to food. Midnight had turned before Darina reluctantly tore herself away, promising to come back soon and go through Simon's recipes with him.

Despite her low consumption of alcohol Darina felt as though she had drunk a whole bottle of champagne. Life suddenly seemed a great deal more attractive than it had that afternoon. She'd write to William tomorrow and tell him she was pleased things were going well for him, she might even mention Simon Chapman, let him know she was having fun as well.

# Chapter Four

'Natasha Quantrell, how dare you slip back here without telling me!'

The thin woman picking parsley straightened and turned. 'Constance!' She stood on the flagstoned path, her hands full of herb, her face shaded by a straw hat, and looked uncertainly at her visitor.

Constance Fry caught her breath as she came up close, hesitated for a second, then gathered the other woman in a fierce embrace. 'Natasha, oh, Natasha.'

For a few moments the two women clung together then Constance drew back and looked again at her friend. 'Why didn't you tell me you were coming back?'

The woman turned away from the intensity of the other's gaze and rubbed a hand quickly across her eyes. 'I'm sorry. Come inside, let me put the kettle on for some coffee.' Then she added, 'I can't tell you how pleased I am to see you.'

Nothing more was said as the way was led up the kitchen garden to the rear of a low Elizabethan house built of golden stone and surrounded by waves of flowering shrubs and plants interspersed with hedges of yew and rose.

In the kitchen, Natasha Quantrell rinsed her parsley under the tap and thrust it into a pottery jug with water. She removed the hat and ran her fingers through short dark hair that was streaked with grey. She filled a kettle and placed it on the large Aga, then fed a small hand-grinder with coffee beans.

Constance sat at the big pine table in the centre of the kitchen and watched the other woman revolving the grinder's handle, forcing the beans through the mechanism, then removing the coffee grounds from the small drawer at the bottom of the machine. She looked at the long sleeves of the dress her friend was wearing, and tried not to stare at the angry scars on the hands that dealt so deliberately with the business of making coffee.

Natasha warmed an earthenware jug then added the grounds. She found a tray, placed china on it then gave Constance a quick glance, removing her gaze as soon as it was met. 'Shall we go through to the library or would you prefer to stay here?'

'Let's stay here, I always did like this kitchen.'

The sun shone through the leaded windows over the sink, caught the gleam of copper moulds on the green-painted dresser and the old knife-polisher standing on a long counter underneath a series of bells, each named for a principal room. The large flagstoned floor gleamed with a soft grey sheen, the sun dappling over its uneven surface. On old wooden draining boards stood the remains of a simple lunch: a plate with apple peelings and cheese rind, a mug. There was the smell of damp wood mixed with some harsh cleaning material, warmed by the peppery scent of geraniums from the windowsill.

Natasha removed the boiling kettle from the stove and filled the coffee jug. She brought a small strainer and the jug to the table and sat opposite Constance, facing the window and the sun.

The light was not kind. It revealed with remorseless clarity the latticework of scars puckering the skin, the purple shadows beneath the fine hazel eyes sunk in sockets of pain, the incised lines that ran from the hawk-like nose to the straight mouth. Constance remembered how attractive the face had once been. Both Natasha Quantrell and her cousin, Natalie Duke, had been striking girls. Natalie's personality was the more forceful but Natasha's quieter charm had been equally attractive. Now her face spoke of nightmare more powerfully than words.

Constance reached out and gently covered one of the scarred hands. 'I was so sorry, so very sorry. I wrote, I don't know if you got my letter, but I didn't really know what to say.'

Natasha bent her head but allowed her hand to remain where it was. 'Yes, thank you, I did but, I'm sorry, I haven't written to anyone. It was impossible.' She picked up the jug, went to the tap and poured a tablespoon of water over the top of the coffee and brought it back to the table. She filled their cups with the steaming liquid. The strength of the aroma plucked at Constance's taste buds, taking her back through so many years, to a Greek island and a sun that turned an arid terrace into one huge cooking surface.

'How did you know I was back?'

'Terry at the shop; he said the postman had delivered letters addressed to you here and Mrs Boult had told him she'd opened up the house. But he hadn't seen you shopping yet.' Constance gave a smile that lightened her face, softening the stern lines. 'Nothing goes on here without Terry and Sally knowing.'

'What happened to the Baxters?'

'Mrs Baxter died some years ago, I think the heart went out of George, he sold up and went to live with his daughter in the north. Terry and Sally have done a lot, installed new freezers, widened the range of goods, seem to be making quite a going concern of the shop and the post office. Didn't your grandfather tell you?'

Natasha closed her eyes in a slow blink that may have staved away tears. 'He probably did. Lamington all seemed so far away to us in France. You sent me a letter, didn't you, when he died? Did I answer that one?'

'Yes, you mentioned the old days, said how he'd liked me.' Constance felt awkward, so much had changed since the old days.

'I find it difficult to remember anything that happened before . . . ' Natasha fell silent then drank some coffee, replacing the cup in its saucer with care.

'Can you tell me what happened? Don't if it's difficult but you can never believe newspaper stories.'

The other woman sighed. 'I think it would help. I haven't talked to anyone about it, not in France, not here. People have been very kind; apart from the officials, no one has asked questions but I think it would do me good to tell someone exactly what happened.'

There was a short pause then she asked, 'What did you read?'

Constance dropped her gaze. She felt that, despite Natasha's words, she had invaded a private area and didn't know how to retreat. 'Just what was in the newspapers, that Natalie had lost her life in a fire.'

Natasha began to speak slowly, her voice low. 'I had just returned from a shopping trip. I'd taken the bags into the kitchen and was going to get lunch ready when there came this noise. An explosion. But it wasn't like a bomb, something blowing up, more a sort of whoomf; there was a vibration that seemed to travel right through the house.

'I ran outside. Natalie's studio, where she did all her writing, where she produced all but that first cookery book, was on fire. Flames were leaping inside, I could see them through the window, and Natalie was screaming. I hear those screams in my dreams, night after night.' The scarred hands picked at a knot in the pine table.

'I rushed over. The handle of the door was burning hot, too hot to hold.' Natasha's mouth worked, she had trouble forming her words. 'I wrapped the bottom of my jumper round it and managed to open the door. I could just see her lying on the floor, her clothes, her hair, all burning, burning with such a flame. Her face was buried in her arm, as though she was trying to protect it from the fire. I tried to get to her but I couldn't. The flames were crackling and leaping, higher and higher, everything in the studio was on fire. The papers were burning, the books were burning, the curtains, the furniture, and the heat was impossible. It was just impossible . . . ' The voice grated to a stop.

Constance had hold of Natasha's scarred hand, gripping it across the table with steady force. 'You did what you could, you couldn't have done more.'

There was great sadness in Natasha's face as she scraped at her weeping eyes with the heel of her free hand. 'No, I know. At least I can never feel guilty over that.'

'There's nothing for you to feel guilty about. For nearly twenty-five years you devoted your life to Natalie. I can guess how difficult it's been at times. I remember telling you in Greece you mustn't sacrifice everything, however fond you were of her. We both know what she was like, how appallingly self-centred she could be. I don't suppose you got much consideration and how you stuck it all this time, I'll never know. But for her to go that way was just terrible. Do they know exactly what happened?'

Natasha seemed bemused, as though she found it difficult to understand what Constance was saying. She gazed out of the window at the gentle pinks and blues set in misty greens, blinking rapidly. After a few minutes she regained her control. 'They think she had been standing on a chair, perhaps to reach one of the high shelves, and overbalanced. A chair was lying on its side and one of her legs was broken. As she fell, her skirt must have caught the gas fire. It was one of those free-standing butagaz affairs. It looked as though she tried to drag herself towards the door but the fire spread too quickly. There was a window open and that must have fanned the flames. And of course there was so much paper in the studio, so much paper.'

'You might have lost your life, too. As it was you must have suffered terribly. We heard you were in hospital.'

Natasha looked down at her hands, then touched one of the scars on her face. 'Yes, well, the burns were nothing, really. But they took a long time to heal. They said it was the shock. At least in hospital I was spared the attentions of the press.'

Constance felt fascinated horror. 'You mean there were journalists there?'

'Of course! Natalie Duke was dead. One of Britain's leading cookery writers, who'd hardly given an interview in all her life. Of course they wanted to talk to her cousin, learn all the details, see the burned-out wreckage, talk to the villagers about 'les Deux Anglaises'. But the journalists didn't have much joy. Nothing can be closer than a French peasant when he doesn't want to talk and the hospital protected my privacy. For weeks I saw no one. There was no one I wanted to see. And when I was finally discharged, what had been our home didn't seem home any more. The fact that the house was intact, that it hadn't been touched by the fire, was almost worse than the charred beams of the studio. So much else was changed it seemed impossible that the house still stood as it always had.'

Constance felt such pity she could hardly bear it. 'You'd lived there together for how many years?'

'Over twenty. After Natalie decided she'd had enough of Greece and wanted to study French food, we thought of the south first, because of the sun, but already development was taking over and we could see what it would be in a few years' time, quite apart from the fact that prices were more than we could afford. So we started travelling around, eating, talking to people, looking at property every now and then when something caught our eye. Then we found this tiny manoir going for nothing in southern Brittany. The weather seemed reasonable and the countryside was lovely, it reminded us both of Somerset, so we bought it. And made it into a home.' She looked round the kitchen. 'It was very different from this but we loved it.' There was another silence.

'When your grandfather died, we thought you'd come back here,' said Constance.

'We were going to. We had everything planned, then the fire happened. Afterwards, it seemed all that was left to me.'

'Natalie must be looking down from somewhere mad as anything, she always loved this house.' Constance tried to lighten the atmosphere but ruined the attempt by asking more sharply than she had intended, 'Who have you seen since your return?'

Natasha gave a small smile. 'You were going to be the first, how could you think anything else?'

Something inside Constance relaxed. She hadn't known until then just how much it had hurt, not having received any word from Natasha.

'I wrote to the lawyers, asked them to get Mrs Boult in to open the house, see everything was in order, and told them I was arriving the day before yesterday. I meant to come over to see you straight away but I found I needed a little time to, well, to settle myself.'

'Verity's driving down this weekend, we're giving a party for her, she's won some sort of cookery competition,' Constance said abruptly.

It took a little time for the information to penetrate the other woman. She looked blankly at her friend, then smiled.

'How nice. She's doing well then?'

Constance gave details of the competition and Verity's doings, conscious she was talking too much but unable to stop herself describing how Verity had practised and practised her dishes, how wonderful she was at cooking, what lots of ideas she had, how successful she was becoming.

Natasha listened intently.

Constance at last managed to make herself stop and wait for a response. When none came she looked firmly at the other woman. 'When I heard of Natalie's death I wondered if . . . ' She let the sentence trail away but continued looking into the other's hazel eyes.

Natasha glanced down at her cup uneasily. 'We had an agreement, everything to each other and the last to go would look after Verity. Maybe if we'd known just how much Grandfather would leave . . . but I always thought his capital would be exhausted, he was so old when he died and always complained he'd end in the poor house.' She looked up and met Constance's eyes. 'Are things difficult? It must have been a struggle since Thomas died.'

'Natasha, you knew how difficult things were when Thomas was alive. No one knows better than you the problems of living with an impossible person when you are fond of them, can't you imagine how much worse it is when you feel nothing for them? There were times I contemplated murder. And that's no figure of speech, I once actually looked at the paraquat and wondered how much I'd need in his tea. But it goes a funny colour and I was sure he'd have noticed.' Constance gave a forced laugh. 'Don't look so shocked, there must have been times you felt the same about Natalie.'

'Connie, I loved her. Yes, she was difficult to live with but she had so much pressure on her, publishers wanting more books, people always trying to visit, both old friends and reporters, and I wasn't always very good at choking them off, she'd have to ring up and say they couldn't come after all. It was just as irritating for her to have someone as inefficient as me around. Yes, we had our arguments from time to time but, believe me, mostly we got on together very well.'

Constance thought how typical of Natasha to plead everything in the garden was lovely. Yet, when she herself had been talking about life with Thomas, there'd been a flash of something in her eyes she hadn't recognised, a glint of steel that had never been part of the old Natasha.

'I know you're going to miss Natalie,' she burst in clumsily, 'but you've got a chance now to make a life of your own. Oh, it'll take time, I know that. Despite the sheer relief that rolled over me when Tom went, it took me ages to get used to being a widow. But then I realised life wasn't completely over for me, that there were things I could do. I started to build up the organic meat side and I can't tell you how satisfying it has been. The sense of achievement has been, well, liberating.'

She reached across for her friend's hand again.

'Natasha, don't ruin things for yourself by feeling guilty you couldn't save Natalie. If it had been me, I think I might have felt justified in not striving too hard to rescue her.' Then she felt she had gone too far for Natasha looked at her as though she'd been accused of putting a gun to Natalie's head and pulling the trigger.

'I didn't mean that, you know I didn't. Come round and see us soon. Pru has been such a help with the farm, I don't know how I ever managed without her.' She rose. 'The party's on Sunday, a buffet lunch, there'll probably be people you used to know and we don't often get a chance to see Verity down here now, she spends most of her time in London. She's got a boyfriend, rather older than she is but very suitable. He'll be there on Sunday as well.' She looked at the scarred face and realised how unlikely it was that Natasha would want to come.

The woman shook her head. 'It's very kind but I don't think so. Perhaps later.'

Constance stood awkwardly, she should be going, Natasha looked exhausted. There was a sense of unfinished business hanging in the air, something more should be said but she didn't know what. How different it was from the old days when she and Natasha had been such friends; a friendship tested to the limit whenever Natalie had appeared on the scene during holidays from school and university. Natalie had the prior claim on Natasha, seemed to take her over like a Svengali with Trilby, Natasha never protesting at the rearrangement of any plans.

Then Natalie had joined a newspaper in London, Natasha started work in Bristol and Constance met Thomas. They drifted apart. But later, much later, there had been that time in Greece. And after that she and Natasha had never lost touch entirely, always exchanged Christmas cards with little notes, Constance including snapshots: Verity as a toddler, Pru leading her sister on a pony, Thomas and Verity on a tractor, so many small moments caught in the amber formed by passing years. Never once in all that time had Constance failed to feel Natasha was still as close a friend as when they had been in their teens and early twenties.

How stupid she had been, she thought as she stood in the kitchen and held out a hand to say goodbye, not to have realised that all those years would make a difference.

Natasha looked at the hand then back at Constance. 'Oh, my dear,' she cried and reached out, enfolding the woman in a warm embrace. 'My dear, I'm sorry, it's going to take time, you must give me time.'

Constance clung to her, recognising that it wasn't time that made things strange between them, it was the effect of Natalie's terrible death. There was just too much for Natasha to cope with at present. She had never been as strong as her cousin.

She patted her friend awkwardly on the shoulder. After a little while Natasha drew away and tried to smile. 'You don't know what it means to see you again,' she said. 'Please, come again soon.'

'I will,' Constance promised. 'But you must come and see us. If not on Sunday, soon.'

'Soon,' Natasha agreed. She led the way to the front entrance and opened the heavily studded door. 'How did you come, on foot or by car?'

'Neither,' Constance laughed, 'I left my bicycle at the gate, look!' The two women walked down the path and Constance took hold of the ancient machine leaning against the stone wall.

'Heavens, it can't be the one you used to ride all those years ago?'

'It is! Can't afford to lash out on new things when the old ones still work. And they don't make them like they used to.' Constance mounted, gave an alarming wobble, then started cycling steadily down the lane.

Once she was well balanced she looked back, but Natasha had already disappeared. She stopped cycling, stood with the machine between her legs looking back at the house, its frontage in shadow, the door closed behind her friend.

Something was definitely different about Natasha. And the money she had hoped for Verity was not to be. She supposed Natalie had felt she owed her cousin something for her years of devotion. And perhaps Natasha felt she had a right to it, there had been no suggestion Verity might have a better claim. But Natasha had her grandfather's money. Though what was it she had said, if they had known how much her grandfather would be leaving her? What then? Would Natalie have decided to change her will? The news of Natasha's inheritance must have come not long before Natalie's death but Natalie wouldn't have felt much pressure to instruct a lawyer, time enough for that, she would have thought.

Could Natasha be persuaded to help Verity? Rich boyfriends were all very well but Constance knew she would feel happier if her daughter had more security and there was nothing she could spare from the farm. She'd already let Verity have more than she should to help her buy her car – there'd be trouble if Pru found out how much – and there had been hints recently that the girl was in some financial trouble. Great things were talked about as a result of winning this competition but Constance doubted instant fortune would be one of them. Carefully she remounted her bicycle and rode slowly home wondering just how she was to introduce Verity to Natasha.

# Chapter Five

Pru scratched behind the ears of her favourite pig. Amelia responded by wrapping her chestnut-brown ears even further forward, obliterating her little eyes, and making a series of low grunts, standing stock-still in ecstasy. 'That's it, I'm afraid, old girl.' Pru took a step back, carefully avoiding the sprawl of piglets jostling for position at their mother's teats, checked that the water level was right in their drinking trough and let herself out of the pig enclosure.

As she made her way through the orchard back to the farmhouse, depression fell on her like winter rain on a sodden meadow. She knew as soon as she entered the kitchen she would be sucked into yet more preparations for that day's party. It seemed to have taken over the entire farm for the last few weeks.

First it had been the guest list to be drawn up, with much agonising over who was to be invited and who not. 'I don't know why you're worrying,' Pru had said to her mother, 'Verity's hardly been here the last year or so, nobody's going to expect to be asked.'

'They all remember her,' protested Constance.

Numbers crept up. The deep-freeze was checked for the special cuts Constance had stashed away as animals had been killed over the last month or so, leaving Pru to juggle the orders, no easy business since demand for the prime cuts always outstripped supply. 'What are you going to do with them if Verity doesn't win?' Pru had asked.

'There'll be something else to celebrate, or we'll just have a party anyway. She's seeing a lot of this Oliver Knatchbull.'

Pru stared at her mother. 'What makes you think he's any different from all the others?' she demanded.

Constance dropped the list she was studying and gave serious thought to the question.

'It's just something about the way she talks, or rather doesn't talk, about him,' she said at last. 'She doesn't make jokes, doesn't laugh about him in the way she has about most of her boyfriends.'

'It's wishful thinking,' Pru said sharply. 'You just want to see her married to some successful City man with lots of money and a nice house.'

'And why not?' Constance asked mildly.

Pru had walked out of the room, shutting the door with unnecessary force. She had behaved exceedingly badly over all the preparations, she admitted to herself now. She had made no concessions over the work to be done on the farm, only grudgingly giving a hand with the mountain of cooking organised by her mother. But at least she had, without being asked, done her special Spiced Beef and a large pickled pork.

Now she just longed for the day to be over so that everything could return to normal.

It was not, she told herself, that she begrudged Verity her party. As long as it stayed at a party and her mother didn't start making noises about letting her have some capital, the money for the car had been more than enough. The child had done well, though, and it was only fair a little fuss should be made of her. It was just, well, just that life didn't seem to have been very fair to herself.

A small boy hurled himself across the yard and grabbed her legs around the knees, burying his face into her jeans, and burst into tears. Sighing deeply, Pru bent and hauled him up. The boy exchanged his armful of legs for a grasp of her neck and continued his howling into the soft cotton of her shirt.

'Hush, darling, hush,' she murmured, pressing her face against his unaccountably damp T-shirt, feeling the warmth of his body rise through the wet material. 'Tell Mum what's wrong.'

'He put the puppy in the tumble-drier and got spanked by Gran.' An older boy had followed the sobbing youngster and now stood uneasily in front of Pru.

'Oh, Alastair, you didn't!' The small boy buried his face deeper into Pru's neck. She looked down at his older brother. 'Did he turn it on, Mark?'

Mark shook his head wordlessly.

Pru roughly dumped her younger son on the ground and crouched down until she was on a level with him. She grabbed his shoulders and shook him, exasperation flooding through her like acid through a battery. 'Alastair, how could you?'

Shock had dried up his sobs. Now he looked at her with his eyes and mouth wide open, his little face red and flushed. For a moment it seemed as though the crying would start again at an even higher pitch then he relaxed and grinned engagingly at her. 'Puppy so *wet*!'

As so often in her dealings with Alastair, Pru melted. She forced herself to ask sternly, 'And how did he get so wet?'

'Mark an' me put him under the hose.'

Pru looked at her elder son. 'Did you?'

He kicked his sandal at a large stone at the edge of the yard, refusing to meet her eye. He was seven, more than four years older than his brother. He pushed his hands into the pockets of a pair of sodden shorts. The sandals, too, were dark with damp. 'The dogs were so hot, they were just lying and panting, they didn't want to come for a walk at all.' He sounded sulky and aggrieved.

'Panting,' repeated his little brother, eyes wide and innocent. 'Hot, it's so hot.'

'Well, I've much too much to do to sort you two out, you know it's Aunt Verity's party today. And look at you both, worse than drowned rats. The dogs couldn't be any wetter than you. Serve you right if I put *you* in the tumble-drier.' She gave both boys a short lecture on proper conduct towards dumb animals then told Mark to take Alastair upstairs to change. 'And stay out of trouble for the rest of the day!' she called after them.

Pru found her depression had lifted a little. She wondered what other mischief they would find before the day was over; Alastair was ever in some pickle or other and where he was Mark could be found as well. Despite the difference in ages, it was the younger boy who led the way. Pru gave a short bark of a laugh and went inside. She supposed what she felt towards Alastair was what Constance felt towards Verity. She must take greater care with Mark than her mother had with her. Why did some children have an enchanted aura? And then she wondered sourly if Alastair would turn out to be just as self-centred as Verity.

Shortly after the start of the party, when the sun was at its hottest and guests were wandering under the orchard trees in a lack-lustre way, the two boys stripped themselves of all clothes and ran naked, threading themselves through the various little groups. Afterwards she had to acknowledge the incident got the whole party going but at the time Pru was mortified. Controlling her temper with difficulty, she grabbed two tiny arms and, ignoring both Alastair's and Mark's agonised whimpers, marched them back into the house and up to their bedrooms, almost threw them on the beds and said in a fierce voice that brooked no argument that they were to remain there until told they could come down.

Then she closed her ears to their cries and went back to the garden, where a happy buzz told its tale of a successful party.

Verity was charm itself and worked as hard as her sister and mother, making sure everyone enjoyed themselves, introducing Oliver to people she had known since childhood, congratulating Pru and Constance on their cooking and pleading, unsuccessfully, for the boys to be allowed back. Then insisted on taking them a plate of their favourite foods. Pru remembered a much younger Verity following her around the farm, trying to help with the animals, lugging pails of feed, attempting to move bales of hay twice her size, so eager to play her part, and felt a sudden wave of warmth towards her young sister.

'I hope on another occasion you will show me round your farm, you seem to have a most impressive operation here.' Oliver Knatchbull appeared at Pru's side.

She regarded him uncertainly. Sophisticated middle-aged men had not played much part in her life. She knew he was rich and successful; Verity had described the penthouse flat to them and the Rolls-Royce she enjoyed being driven around in. He'd arrived in a Volvo today, though, small but powerful-looking, much less pretentious amongst the Fords, Fiats and Rovers of the other guests than the luxury car would have been. It suggested a sensitivity that did him credit.

How seriously involved was Verity with him? She talked of being engaged but there'd been no announcement, no ring. He must be all of forty, perhaps more. Tall, lithe for his age, but definitely going thin on top with his fair hair brushed back without the slightest attempt to conceal its deficiencies. His regular features were certainly handsome and his blue eyes had startling depth. They were looking at her warmly and he appeared sincerely interested in her farming activities, questioning her on the stock, asking how it was raised and looked after, what their marketing and future plans were.

Pru found she was chatting happily, it wasn't often she had an opportunity to discuss the subject nearest to her heart with someone of such intelligence. Well, she corrected herself, the subject almost nearest to her heart.

When he disengaged himself to move on elsewhere, it was with such tact and discretion she was left with the impression that he really regretted not being able to continue talking with her longer.

'Now there's a man of considerable charm, your sister's a lucky girl.'

Darina Lisle came up to Pru, with a spoon in one hand and a glass of syllabub in the other. Pru looked despairingly at the floating dress of lemon-yellow muslin, the floppy hat elegantly sitting on fair hair loosely knotted at the nape of a long neck, and scowled. For once she herself had put on a dress, a three-year-old blue linen. She hadn't liked the effect in the mirror and now felt dowdier than ever.

'Verity always has been lucky.'

She received a keen look. 'Life seems very unfair sometimes. Look at my height, for instance. What wouldn't I give to be petite and pretty like you and your sister.'

At five foot seven with shoulders as broad as a gentleman's coat-hanger, Pru thought she could hardly qualify as petite but beside the tall cook she could almost feel small. She muttered something about Darina not having to worry much. The other girl laughed. 'You have no idea what agony I go through. At dances all the tall men seem to go for midgets and I get left with embryonic Napoleons who treat me as though I'm their key to success. This is the most wonderful syllabub I've ever tasted, is it your own cream?'

For the second time during the party Pru found herself in an intelligent conversation. It took something like this afternoon to make her realise just how cut off she was here on the farm with Constance. Of course there were the customers, and every now and then she manned a stall at an agricultural show when she did meet all sorts of people, but she didn't have any friends, not that she could really talk to. It wasn't just the demands of the farm, there were the boys as well.

'Do let me show you round some time, I didn't really mean what I said at the Savoy about writing us up.'

Darina appeared delighted at the invitation. 'I'd love to, if you are not too busy. One day next week?'

'Sure, give me a ring tomorrow and we'll make a date.'

A little later Pru saw Darina Lisle talking with Oliver Knatchbull in the shade of some old apple trees. What a much more suitable couple they made than Verity and Oliver. Nearer in age and nearer in height, too. She looked round for her sister, then froze.

The party's heroine was in a corner of the orchard talking to Simon Chapman. Both of them were laughing and looked as though they hadn't a care in the world. How dare he come here! He'd promised he wouldn't.

The chef had turned up on Friday to collect his meat order bearing an enormous version of his famous apple and Armagnac tart, a huge container of lemon ice-cream and a box of langue de chat biscuits, specially sealed with sellotape to keep them fresh. 'I thought they might help,' he had said nervously, handing them over. Pru had rushed her thanks, hustling the ice-cream into the deep-freeze, talking too quickly, hoping Constance wouldn't come through and spoil this moment. Of course he had done it for Verity but it was so rare to have any contact with him beyond the brief handover of meat. She had wanted to keep him there and for once he seemed happy to be with her. She'd scoured her mind for conversational topics, related some funny stories about Alastair, told him Mark's latest doings at school. He had seemed very interested in the activities of the boys but contributed little himself. They had stood in the old outer kitchen beside the long deep-freeze, no glimmer of his usual bantering smile lighting his dark eyes, until her talk all dried up and she could only look at him.

Then he had launched into the story of how his restaurant was all washed up unless he could find another backer and would she consider putting some money into it?

She had gazed at him speechlessly.

'You know it's a success. It wouldn't be a risk and I could make over the lease to you. If I had the backing of a place like this, the bank would be a bit more co-operative.'

'But I haven't any money,' she had said slowly at last.

'You're a partner in the farm. You could raise a mortgage with no trouble.'

She had been torn between bitter disappointment that this was the reason for his unusual company and a deep longing to be able to help him. Then she had been spared any necessity to resolve the conflict by Constance erupting upon the scene. She must have been listening in the kitchen for she left Simon in no doubt that his looking for backing from Fry's Farm was like expecting the goose on the back pond to lay golden eggs.

'I've not spent the best part of my life building this place up, without help from bank or any other, to have you squander it all in two seconds. You know what I think of you!'

'Only too well,' he'd muttered.

'And how you have the gall even to suggest it, I cannot imagine.' Her look of cold dislike deepened into hate. It flicked contemptuously over him then Constance disappeared back into the kitchen, slamming the door behind her.

Pru looked at the disappointed man. He sagged against the deep-freeze and gazed back at her with miserable eyes.

'I'm sorry,' she said at last. 'But you see how it is. There's nothing I can do.'

'Would you, if you could?'

She looked into the coal black eyes. 'Yes,' she said without equivocation. 'Yes, I would.'

They continued to stand there in silence for a long moment. 'Verity's sent me an invitation for the party,' he said. It seemed to be a question.

'You're not coming?' Pru replied with instinctive horror.

He gave her a twisted smile, so unlike his usual grin.

'I suppose it hardly seems the best of ideas.'

'You mustn't, you see how mother is!'

He nodded, then leaned forward and gave her a swift, hard kiss. 'Say hello to the boys,' he said and disappeared.

She had gazed speechlessly after him. Then shook herself, picked up the tart and went into the kitchen. Constance wasn't there. Pru had put the tart in the larder and gone to prepare feed for the animals, thrusting any consideration of the encounter with Simon to the back of her mind.

Now, after all that, here he was, bold as brass, amiable grin in place and looking at Verity as though she was some Salon Culinaire prize dish.

Then there was a small whirlwind as Constance appeared from

nowhere, hurling words at Simon in a furious undertone. Pru heard: 'You've caused enough trouble already, I never want to see you here again, never, do you understand? You can buy your meat elsewhere.'

There was no smile on Simon's face now. He was suddenly toweringly angry. 'You interfering old witch,' he said with a venom Pru had never heard in his voice before. 'You're the one who's always causing the trouble. If it hadn't been for you—' he broke off abruptly as Pru came and stood beside her mother.

'Yes?' she said, challenge ringing in her voice. 'Just how did mother interfere with your little games?'

Simon took a visibly deep breath. 'If you don't know,' he said, then stopped himself.

Verity was almost crying. 'Don't, don't,' she wailed. 'Oh, please, why can't you all be friends!'

Simon turned on her. 'Be your age, girl. You, of all people, should know exactly why that is the last thing any of us can be. Except, perhaps, you and me.'

'Why did you come?' Pru was as near tears now as Verity.

Simon's shoulders sagged. 'Because I wanted to ask Verity if she thought Oliver Knatchbull might come up with some finance for the restaurant; she said it was the only opportunity she'd have to talk about it. And,' he straightened his shoulders and looked at Constance and Pru defiantly, 'she wanted me to be here. It's her day, after all, why shouldn't she have what she wants, be happy?'

'And now that you can see it's making her miserable, perhaps you'd be good enough to go?'

Unnoticed, Oliver had joined them. He placed a protective arm around Verity. Pru thought how calm he seemed and envied the way he could make his request so quietly and dispassionately – almost as if he was simply asking a clerk to remove a file he had finished with.

Simon however was by no means as calm. 'Oh, I'll go,' he said. 'But don't think you won't see me again. I'll be back, you can count on that.'

'Not if I've got anything to do with it, you won't,' Constance hissed after him; she was holding Pru by the arm, her fingers digging mercilessly into muscle, a physical expression of her deep, hard anger. Pru hardly noticed the pain, to her shame she could feel hot tears sliding down her face.

'Well, now,' said Oliver comfortably, giving Verity a small squeeze with his encircling arm as Simon strode furiously away. 'Constance, you can rest assured I shall not be backing that young man.' He looked down at the girl he held. 'Why don't we do something to cheer your mother and sister up, make them forget this little incident?' They exchanged a glance of perfect understanding.

Even before Verity spoke, Pru knew what she was going to say, saw the enormous sapphire ring, and a wave of piercing envy swept through her. Not, a tiny detached part of her mind noted with relief, jealousy. She didn't want Oliver for herself, didn't want Verity's life for herself. But, oh, how she wanted the comfort of the love they so obviously had for each other.

She watched with a certain wry amusement the way Constance hugged her younger daughter. 'Engaged! Girl, I'm so happy. And what a ring! You'll be so happy, both of you, so very happy. Come along, we must tell everybody.'

But Verity hung back and turned to her sister. 'I hope you're pleased for me, Pru?'

She looked wistful, as though she needed this final seal of approval and the older girl couldn't find it in her heart to say anything but, 'Of course. I wish you all the happiness in the world.' She knew, though, how flat the words had sounded. 'Welcome to the Fry family, Oliver.' She held out her hand but found herself drawn towards him and a warm kiss placed on either cheek.

'I'm a lucky man not only to have found Verity but a lovely sister and mother as well.'

It was a clichéd speech but his obvious sincerity made it acceptable. Pru watched the couple following Constance through the orchard to the plundered buffet table. As her mother climbed on a chair to get the attention of the guests, Pru thought that maybe, just maybe, Verity had got it right this time.

The last guests were finally making noises about going and Pru was clearing away the worst of the debris and loading the dish-washer. As she filled the sink with hot, soapy water to deal with the large serving plates, she was hugged from behind by her sister.

'Darling Pru, I really am so happy. It's not just that I love Oliver, he's what I need as well. He knows how to handle me and he understands I can't give up my career.'

Pru removed her soapy hands and found a towel. 'I meant what I said, I really do wish you every happiness but don't think it's all going to be plain sailing. You're going to have to work just as hard at marriage as you do at your cooking.'

Verity looked at her sister more closely then gave her another warm hug. 'I'm so sorry, I really am, and I know I shouldn't have persuaded Simon to come to the party. I swore it would be all right. After all, he gets his meat from you and you seemed to be talking at the Savoy. It really wasn't absolutely my fault, you know? Say you forgive me, please! I won't feel really happy until you do.'

Pru stood very still. So many emotions surged through her. She wanted to throw her arms round her sister and feel again the pure love there had been between them when Verity was a little girl. And she wanted to tell her, really explain to her, what being deeply in love could mean, how it was such a whirlpool of feelings and there were so many ways a couple could hurt each other even while they were in love. And she wanted to ask her if she had any idea what bringing children into the world meant? And had she given thought to what Oliver might need from marriage? She wanted to tell Verity, in fact, that it was time she stopped thinking about Verity and started considering other people. Like Constance, for instance. Had she noticed how thin her mother was getting and how forgetful she was at times? How she found it more and more difficult to do tasks she had once carried out without thinking?

Pru checked her thoughts. Verity was still looking at her, her face a mixture of hope and anxiety.

At last she said, 'Forgiveness is a lot to ask. I've said I'm happy for you and I mean it.' The words sounded sour even to her and as she turned back to the washing up she saw her sister droop. Then Constance entered the kitchen with Oliver and swept Verity into a whirlwind of plans for the wedding.

It seemed that the couple were thinking of getting married quite soon. If this party had caused havoc, Pru thought with wry dismay, what was a wedding going to do?

# Chapter Six

Darina looked at the lambs. 'I wouldn't mind coming back in another life as an animal on your farm,' she said. 'There are far worse fates.'

'Quality of life, that's what it's all about.' Pru gently pushed away an inquisitive nose. 'Happy animals are healthy animals. Their flesh reflects their life here.' She gave a wave encompassing the softly rolling hills that provided a backdrop to the farm, the neat hedges, the deep green grass dotted with grazing animals. 'And everything we give them is just pure goodness. No grain grown on land fed with chemicals so it's stuffed full of chemicals itself. No growth-promoters, no meal made from fish caught in waters polluted with heavy metals. What cocktail is that to wash down with a chicken dish or feed children on? No pharmaceuticals to ward off illnesses that nature herself provides an immunity system to.'

The girl had pushed a hand through her dark curls as she stood protesting her farming philosophy, and Darina thought how attractive she looked with her hair awry and a flush of enthusiasm on her face.

'Where do you get your organic grain?' she asked.

Pru turned to lead the way back to the farmhouse. 'We tried to grow some of it ourselves but the soil isn't really suitable, it's heavy clay, ideal for pasture and that's what we've decided we have to concentrate on. We've got twenty acres of weeds that we hoped would be barley. Going to be a hell of a business getting it back to grass. So we buy from an organic grain mill in Lincolnshire, one of the original members of the Soil Association. They guarantee to supply all we need but we have to estimate a year ahead. I think that's why most supermarkets aren't moving into organic chickens yet, the feed supply is too difficult.'

'Would you like to supply your poultry to a supermarket?'

Pru laughed. 'We couldn't begin to produce the numbers they need. And we sell everything we can rear anyway. I've got to prepare the orders for mailing this afternoon. Would you like to come and see the kitchen and shop?'

'You bet!' Darina followed her guide. 'Are you sure I won't be in the way?' She was keenly aware this was a hard-working operation and that her visit must be interfering with the routine. But Pru seemed delighted to show her around. And during the tour Darina had developed as keen an interest in the girl as in her farm. There was a spontaneity about her, a directness in the way she spoke and dealt with life that was very attractive. But, oh dear, how difficult she could be. There had been a passage with her mother shortly after Darina had arrived.

Constance Fry had welcomed her warmly. 'Make sure Pru shows you everything then come back here, I'm in the middle of checking the orders and ringing suppliers at the moment but I should be through by then and we can have some coffee and a chat. And Verity is coming down some time this morning, she'd love to see you again, perhaps you could stay to lunch?'

Pru scowled at her mother. 'What do you mean, coming down? Why isn't she working?'

Constance hardly seemed to notice the change in her daughter. 'It's so exciting! She's given up her job. Apparently she's received several offers since this competition and Oliver says she should concentrate on building up her career and organising their wedding. And, Pru, if she's not here by twelve, I won't be able to collect Alastair from nursery school, you'll have to.'

'For heaven's sake, Mother, what does it matter if you're not here when Verity arrives?' Pru had burst out, then stumped off in a sulky silence, seeming to expect her visitor to follow.

Darina decided that it would be tactful to make sure she disappeared before twelve. She wondered briefly what had happened to the father of Pru's children. She understood that Pru was known by the Fry surname. Had she been married? One child as a single parent was all too common these days but two children was rather more unusual.

Now she noticed that the tour had taken longer than she had realised. It was approaching twelve and she hadn't had a chance to chat with Mrs Fry yet and find out exactly how the whole organic enterprise had started.

'Damn,' said Pru, 'Alastair will have to be collected soon but there's time to show you the shop before I have to see if that little sister of mine has arrived or if I have to fetch the brat.' She seemed in a better humour over the prospect. 'I take the two boys in the morning, Mother is supposed to collect Alastair before lunch, he only goes for a few hours, and I share the afternoon run with a friend.'

'You and your sister are very different,' commented Darina as she followed her back down the lane to the farm.

'Ah, you don't know, then.'

'Don't know what?'

'That Verity was adopted.'

Did that explain Pru's bursts of resentment? It was certainly why Verity's quicksilver quality was in such contrast to her mother's stoic acceptance of life's cut and thrust and her sister's air of brooding intensity.

'Was that difficult for you?' Darina asked carefully.

'Difficult?'

'You must have been at least seven or eight when it happened, not an easy age to find yourself sharing your nest with a cuckoo.'

Pru stopped without warning beside an enclosure of guinea-fowl set under a wide oak tree and gazed at the little birds, fat ovals of finely marked grey feathers, pointed tails at one end, small, delicate heads at the other.

'I was ten years old when she arrived. And, yes, it was difficult but not in the way you mean. You see, I gradually realised that even though she was adopted, Verity *was* Mother's daughter, is my half-sister.'

Pru paused and the two women watched the guinea-fowls making nervous, tittupping steps before breaking into a collective run like middle-aged women in hobble skirts being chased. Then she said, 'I've never discussed this with anyone before but there was a man, years ago, that Mother had an affair with. He was a schoolmaster. She worked with him to raise funds for a new school building or something. I don't know exactly what happened, I was too young. I just know Dad was desperately unhappy. They had terrible arguments, she and Dad, when they thought I was in bed and asleep. I used to creep down and listen, sit on the stairs outside the living room. Several times I heard her say she was going to leave him, she couldn't stand it any more. That he'd ruined her life. Then he would burst into tears and beg her to stay. And she'd get even more upset and tell him he meant nothing to her and she had to get away from him. And then he'd tell her if she did that, she needn't think he'd let me go and live with her. He'd keep me here.' Pru gave an awkward toss to her head. 'I didn't want her to leave but I would have hated losing Dad much more. He needed me in a way she didn't. We really loved each other, you see, him and me. She didn't love him, or me really.'

'What happened?'

'The man died, he had some sort of accident, and Mother, well, I suppose she had a sort of breakdown. She went to Greece, to stay with Natasha Quantrell, her great friend, who was there with her cousin, Natalie Duke. She stayed for three months. When she came back she was a different person. She was happy in a way I'd never seen her before. And she told me I was going to have a little sister. Then Verity arrived.'

'Arrived?'

'I can't remember exactly how, it seemed one moment she wasn't there and the next she was.'

'And you think your Mother gave birth to her in Greece?'

'Doesn't it make sense? 'Course, I didn't think that at the time – I was too young to understand anything about it all. No, I put it together as I grew up and things sort of gradually fell into place.'

'What about your father, how did he react?'

'Dad? Dad just seemed happy to have Mother back.'

'He didn't resent Verity?'

'Oh no, he loved her, we all did. She was such a lovely baby, never cried, always laughing.' Pru's voice softened. 'When I get cross with her now, when she's being particularly self-centred, I remember how she was then. In the end, you forgive her anything. She never means any harm, it's just that she doesn't think. She doesn't seem to realise that mother is getting older and can't do what she used to. I don't think she'll be able to manage looking after the stock for very much longer. We shall have to try and get some help. I did think at one time that Verity might join us but that's quite out of the question now, what with winning this competition and getting engaged to Oliver. I don't suppose we shall see much of her down here in the future.'

Darina tried to imagine what it must be like to have a completely adorable baby sister who was the light of your mother's life, a mother you felt had never really loved you.

'Do you think Verity takes after her father?' Darina said after a moment.

'Must do, she certainly isn't anything like mother or me. I don't remember much about him but I think he laughed a lot and was rather handsome, bit like a film star. The other girls were always saying their mothers thought he was wonderful.'

'What was your father like?'

Pru was leading the way towards the farmhouse again. 'Dad was quiet, like me. Kept everything inside himself. But it didn't mean he didn't feel things. I think people like him and me, we feel more than other people just because we find it so hard to express ourselves.'

They walked through the farm yard, which was surrounded on three sides by a number of buildings. In the main these were open barns or somewhat rickety-looking outhouses. But those extending on from the farmhouse itself were more elaborate, and a stable-type door bore a notice saying SHOP. There was a window with a bright flower box then another door. Between them stood a couple of white wrought-iron tables with chairs and red and white striped umbrellas. Pru opened the further door and led the way in.

'The stock is really Mother's province. This is where I operate,' she said.

Darina found herself in an area that was divided by a refrigerated shop counter. The far side was obviously for the customers and contained a couple of deep-freezes and a display of organic wines and some prepacked vegetables. On their side of the counter were a very modern-looking digital scales and cash register and a small stainless-steel kitchen area with a commercial oven topped by electric hobs. On it was a huge pan filled with gently steaming minced meat, which gave off a wonderful smell, rich and complex.

'The faggot mixture,' Pru said briefly. 'And there's a ham cooking.' She indicated a square stainless-steel commercial boiler beside the oven then went through an open doorway at the back into a further area. 'Do you want a quick look at the chill room?'

Pru opened a heavy door and cold air fell out. Inside was as big as the room outside. Down one wall were hung quarters of beef, sides of lamb and a pig. On the opposite wall were shelves stacked with cooked gammons, smaller cuts of meat, vacuum-packed slices of bacon and ham and a tray of cooked pies.

'All ready to start packing the mail orders,' she explained.

'Do you use Datapost?'

'No!' Pru was scornful. 'They just aren't geared up for this business. We use a private service that collects and guarantees delivery anywhere in the UK within twenty-four hours.'

'What about temperature control?' Darina moved gratefully from the chill of the refrigerated room to the warmth outside.

'The boxes are all lined with insulating polystyrene and once they leave here they are constantly on the move. It all seems to work very well.'

Darina looked round at all the equipment, at the butcher's block, the commercial mincer, meat-slicer, vacuum-packer. She thought of the stove and boiler in the area behind the shop. 'Quite an investment you've got here.'

Pru gave a grimace. 'I'll say. The vacuum-packer alone cost two thousand pounds. But it's worth every penny. We've built it all up gradually. You should have seen it when we first started, talk about cottage industry. But you can't do things like that now. All the new EC regulations are enough to frighten anyone off. For a time we wondered if we would be able to afford to comply with them.'

'But you did?'

'We asked the Environmental Health Officer round to look at our operation and tell us exactly what we needed.' Pru grinned suddenly. 'He was stunned, I don't think anyone had ever done that before, usually he's following up complaints, not being asked for his advice.'

'And?'

'And he said there was really very little we needed to change in order to be within the present parameters. But we have to watch new directives. Let's see if Verity's car is here.'

Standing on a concrete area in front of a large barn was a small Metro. 'Verity's,' said Pru briefly. 'And Mother's car isn't here so she must have gone to collect Alastair. Heavens, has our fame spread to the Continent?' Beside the smart Metro was a battered old Renault with a French registration. 'If it's a customer, I can't think where she can be, unless Verity has taken her inside.' Pru went towards the farmhouse. Darina said she ought to be going but Pru wouldn't hear of it. 'Mother will be so disappointed if you're not here when she gets back, she's been looking forward to talking to you.'

There was no sign of anyone in the large farmhouse kitchen. Pru moved along a passage and into a pleasant room with a conservatory at one end. Sitting in the cool shade of the room were Verity and the visitor from France.

As Pru and Darina entered, Verity sprang to her feet and her guest looked round. Darina had to exercise fierce control not to betray her shock at the dreadful scars on the woman's face.

'Pru, have you met Natasha Quantrell?' Verity said, her voice almost squeaking with excitement. 'She's Natalie Duke's cousin! They lived together in France. She's going to tell me all about how Natalie wrote her books and about her cooking, everything!'

The woman's hands trembled on the arms of her chair, drawing attention to scars even more horrific than those on her face. She seemed to have withdrawn inside herself. Darina thought what an ordeal it must be for her to have to meet so many people. She ought to leave but that might suggest to Natasha Quantrell her looks had proved too embarrassing to cope with. And Darina was as fascinated as Verity with the Natalie Duke connection.

She went forward. 'I'm so delighted to meet you. I'm afraid I'm another great admirer of your cousin's work.'

'Darina Lisle is a cookery writer too!' Verity danced towards her, full of life, looks and enthusiasm, a bitter contrast to the scarred woman. 'She was one of the judges in that competition I was telling you about.'

Natasha Quantrell's facial muscles moved, impossible to tell if it was involuntary or an attempt at a smile, then her head jerked and her hands twitched restlessly.

'And this is my sister, Pru.'

'Prunella, isn't it?' Natasha Quantrell said with sudden interest, her body stilled for a moment.

'Nobody has called me that since Dad died.'

'I met you often when you were a little girl. Before,' her voice broke for a moment then she drew a quick breath and tried again. 'Before Natalie and I left England. Do you remember?'

Pru nodded. 'And I remember what friends you were with Mother.'

'Still are!' came Constance's voice from the door. 'What a grand surprise, Natasha. Sorry I wasn't here when you arrived, I had to pick up my grandson. Verity wouldn't come with me, said she wanted to wait and see Miss Lisle.'

A little boy dashed in, then stopped short at the sight of Natasha and looked at her closely. Pru moved swiftly but too late.

'Why's that woman's face funny?' her son asked in a piercing whisper. Pru grabbed at his shoulder.

'Off to clean your hands, my lad, now!' She marched him out of the room. From the corridor could be heard Alastair's louder repetition of his question followed by a cry of protest.

It was impossible to know if Natasha Quantrell had absorbed the small scene or not, nothing registered on her mask of a face. 'I must go,' she said baldly.

'I was just going to ask you to stay for lunch!' Constance protested.

'Yes,' cried Verity. 'There's so much I want to talk to you about.'

Natasha took the girl's hand. 'Come and visit me and I'll tell you all about Natalie and how she wrote her books. Come soon, come tomorrow.'

Verity smiled at her. 'I will, promise.' She leaned forward and gently kissed one of the scarred cheeks. Natasha's hand came up towards the girl's face but then, with one of the nervous movements that seemed characteristic of her, she jerked it away.

Constance came forward. 'I'll see you to your car if you are sure you won't stay. Did you come over for anything special, or just to see us?' Her normally abrupt manner had softened, she slipped a hand under the other woman's arm.

'Why did I come?' her friend asked vaguely. 'I don't know. There was something but I can't remember what, talking with Verity has made me forget. Constance, I have to talk to you but not now. Now there's something else I've got to do, something I must check.'

The two girls watched Constance Fry steer her friend through the door.

'How awful!' breathed Verity as the two women disappeared down the corridor.

'What happened?' asked Darina.

'Oh, Mother told us the other day. You remember Natalie Duke died in a fire at her home in Brittany? Well, Natasha got burned trying to rescue her. Imagine how brave she must have been!' Verity flung herself down in a chair. 'It must be so terrible for her now, looking like that and being alone, without her cousin, they'd lived together for years, you know. Oh, how wonderful to be able to talk to her about Natalie Duke! Do you think I can absorb some of her genius through Natasha?'

'You really want to be a cookery writer, don't you?' Darina was both amused and impressed by the girl's intensity.

'I want to do it all, write, demonstrate, make television programmes, everything.'

'And you can combine all that with marriage?'

'Oh, yes,' the girl said blithely. 'That's what girls do these days. Husbands don't expect you to run round them any more. I was telling Natasha all about Oliver and how much he encourages me. I will work from home, you see, and recipe testing means there should always be lots of food to eat.'

Darina forbore to mention that recipe testing didn't always provide the sort of meal husbands expected. Six fruit jellies and an old English trifle, the starting point for an article on summer puddings, wasn't exactly what a hungry man needed for supper, nor would it provide a three-course dinner party.

'Anyway,' continued Verity, 'he likes to eat out, which helps me because I can get ideas and it means I don't have to wash up! And he really does want me to follow my own career. He's quite often abroad, you see, and he thinks I might get bored if I'm just on my own.'

'You can't travel with him?' Darina thought Oliver sounded a canny fellow but that he mightn't quite appreciate how much Verity could be taken over by a successful career.

'He says he works so hard it wouldn't be any fun for me, it's a couple of days here, a couple of days there, you see.'

Constance came back into the room. She was upset. 'I tried to drive Natasha home, she looked so dreadful. Much worse than when I saw her the other day. But she wouldn't hear of it, said she was fine. I don't think she's recovered nearly as much as she thinks.'

Pru came running into the room. 'The pigs are out. I saw them from the bathroom window!'

'Oh, no!' said Verity. 'Not again!'

'Come on, quick,' said Constance. 'After them!'

# Chapter Seven

'I never knew pigs could be so wily!' Darina finished her tale of their Houdini feats with Simon in fits of laughter.

'They are intelligent, intensely curious and have absolutely no herding instinct at all.' He sounded deeply appreciative of the pigs' independent attitude and the dark eyes sparkled above his chef's whites.

There's a particular glow of satisfaction that comes from making someone laugh, really laugh. Darina felt it begin to warm the cold space that had lived under her ribs since William had left. 'You can say that again! We had to catch each one separately. According to Pru this hot spell has dried out the ground so much and their little trotters are so dry themselves, the electric fence isn't earthing when they touch it, so, bingo, no electric shock and they're off.'

They were in the restaurant's private sitting-room upstairs, an attractive room cluttered with paper. Sheaves had moved out in a pincer movement from the desk in one corner to cover sofa and chairs and end in a reckless pile on a low coffee-table. Even the walls seemed to have been invaded; they sported a rash of framed menus and certificates attesting to Simon Chapman's skills.

On a round table in front of one of the dormer windows was his draft cookery book. The idea had been that Darina would go through it while he organised his mise-en-place for the evening meal then they would have a couple of hours' discussion before he needed to start cooking.

Darina had bumped into Simon at Fry's Farm that morning. She had gone over to collect some meat she needed. After her tour of the farm the previous week, she had gone home with several cuts and had been so impressed with the quality of the meat, its taste and texture, she couldn't bring herself to buy any other. The shop wasn't open but Pru had said she could always ring and pick up meat at any time by arrangement. The farmer met Darina in the yard.

'I've just finished preparing a mammoth meat order for a caterer with a rush job. I packed up most of your requirements at the same time but you said you wanted some garlic sausages and I shan't be able to get round to making those until this afternoon, will a packet from the freezer do as well, I only put them in last week?'

Darina said they would do fine. Pru fetched the sausages then invited her in for a cup of iced coffee.

She accepted gratefully; without any wind it seemed unfair the way dust got in the lungs, just as it seemed unfair to complain about the continuing heat.

In the kitchen Verity was making notes at the big table. She welcomed Darina with an excited squeal, not unlike the pigs they'd chased. She wore the same look as when she gave her triumphant boxer's salute after winning the cookery competition. 'I had the most fabulous day yesterday,' she cried.

'She'll talk your head off if you're not careful,' said Pru with some asperity. 'She's spent practically all the last week with Natasha Quantrell discussing cooking and food.'

'Oh, it has been wonderful! She's told me all about how Natalie Duke worked, how the two of them would go round the countryside eating local food and going to markets, talking to the women selling produce, asking what they did with it, getting invitations to homes to see dishes being cooked. Natalie used to make notes the whole time and Natasha would take photographs.'

'Did she always accompany her cousin?' Darina took the glass of iced coffee topped with a generous spoon of double cream that Pru offered her and sipped at it slowly.

'Nearly always, she said. Sometimes Natalie wanted to be on her own and sometimes Natasha said she couldn't face another food trip but mostly she enjoyed it. She said Natalie had such an instinct for getting on terms with all these women. Even in Greece, though she couldn't speak much of the language, she knew just what was the right question. And Natasha said she and Natalie would talk about the food together, that helped Natalie crystallise her thoughts and information. Often they were offered hospitality, which helped with the expenses, but other times they stayed at sleazy little pensions and hotels. On your own, Natasha said, it would have been dreadful but when there were two of you together it wasn't too bad.'

' "Natasha said" is now a dreaded phrase in this household,' Pru commented drily.

Darina had every sympathy with Verity's enthusiasm. Natalie Duke had had a unique talent for conveying the spirit of a nation's taste-buds as well as the basic details of the cooking that had sustained its inhabitants for centuries. Talking to her cousin would be almost as good as talking to her.

'I hope you don't tire her, you know what Mother said.'

'Of course I don't, Pru. She says she enjoys talking to me, that it relaxes her. And she's much better than when she came round here that day I first met her.' Verity paused and frowned, a puckering of her face that threw into sudden prominence her bony nose, unbalancing the classic sweep of cheek-bones and jaw line. 'Except yesterday. We had the most marvellous cake for tea, Darina, basically honey but there was another flavour I couldn't identify. I was just going to ask her what it was when the telephone rang and by the time she came back, I'd forgotten because I'd found a copy of a Natalie Duke book on the kitchen dresser that I'd never seen before and I had to ask about that. Did you know she wrote some little books for a firm of spice merchants? All about the different ingredients they imported? With marvellous recipes. I must try and collect them. Natasha said it might be possible to get them from cookery book specialists who sell secondhand books, they're out of print now. She said she would try to find me some catalogues, Natalie used to collect cookery books. Isn't it awful, they were all burned in that dreadful fire! But next time Natasha's in France she said she'd look and see if there were some in the house, she thought there might be.'

'I'm not surprised she gets exhausted if you grill her like that,' protested her sister.

'I don't grill her,' Verity was indignant. 'I told you, she enjoys talking to me, discussing Natalie and cookery writing with someone intelligently interested. She says I obviously know a great deal about food. But she did look tired during tea. Her face was sort of drained and the scars all prominent. I'm sure she misses Natalie.' Verity started chewing on her pencil, her face dreamy, obviously thinking of some detail Natasha had told her about her new role model.

Darina thought of the cookery writer and her devoted cousin. What an idyllic relationship it sounded as though they had enjoyed. Happier than most marriages! She wondered just how memory was adjusting the truth for Natasha, surely it couldn't have been easy for the two of them to live together all those years? Surely claustrophobia would have set in? Natalie had her work but Natasha seemed to have had nothing but her cousin. If she really had devoted herself entirely to the cookery writer, no wonder she was so devastated by her death.

Verity stopped chewing. 'Oh, Pru, I forgot, did you know Simon is here?'

'Simon? I thought he wasn't going to get his meat at Fry's Farm any more.'

'Oh, he didn't mean what he said at the party, you know he can't get your quality anywhere else round here. In fact I've been delivering his orders for the last week to give the aggro a chance to quieten down. But he hasn't come for meat, he wanted to talk to Mother.'

'Damn and hell! I told him it was no go! What on earth is the point?'

Verity looked unusually sober. 'I think he's getting desperate, he said something about his partner being really up the creek now. I failed completely to interest Oliver in backing the restaurant, not surprising I suppose, he knows nothing about Simon.' Verity was all reasonableness, Pru full of sulky ire.

Then from down the corridor outside the kitchen came Constance Fry's voice, dismissive and contemptuous.

'I've told you, Simon, you have no right to ask me and I won't do it. Now, I would be grateful if you would drop the subject. You know how I feel about you and your treatment of this family and I'm surprised at your gall. See yourself out!'

A door slammed in the distance. After a moment or two Simon Chapman entered the kitchen, a little patch of white beside each nostril flagging a barely contained anger. He stopped as he realised he wasn't alone but almost immediately had himself under control and flashed a quick grin. 'Well, my three favourite girls! Pru, I'm afraid you were right, don't bother saying I told you so. Darina, this is wonderful, I was going to give you a ring and ask if you couldn't take a serious look at the awful mess I'm making of this book.'

So then she'd agreed to go over that afternoon. Any excuse to put off working on her own book for a few more hours; the strain of undiluted effort was telling on her.

While Simon was in his restaurant kitchen preparing his ingredients for the evening's meals, she gave her attention to the badly written pages. At one stage she had gone down to ask him to sort out a particularly tangled set of instructions but found the kitchen empty, a half-chopped bunch of parsley on a board, hazelnut meringue rounds cooling on a wire rack. She had stayed there for five or ten minutes, looking through more of the recipes, thinking he'd be back any moment, then returned to the sitting-room. She went back a little later just as he entered the kitchen carrying some boxes of eggs.

'Ran out,' he said simply.

'I could easily have gone, why didn't you send me?' protested Darina.

'And interrupt your work? Your time is far too valuable!' He gave a wide smile, interpreted the puzzling scrawl then pushed her upstairs again.

Finally she sat back in her chair, impressed with the imagination behind the recipes, daunted by the expertise called for and appalled by the slapdash way they had been caught on paper. But she could understand his difficulties.

Writing a cookery book, Darina had found, was not the doddle some people seemed to think. 'Oh,' they said, 'you won't have any trouble with that. Just got to find enough recipes and string them all together. I've always thought it's something I could do, you know? Write a really sensible cookbook with recipes people actually want to cook. If only I had the time!'

After a few months of this, Darina stopped telling people what she was working on. If only, she thought grimly, they would actually try to sell a book with all those recipes they thought people actually wanted to cook. First they would find that publishers didn't want 'general' cookbooks, they wanted 'expert' books, 'specialist' books, books by celebrity names. *Microwave Gourmet Vegetarian Dishes from Tibet* by a TV chat-show host she was sure would find an instant publisher.

And once having sold your idea for the cookbook you felt the public really needed, your hard work started. The refining of recipes, the testing, the careful setting out of the ingredients and instructions, the mind-wringing business of finding something interesting and different to say to introduce each dish or place it in context. She was sure it wouldn't take much more imagination to write a novel.

'I love your ideas,' she said to Simon when he joined her carrying a pot of strong tea and two mugs.

'You're giving me the good news first, I know.' He filled the mugs and sat down, flicking dispiritedly at the piles of loose paper.

'The dishes sound great and I bet all the recipes are ones you've used again and again so you know exactly how they work?'

He nodded, sipping the tea, his dark eyes watching her as she talked.

'I'm creating half mine as I go along. Recipes that work well for two, trying to use inexpensive and easy to get ingredients for dishes that don't need long preparation, will cook quickly and not leave lots of left-overs. Or can combine preparation for two meals.'

He looked interested. 'Lots of these recipes could qualify.' He tapped the pages.

Darina laughed. 'You think so because you cook to order and can produce the dishes quickly. But you forget the hours of preparation, the care that's gone into finding the right suppliers, the variety of ingredients you have at your fingertips, the stocks you prepare. No housewife wants to buy five different vegetables and three sorts of fish to produce one meal for two!' She picked up a recipe for a Seafood Pot-au-Feu.

The chef sighed. 'I knew the whole idea was hopeless from the start. I can't think why the publishers approached me or why I was stupid enough to take the money they offered.'

'Don't get depressed, your approach isn't wrong, it just won't fit into the sort of book I'm writing. What I was trying to get across was that I am having to spend a lot of time making sure that I've got the recipes absolutely right, doing lots of testing. You've already done that. All you need now is to write them down in an accepted form and work out the alternative measurements.'

'You mean I have to use both imperial and metric?'

'I'm afraid so. I keep expecting imperial to disappear altogether, some schools now don't use it at all, but for the moment there are still women clinging to their old-fashioned scales and publishers daren't ignore them. Has the American market been mentioned to you?'

'I don't think so.'

'That's a relief, they use volume measurements over there, cups and spoons, and working those out is a real pain. I hate it. Chopping mushrooms and measuring their volume instead of just weighing the things! And I always think it makes the shopping so much more difficult. Why not just say a hundred grammes or four ounces?'

'Much simpler on the equipment, though, every household has a cup. It must be a hangover from pioneer days, I can just see the covered wagon and Mrs Overlander measuring out the flour and water for the buckwheat cakes cooked on the open fire.' His enthusiasm had returned, the black eyes snapped with interest. Then he glanced at the paper-strewn table and sighed deeply again. 'I can't see your average housewife being interested in these, Mrs Overlander wouldn't give them the time of day.'

'Ah, she now lives in a modern house with a space-age kitchen, eats out in expensive restaurants and wants dinner parties that will be a knock-out. She is going to buy this book in the sure and certain knowledge that it will equip her to get one over all her rival hostesses.'

'And will it?' Simon eyed her with fascination.

'It will give her lots of ideas, perhaps three recipes she will attempt and maybe one that will go into her repertoire. But she will place it in a prominent position on her coffee-table to start with, then on her cookery bookshelf, and every time she glances at it, she will be filled with desire and confidence.'

Simon read slowly through a couple of pages. 'What about introductions to the recipes. The publishers said I could write what I wanted.'

'And what would you like to say about them?'

'Not a lot!'

'Then don't. It's nice if you can give an idea of a recipe's background, or a comment on a particular technique that will help the amateur, or offer a hint on preparation, but with a book like this it's the recipes that matter.'

'And you think they're all right?'

'I think they look absolutely marvellous. And judging by the meals I've eaten here, I'm sure they will taste as good as they read.'

'Ah, there's the rub. As you say yourself, they don't read good.'

'A minor detail.' Darina lied through her teeth. All the recipes needed complete rewriting. Simon had no conception of the average housewife's ignorance of cooking techniques. No idea how they could misread seemingly straightforward instructions. But it wouldn't be difficult, just tedious, unless, like her, you rather enjoyed creating clear-cut instructions that read well. It was to cheer Simon up that she launched into her account of the pig-catching activities she had become involved in the previous week.

'And you even got Verity chasing them?' he asked as their laughter gradually subsided.

'Absolutely. She was quicker than any of us!'

'Definitely a fast little number,' he said slyly.

Darina looked at his twinkling dark eyes, the amused creases in his face, her head slightly on one side.

Before she could speak, the telephone rang. Simon picked up the portable instrument he'd placed on the table with the tea. Almost immediately the humorous lines disappeared and his expression became one of concern. 'Hang in there,' he said finally, 'I'm coming right over.'

He replaced the receiver on the table. For a moment he said nothing, a mixture of shock and something indefinable in his eyes. Then he looked at Darina. 'That was Pru, Constance has been killed.'

# Chapter Eight

Detective Constable Pat James accompanied Detective Inspector Grant to the scene of the accident.

They crouched beside the crumpled pile of clothes topped with white hair, now dark and sticky with blood. The policewoman watched as the inspector checked there was no pulse. Her face was calm and her manner matter of fact but inwardly she raged.

Hit-and-run drivers made her angrier than almost anything else. It was the cowardice, the inability to face up to the consequences of their carelessness rather than the carelessness itself that got to her. Anyone who spent large amounts of time driving around knew that for many accidents it was a case of there but for the grace of God. Especially in these narrow lanes.

'We'll have to wait for the doc but there's no doubt she's dead,' said the inspector. They both rose. Pat wiped the sweat off her forehead – the sun was still fierce despite the fact that it was late afternoon – and looked around, assessing the scene.

The road was more than a lane but could hardly be termed a highway. It connected various small settlements with Lamington and Charlton. Both hovered between qualifying as a large village or a small town. As a direct route from one place to the other the road was useless, meandering as it did round nasty bends and including a dog-leg that doubled the distance between the two places. Local traffic was not great. More than four cars an hour meant it was the rush hour.

A bicycle lay a little way from the victim, one buckled wheel sticking up in the air. It was a large, old model. The inspector looked carefully at it. 'Seems to have met something coming face on, it's the front wheel that's suffered the damage. The victim was probably flung from the machine by the force of the impact and landed on that verge.'

Both officers inspected the surface of the road, paying particular attention to its edge. 'The weather's been too dry,' said Pat. 'There's no mud that could capture tyre marks, the earth is like concrete. Could just be a chance of a dust print but I can't see any.'

'That'll be for the SOCO boys to check. They should be here shortly.'

Together with the doctor to certify death, the scene-of-crime officers had been sent for; shortly the quiet lane would be swarming with officials. But for the moment it was just her, the inspector, and the police constable who had first been alerted to the accident and was now roping off the road. Grant set off towards him, telling Pat to wait where she was and stop any traffic coming down the road the other way.

'You found anything?' A middle-aged man in short-sleeved shirt and faded lightweight trousers secured with binder twine came round the bend in the road, a black and white collie at his heels, a stick in his hand.

'It was I found her,' the farmer said helpfully. He stood patiently by the side of the road, his dog looking curiously at the limp figure on the grass. 'Them's my cows.' He pointed over the hedge at the herd of dark cattle gathered round a gate further down the road, beyond the body. They were lowing, heads being lifted and lowered, heavy bodies slowly pushing against each other, tails swishing at flies. 'Time for their milking, see. Came along here and saw her.' He regarded the body doubtfully. 'Looked dead to me but thought I better tell someone.'

'Yes, right,' said Pat, slightly mesmerised by his slow but steady flow of words. 'Did you see any vehicles on the road?'

'Vehicles? Cars, you mean? Tractors?'

'Anything.'

The dog's curiosity got the better of him and he advanced towards the crumpled figure on the verge. 'Come back here!' Nothing slow about that command or the way the stick was raised. The dog slunk back to his master and crouched down by his legs, eyes flicking nervously from side to side.

'Vehicles.' The word was rolled round the mouth as though it was a piece of food that could be tasted. 'Can't say I did. Nothing much goes along this road, see. Only us as lives here uses it. Main traffic between Lamington and Charlton takes the A road.'

'Where's your farm?'

He pointed back down the way he had come and Pat could just see the chimneys of a house rising above the hedges.

'What were you doing before you came down to see to your cows?'

'What was I doing?' More thought. 'I were up the forty-acre field.'

'And where's your forty-acre field?'

'Up beyond.' He indicated an area behind a small copse.

'Can you see the road from there?' The answer seemed obvious but the question had to be asked.

'See the road? Nah, don't suppose I could.' The farmer scratched his head but failed to stimulate further thought.

'Do you know the victim?' Pat asked, hoping this time he would manage to refrain from repeating the gist of her query.

'That's Mrs Fry.' There was faint surprise she had to ask.

Pat waited a few minutes but no additional information came forth. 'Does she live near here?'

'That's her farm, back along. 'Bout half a mile down the lane.'

'Does she have any family?'

'Family?' Pat held on to her patience and was rewarded. 'There's Pru, her daughter. Run the farm together, they do. Don't know what Pru's going to do without her ma, team they are.'

'So she's a widow?'

'Widow? Pru? Nah.' Then light dawned. 'Oh, ah, see what you mean. Well, you're right there. Tom died 'bout fifteen year back. No,' he paused and scratched his head again, thinking deeply, 'I tell a lie, can't have been more 'n thirteen year. I remember 'cause that were year I won ploughing competition 'gainst Tom at Show, not more 'n six weeks afore he died. An' I were saying to Mary only a few weeks back, it would be a bloody miracle if I won again and it were thirteen year since I won last.' He paused once more. 'Shock it were, Tom going like that.'

'What is the name of Mrs Fry's farm?'

He looked at her in astonishment. 'Why, Fry's Farm.'

Of course, why on earth had she thought it would be called Meadow Farm, or Hillside Farm or any one of a number of other location-based names?

The farmer started walking off down the road towards his cows, the dog following, skirting the dead body but still sticking out an inquisitive head towards it.

'Excuse me!' Pat called after him as she finished scribbling in her notebook and noticed his retreating back. 'Can you please give me your name and address?' She added these to her notes. 'And, look, I'm sorry but you can't bring your cattle along here, not yet.'

'Eh, I can't? They gotta be milked, you know. They're late as it is, what with me going home to phone and having to come back again. Need one of these here car phones, could call it a cow phone!' He cackled heartily.

Pat gave a polite smile. 'Well, as I said, I'm sorry but you can see that we can't have a whole herd of cows charging down this road, not before we've had a good look at it. Can't you?' she ended doubtfully.

'Unnerstand what you're saying but cows gotta be milked. Can't do it in a field, not these days.' He was resolute in his insistence.

'Isn't there some other way you can take them to your farm?'

More scratching of his head and a long look around the terrain. 'Well, could take them up the lane.' He indicated a turning beyond his field which seemed to lead to a clump of trees before petering out. 'Back through the wood and along river. It's a tidy step round, though.' He was clearly reluctant to have to drive his cattle home that way and, looking at the route he had outlined, Pat could understand why.

'We really would be most grateful.' She tried to make her eyes look as large as possible and hoped her diminutive stature would have its usual effect of bringing out any chivalrous instincts that existed in the opposite sex. She didn't want to have to call to the inspector to add his authority to hers. 'There could be evidence here of who hit Mrs Fry and I'm sure you're anxious to see whoever was responsible caught!'

At that his face lightened. 'You're right there, lass. I'm right sorry it were Mrs Fry. Think a lot of her we do.'

And it was 'Mrs Fry' but 'Tom' for her husband, Pat noted, watching the figure walk steadily off towards the cows. She turned back to the corpse and wondered how long before the doctor appeared on the scene. It was then she saw the hat. A supple straw with a large brim, it was lying at the bottom of the dry ditch beside the grassy verge, as though it had floated off at the moment of impact. Pat left it where it was.

Soon the quiet country road was crowded. There were numerous police vehicles, an ambulance and the doctor's car. Distances were measured, the ground scoured for betraying marks, a video record taken. A little while later the pathologist was giving Detective Inspector Grant the results of his preliminary examination of the dead woman.

'Look at this stone.' He pointed to a jagged rock more than half concealed by long grass. 'And feel the dent in her head.' The doctor's hand gently probed in the sticky mass of hair.

'I think I'll leave that to you,' said Grant with distaste. 'But let me see if I understand exactly what you're saying. She hit her head on that stone, that's what actually killed her?'

'Have to leave it to the autopsy to confirm, of course, but I'd say it's almost certain.'

'Hmm . . . ' Grant looked around him. 'The bike definitely appears to have received a blow but you say she doesn't seem to have been hit herself?'

'Not as far as I can see at the moment.'

'So if it hadn't been for that stone, she might well have got away with nothing more serious than bruising?'

'Can't say that,' the pathologist protested.

'How about when it happened?'

'About an hour and a half ago, as far as I can judge at the moment, but it's a very hot day and it could have been earlier.'

Grant looked at his watch. 'So that would have been around three thirty p.m.' He glanced round and called Pat James over. 'Constable, you've got the name and address of the victim, haven't you? And the next of kin? You'd better inform her.'

Pat drove slowly down the road. It was only a few minutes before she saw a large sign for FRY'S FARM – ORGANIC MEAT. She turned up the long drive and eventually reached the farmhouse and its attendant buildings.

She sat for a brief moment after turning off the engine, looking at the wisteria hanging from the front of the old stone house. This was the bit she hated more than anything else. But Pat wasn't one to agonise over what she had to do. The thing was to get on and do it, the sooner the job was tackled, the sooner it would be done.

No one answered the doorbell. She looked around and then

noticed a signpost pointing the way to a shop. Pat walked round, fishing out her identity card and skirting a tricycle and boy's bike left carelessly on the ground.

There were no customers in the small shop nor was there anyone behind the counter, a chilled cabinet packed with appetising-looking meat goods. But from a room off to the rear came the sounds of a fierce argument.

'And I can't see why you can't help more. You've given up your job, you've nothing to do as far as I can see, and Mother really needs to take things more easily.' The voice was brusque, insistent.

'You don't understand,' came a tearful response, 'I've got to get together some ideas for a book, there's the wedding to organise and I could be needed for a promotion at any time. Of course I'll help when I can but I can't promise to be constantly around.'

Pat James looked at the message on the counter asking customers to please ring. She put out her hand, then hesitated and held back from picking up the little brass bell.

'You're selfish through and through, that's your trouble. You never have thought about anybody else and I'm beginning to think you never will. Here's me trying to handle the shop as well as the meat preparation side because Dottie's mother's ill and there's Mother working her fingers to the bone with the animals and all you do is swan around with high-faluting ideas about writing books and promoting plastic spoons. Just where have you *been* all afternoon? Oh, you make me sick!'

'I do want to help, Pru, really I do! I just didn't realise. Let me do those sausages for you.'

Pat abandoned any thought of ringing the bell. She edged her way round the end of the counter towards the open doorway leading to the rear room.

'OK, then.' The bitter voice lost a little of its bile. 'And perhaps after that you can collect the boys, they're swimming with the Nolans.'

Two young women were standing either side of a large mincer that was spewing its contents into a long skin snaking off its nose. Pat could see immediately it was the older who had been tearing off such a strip. A white cloth hat covered her head, a little peak softening the severe effect but doing little to shade the tired eyes. Her mouth was firmly folded away, the thin lips pressed together.

The younger woman, a girl really, looked tearful, her eyes full of moisture, a pink flush round the nose, the lower lip pouting slightly. Pat's presence went completely unnoticed.

She cleared her throat.

'I'm sorry,' she said. Before either could speak she held up her identity card. 'Detective Constable James, I'm looking for Pru Fry?' She looked towards the older girl, confident of the identification.

'That's me. What's happened, the pigs aren't on the road, are they?' Anxiety sharpened her voice again.

Pat shook her head. 'Is there somewhere we can go?' she asked, glancing around her at the butchery equipment and the obscene length of sausage. The last thing she wanted was to have to break her news in these surroundings.

Pru Fry seemed about to say something then shut her mouth. Without a word she pushed past Pat and led the way out of the shop and towards the farmhouse, the policewoman following. After a moment's hesitation, the other girl abandoned the sausage-making and brought up the rear.

A few minutes later they were in a big country kitchen. 'Take a seat,' said Pru Fry. She pulled out a pine chair and sat herself at the scrubbed table, waiting for Pat to do the same. 'This is my sister, Verity,' she added as the other girl pulled out another chair. 'Now, perhaps you'll tell me what all this is about.' She pulled off the white mob cap as she spoke, releasing short dark hair that curled strongly, giving a new life to her face. A fresh and disturbing thought struck her. 'It isn't anything to do with the boys, is it?'

Pat said no, it was nothing to do with the boys. She looked around for the kettle, saw it on the back of an Aga and went and fetched it without permission. As she filled it, she wondered how they could bear to have the stove going in this heat. But the kitchen, facing north, wasn't overly hot. She lifted one of the heavy lids and placed the kettle on the hob. Only then did she turn back to the two women. Pru Fry's fingers were drumming on the table, Verity Fry sat quietly, her eyes following the policewoman's every action.

'I'm afraid your mother has had an accident,' Pat said gently.

'Accident?' Whatever they might have been expecting, it wasn't this.

'It looks like a hit-and-run driver. She was riding a bicycle.'

'Oh, God!' Pru Fry rose urgently from the table. 'Where is she? Has she been taken to hospital? I must go to her.'

'I'm afraid,' said Pat again, 'it's worse than that.'

'Worse?'

Both girls looked at her blankly, then Verity gave a brief cry and buried her face in her hands. Pru's face set in hard lines, her lips thinned to vanishing point. 'You mean, she's dead,' she said flatly. It was a statement of fact, not a query.

'I really am very sorry.'

Pat looked around again, saw cupboards near the sink, found a teapot and a packet of tea and made a strong brew. She brought it with a bag of sugar to the table, found spoons and milk then poured out three mugs, adding a generous helping of sugar to each. 'Have some tea,' she said, placing a mug in front of each girl.

The girl called Verity was crying softly, the older daughter, Pru, still seemed to be in a state of shock. She picked up the mug automatically, looked at it, replaced it on the table, then changed her mind and drank some of the sweet steaming liquid. 'Mother?' she said at last. 'Oh, Mother!' Dry-eyed she looked across to where Pat had now seated herself at the table. 'She only went down to the Bailey, I don't understand, there's never any traffic on that road.'

'Where's the Bailey?' asked Pat gently, getting out her notebook.

Her question was ignored.

Pru pushed back her chair sharply. She rose as though it was impossible for her to sit still and walked over to the door then came back to her sister, putting a hand on one of her shoulders. 'Oh, Verity, what are we to do?'

Verity raised a tear-stained face. 'I wish Oliver was here!' she cried. Then, 'Ring Simon, tell him. He'll come, I know.'

'Simon? I can't!'

'Then I will.' Verity half rose in her chair but was immediately pushed back by her sister.

'No, I'll do it.' Pat watched her go to a wall telephone, dial a number and without introduction give the bald facts.

'He's coming right over.' The girl sagged against the counter that ran along the wall beneath the telephone. It was covered with papers, piles of files and account books.

Pat took over the mug of tea, placed it in Pru's hands, waited while the girl took another drink, then gently steered her back to the table. But when she tried to seat her in the same chair, Pru seemed to take hold of herself and went instead to her weeping sister and took her in her arms so that Verity was sobbing awkwardly against her shoulder.

Pat sat herself down, quietly sipped her tea and looked round the kitchen. It seemed to have been modernised at the height of the craze for stripped pine. Units had been made of new wood but the long counter and a large old dresser seemed antique. They and the table and chairs looked as though they could have been here for many years. But what should have been a flagstoned floor was finished in a chequered vinyl. Easier to clean, thought Pat approvingly, her own little house on the outskirts of Frome had been modernised to within an inch of its life before she had bought it at a rock bottom, building society repossession price. She loved its easy to maintain features and felt no regret for the loss of the Victorian cornices or the original fireplaces. Yes, wood fires were nice but they caused a lot of dust and the gas central heating was so much more convenient. The last thing Pat did each morning before leaving for work, the first thing she did after she returned, no matter how late, was to complete a piece of housework. Only by constant attention could the house be kept to the level of cleanliness and tidiness she felt comfortable with.

It didn't look as though the Fry house was run with the same efficiency. The wooden units had lost their surface sheen, dust lay on the dresser and the only free surface in the whole kitchen was the table she was sitting at. Windowsills were crammed with plants, bits of china and the odd cat. The draining-board carried a load of dishes, clean but left to dry. The worktops had a fringe of free area in front of ranks of canisters and storage jars, processors, mixers, grinders, tins of this and jars of that. Pat longed to strip and reorganise the whole lot.

She glanced down at her notebook. The victim had been on her way to the Bailey, Pru Fry had said. Now, where was the Bailey? She looked towards the grieving daughters. Verity Fry's sobs were subsiding. In a few minutes she might be able to get the basic details, the main questioning could be left until later but there were some facts that needed to be established now.

There was the sound of a car in the yard. Bother, thought Pat with irritation, this was no doubt the Simon that had promised to come. A dark man in his middle thirties entered the room. Then, following him, Pat recognised with disbelief the girl that had once before dogged her detecting footsteps, Darina Lisle.

# Chapter Nine

They had to drive the long way round to the farm; a Diversion notice blocked the direct route from Lamington. They were in Darina's car because Simon's was playing up. He directed Darina along the main road then up an extremely narrow lane so that they came out on the minor road just beyond the farm. Apart from giving the directions, he sat silently, biting his underlip.

Darina drove competently and quickly. As they arrived at the yard, she suggested perhaps it would be better if she dropped Simon and left, she didn't want to intrude on the Fry girls' grief. He clutched her arm, an accident victim holding his life-support system.

'Don't go, Pru will need a woman around, I don't know how she's going to manage without Constance.'

Pru had struck Darina as an extremely capable and resilient young woman but Verity could well collapse completely. She followed Simon into the kitchen.

It was with a sense of inevitability she recognised Detective Constable Pat James.

The policewoman had formed a team with Sergeant William Pigram on several occasions, the first when murder had touched a hotel Darina had become involved with. For a time she had suspected the girl of making a play for the sergeant's affections. William had laughed but there was no doubting his respect for her abilities. Darina didn't often feel jealous but she had to acknowledge that the constable got under her skin.

She saw with a certain grim humour that her appearance was no more welcome to Pat than the policewoman's was to herself. A brief bob of the head acknowledged her presence. Darina gave her a small smile in return.

Simon had gone straight over to the Fry sisters. Verity first flung herself into his arms then almost immediately disentangled herself again, gasped out, 'I must ring Oliver,' and disappeared from the room.

Then Pru and Simon faced each other, her eyes held his gaze and she seemed to be waiting for something. He put out a hand. 'I'm sorry, I wouldn't have had this happen for anything.' The phrase struck Darina as a little strange, what could he have done to prevent it? But it appeared to be what Pru needed. She gave a gasping sob and grabbed at the outstretched hand. Simon allowed himself to be drawn towards her. 'What you need is a drink, a brandy.' He rearranged the arm she was clutching so it was round her shoulders and steered her out of the kitchen.

Darina watched them go and felt rather than heard Pat James give a sigh. 'Just as I was about to get the details of where Mrs Fry was cycling to when the accident occurred!'

Darina quelled a sudden irritation, told herself the girl was only doing her job and asked exactly what had happened.

Pat gave her brief details.

Then Darina said, 'I can tell you where Constance Fry was cycling to.'

The policewoman regarded her uncertainly.

Darina thought back to the scene in the kitchen that morning; the telephone had rung just as she and Simon were arranging her visit to him that afternoon. Pru answered and called her mother. Darina saw again Constance Fry enter the kitchen and take the receiver.

First she had been pleased with the call. 'Natasha!' she'd cried warmly. Then puzzled, 'But I don't understand!' Then astounded, 'You can't possibly mean that . . . ' Finally distressed, 'Yes, yes, I'll come. But, Natasha, I can't believe . . . all right, I won't say anything for the moment . . . yes, three thirty, I'll be there. But, look, Nat, Nat!' She spoke with increasing urgency but the caller had disconnected. Then Constance had replaced the receiver and repeated the name with a note of despair.

Such had been the intensity of Constance's reaction to whatever it was Natasha had said, none of those present in the kitchen could help but give their whole attention to the one-sided conversation.

They stood looking at the white-haired woman. It was as if she had retreated into a world of her own. Then something snapped her back to an awareness of her surroundings. 'I shall be going over to the Bailey this afternoon,' she said, her voice not quite steady, and left the kitchen.

Darina repeated the gist of this incident to Pat James. The policewoman made notes. 'You say she seemed upset by the call?'

Knocked sideways had been Darina's impression, but she said with care that Mrs Fry looked as though she had received a shock of some sort.

'In which case,' said Pat, 'she might not have been too steady on her bicycle.'

Darina had a swift mental picture of Constance Fry just before she left the kitchen. Old and frail beyond her years.

'But she had had several hours to recover from whatever shock it was, if indeed it was a shock. I might have been completely mistaken.'

'Your impressions are usually reliable,' Pat commented drily.

'Not one to let personal feelings affect her judgement,' William had said of Pat James at one stage.

'Natasha Quantrell,' she continued slowly, looking at her notes. She glanced at Darina again. 'Do you know where the Bailey is?'

'I'm afraid not.'

There was a pause.

Darina said, 'Haven't seen you for some time. How are things going?'

'Fine,' Pat responded heartily. 'We miss William, though.' She was the only one of his colleagues to call him that, everyone else used Bill. The sergeant amiably accepted the shortened form but the constable had somehow discovered he preferred his full name. 'I gather he's having an interesting time in New York.'

The statement was alive with undertones. Darina gave her a sharp look. 'Yes,' she said.

'Soon be back now,' Pat added cheerfully.

Darina could not bring herself to ask if she had some definite information about his return.

'Who is this Simon?' Pat asked, her official role taking over. But it was with no feeling of relief at the change of subject that Darina tried to explain that he appeared to be a friend of the family.

She found herself increasingly puzzled about Simon's role in the family structure. He had come to the Savoy to see Verity in the final of her cookery competition and they obviously had a close relationship. He had been shouted at by Constance at both the celebration party, at which he had appeared to be an unwelcome gate-crasher, and this morning when, for some reason, he had felt there might be a chance she could be persuaded into backing his restaurant. Well, he'd been left in no doubt there was no hope of that. Yet he had been the person Pru had turned to in this crisis.

'Did you drive over here in Mr Chapman's car?' Pat was asking.

'No, mine. He said his was acting up, needed a service.'

A note was made in the constable's book.

Then Simon and Pru came back into the kitchen. Both were carrying glasses containing generous amounts of brandy. Pru put hers on the table and sat down. The blue of her eyes had darkened like sea reflecting a thunderstorm and her body was as tense as a newly strung violin. But she was composed.

Simon hovered at her side. 'It's all right,' Pru said, 'I know you've got to get back to the restaurant, I'm OK now.'

'What about the boys?'

'I'll ring the Nolans, ask if they can stay the night, they won't mind, we've had their two over here often enough.'

He hesitated doubtfully.

Pru closed her eyes briefly. 'Oh, do go,' she said irritably. 'Can't you see I can't take you hanging around like a waiter who doesn't know what to serve?'

All Simon's aplomb and good humour had deserted him. He looked helplessly at Pru as Verity returned to the kitchen, her eyes red, nose sore but the tears under control. She went and sat beside her sister and took her hand.

'I got hold of Oliver, thank God for car phones, he says he'll be right down. He'll know exactly what to do.'

Darina didn't think it had been said to hurt Simon but she saw him flinch, give Pru another look then drain the glass he was holding in one gulp.

'If you're sure there's nothing I can do, I'll be off,' he said.

'Can I help in any way?' asked Darina.

Pru looked across as though she hadn't noticed the girl before. 'Thanks but we're all right.'

'What about the business?' Without Constance Fry, Darina was thinking, Pru and Verity were going to have a hard time keeping the farm going as well as cope with all the issues surrounding their mother's death.

It was obvious Pru found the effort of turning her mind to anything beyond the fact of her loss visibly taxing.

'I'll come over tomorrow morning,' Darina promised. 'I don't know much about rearing animals but I can cut meat and prepare sausages and faggots. If you decide you can cope, just give me a ring, here's the number.' She fished a card out of her bag and put it in front of Pru. 'Simon, I'll run you back to the restaurant.'

He moved reluctantly towards the door, it was as though he wanted to go yet couldn't quite bring himself to leave. 'Ring me if there's anything, anything at all.' He looked at Pru not Verity. 'And I'll be over in the morning.'

He said nothing as Darina drove down the farm lane.

Then, 'God, it's dreadful. I still can't take it in, Constance dead!'

After a moment she asked, 'How close are you to the Fry family?' She hadn't meant it to sound quite so pointed but that was the way it came out.

The look he gave her was pure astonishment. Then he uttered a short laugh. 'I didn't think there was anyone who didn't know. Pru and I, my dear Darina, are man and wife.'

The car swerved and swiped a glancing blow at the grass verge.

'You'll have to forgive me for not realising,' Darina said as the car resumed its more usual driving mode.

Simon laughed again without humour. 'Quite, I wouldn't have guessed in your position either.'

'Do you want to tell me what happened?'

'It's a long story and I don't really want to go through it. Perhaps I can best sum up by saying Pru has never really wanted to leave the farm and Constance never accepted me as a son-in-law.'

'And Verity?'

'Ah, Verity.' There was a pause. 'Yes, well, shall we say she caused complications for a time?'

'That time now being over?'

'God, yes.' There was a heartfelt sincerity in his voice that carried conviction.

'And Mark and Alastair are your sons?'

Simon sighed. 'For their sins.' Then he added, 'They're the ones who get the really rough end of the deal.'

'Do you see much of them?'

'In the school holidays they sometimes come round or I collect them from the farm for a picnic, running the gauntlet of Constance's disapproval.'

'Perhaps that side of things will be easier now,' Darina said quietly as they slipped into the traffic on the main road.

'I hadn't thought about that.' Simon silently considered the new factor in the situation.

'But you're not divorced?'

He shook his head. 'Pru's never asked for one.'

'What about you?' Darina thought she might as well try for the full picture.

'I? Oh, I'd like to have my wife and family back,' he said savagely.

Darina thought about the way Pru had sent him packing from the farm, how on their arrival the two sisters had been sitting together, sharing their grief in a way that defied outsiders to enter their familial closeness, until Verity had flung herself into Simon's arms. But Oliver would arrive that evening to look after her. Who was going to look after Pru?

'Would you like me to pick you up tomorrow morning?' she asked as the car drew up outside the restaurant.

'Tomorrow?'

'Yes, you said you'd be over in the morning. And your car . . . '

'Oh, the car. Don't worry, I'll take it into the garage first thing and get them to lend me another. But thanks for the offer.'

He gave her a quick smile, got out, slammed the door and was gone. But then he suddenly returned and came round to the driving side, leaning his head inside the car window. 'And thanks for your help this afternoon on the book. No chance you'd come in with me to help write it? I'd give you a share of the royalties.'

'I've got my own book to write.'

'Couldn't you fit this in as well? It doesn't have to be done immediately, the publishers aren't pressing me to deliver.'

He smiled at her persuasively like a sommelier pushing a dodgy vintage.

Perhaps if he'd asked this afternoon she might have jumped at the suggestion. But now?

'I don't know,' she said slowly, 'I'll think about it.'

'That's wonderful!' He sounded as though the suspect wine had been sold, gave her one of his wide smiles and disappeared into the restaurant.

Darina drove back home, deep in thought. But not about Simon's offer.

# Chapter Ten

A week later Darina stood in the Fry kitchen supervising the refreshment arrangements for Constance's funeral.

She thought how strange funeral catering was. No invitations, no official acceptances and refusals. You took a leap in the dark and made a guess at the numbers who would want to return after the service. Yet in her experience it was extremely rare either to run out of food or drink or to be left with extraordinary amounts. Some internal monitoring device could assess the numbers with a fair degree of accuracy. Or did the mourners adjust their intake to the amount of food on offer? Darina had taken Pru's estimated total and planned and executed with the skill of a field officer, assisted by various of the dead woman's friends.

Cakes had arrived all morning to supplement the savoury items Darina had prepared, there could hardly be a farm within a ten-mile radius that hadn't made a contribution. 'Mother knew most of the county,' Pru said, 'her family has farmed locally since for ever and Dad's was the same.'

Helping Darina put the finishing touches to the refreshments while the funeral service was in progress were two older women. 'We don't go to funerals,' they had said. 'We alus look after the tea.' Comfortable-sized, dressed in flowered sleeveless overalls over cotton frocks, they looked with satisfaction at the loaded kitchen table.

'Connie would have been proud of that,' said June, the older, at least if her white hair was anything to go by. It framed her brown face in an aureole of fine frizz.

'What a change in this kitchen,' said Jackie, her round, equally sunburnt face sporting a dark pudding-basin of a haircut. 'Remember what it was like when she and Tom were married? Don't think it had been touched since Tom's father married. When was that,

June?' The slow-paced Somerset voice was infinitely soothing on this fraught day.

'Must a been back a ways. Some time in the twenties?' An exhaustive analysis of the timings of various local births, marriages and deaths, finally placed the event during the First World War.

'When Connie and Tom were married, the old pump were still in here. And the floor was flagstones. That dresser were all brown varnish. All dark the house was, Connie said it gave her the creeps.'

'Yes, an' old Mrs Fry sitting in her rocking-chair. When she wasn't wandering round the countryside. Sad that was. Hope I never come to such an end. What is it they call it these days? Enzymers Disease?'

'Alzheimer's, I think,' Darina contributed quietly.

'Ah, thass right, Alzheimer's. Well, we didn't know names for it then, just called her barmy. Reckon if Connie hadn't been so pretty and popular, folk might a thought Tom married her to get his ma looked after proper.'

'No thought a that. It were a love match all right. Remember how soon young Pru appeared?' Joint giggling over this. 'An' remember how cheerful Tom was in those days? Oh but he was a surly bugger by the end.'

'Felt right sorry for Connie, she were an angel with that mother-in-law, what she had to do for her. Tom just handed her over, I reckon. Well, men never can cope with that sort of thing, can they?' Not a question calling for an answer. 'An then there was that tragedy with, what was the name of that teaching feller, the one that died that there was all that fuss about?' Jackie couldn't help.

'But,' she said, 'I don't think there was anything in it. Folk'll always make a haystack from a few straws. Connie would never've left young Pru.'

'And her dad would never've let her go. He and young Pru together on the farm were a sight. She tagged after him everywhere.'

'Aye, adored her dad she did. An' he her. Never took to the second in the same way. Well, only natural, her being adopted an' all. Now they're both orphans, poor little lambs.' Indulgent sighs.

'Shall us check the ashtrays?' Jackie asked Darina. 'Never have enough ashtrays at a funeral.' They drifted with quiet purpose from the kitchen.

Darina had found herself spending a lot of her time at Fry's Farm over the previous week, mostly helping Pru with the meat preparation side. She had watched with interest how the relationship between the two sisters had developed. Verity had revealed a depth of feeling that brought the two of them together. Her fiancé had arrived in the late evening after Constance's death. His immaculate Rolls-Royce, looking as out of place as a tiara on a milkmaid, was the first thing Darina had seen when she pulled up in the yard next morning.

Quietly authoritative, sitting at the kitchen table as naturally as if it were a brilliantly polished office desk, he had been organising newspaper announcements and contact lists for funeral directors, vicars, solicitors, bank managers and all the other terrible details that surround a death, particularly when it is sudden. Verity had sat as close to him as a baby chicken nestling by its mother's feathers.

He hadn't been there for long, though. The next day Verity limply told Darina he had had to return to London. 'Business. But he's coming back in a few days and then he says he'll stay a little while.'

Much as she obviously missed him, it was doubtful the two sisters would have become so close if Oliver had still been offering his comfortable shoulder for crying on.

The police had released Constance Fry's body for burial but little progress seemed to have been made in their investigations into her death. Pru worried obsessively about the absence of information. Day after day she rang the police station to check on the investigation. When four days had gone by without any definite news, she had approached Darina.

'You know that detective who came round to tell us about Mother. Can't you ask her what's going on? Every time I ring I get the same message, inquiries are proceeding but there is no information as yet. They must have found out *something*.'

Reluctantly Darina had put through a call to Pat James and asked if they could have a drink together. Rather to her surprise, Pat had agreed immediately. Not only that but she said she'd come round to the cottage instead of suggesting they meet nearer to the station or her home.

'Thought it would be more relaxing,' the constable said as they sat on the little terrace outside the kitchen window sipping chilled white wine, watching the evening sun showing off behind the fruit trees. 'I've been wrapped up in this hit and run without a break. I was having the evening off anyway and you're on the way to my date.'

'Well,' Darina tried to sound welcoming, 'it's good of you to spare the time to drop by, I know just how busy you must be.'

'We've covered a great deal of ground but I'm afraid we've got nowhere.' The constable put her glass down and ticked off the points on her fingers as they were enumerated. 'First of all, there have been almost no sightings of any vehicle going along that road. All the farmers were busy in their fields, not one of them alongside the road; most of the other inhabitants say they were trying to keep cool indoors, a few had gone out shopping or visiting. One woman thought she saw a small car, driving much too fast, she said, at about two forty-five. We managed to identify that and have eliminated it from the inquiry. The driver had reached his destination by the time Constance Fry, according to her daughter's evidence, started cycling to the Bailey, and he has several witnesses for the next couple of hours. There was another report of "the roar of an engine" at about the right time but the witness didn't see the car.

'Secondly, we have examined the vehicles of her daughters and son-in-law' – so, thought Darina, they'd picked that one up then – 'as well as those of others in the area, and have failed to identify any scratches that could relate to the damage done to the bicycle. Forensic examination could possibly help here but without some evidence to suggest one of the cars could have been involved, we can't bring any of them in. Third, the autopsy has shown Mrs Fry died from striking her head on a large stone in the grass verge where she was thrown. It is thought that without that she would probably have escaped with bad bruising. It may even be that the driver thought no great damage had been done.'

'No great damage! Even if he'd only grazed her, surely in law he was bound to have stopped?'

'I'm not excusing the action,' Pat protested mildly, 'just telling you what our investigation has revealed to date.'

'Not a great deal so far as finding the driver is concerned.'

'No,' admitted the policewoman and a note of justification crept into her voice. 'But we shall be appealing to the public through the press for information regarding the incident. Very often in these cases that stimulates the driver involved to come forward with some tale to the effect that he hadn't been aware there had been an accident but his car was in the area at the time. Then the case becomes a straightforward one of dangerous driving and Traffic will take it over. But until then we are still examining vehicles belonging to neighbouring farms and other dwellings. A long and tedious job it is, too.'

'You think it was a local driver then?'

'Who else would have been using that road?'

'A visitor to one of the farms?'

'That is a possibility we are not overlooking. A list has been prepared of all visitors to the area and farmers have been asked about sales reps. They are gradually being eliminated.'

'You seem to be covering it all most comprehensively.' Darina wished she could feel happier about the fact.

Pat gave a small smile of satisfaction and picked up her glass again. 'As you know,' she gave the phrase a slight but irritating emphasis, 'police routine is painstaking. Dull but painstaking.'

'What about the reason for Constance Fry visiting the Bailey, could that have any bearing on the matter?' Darina was intrigued to hear what Pat James would say. Pru had told her Natasha Quantrell had refused to explain why she had asked Constance over, had only said that it would be made clear in due time. Pru had been fiercely resentful of what she termed a 'stupid mystery' but Verity had seemed to accept the promise of future elucidation with equanimity.

The policeman's poise was disturbed for the first time. 'Miss Quantrell has said it was a private matter and could have nothing to do with Mrs Fry's death. She refuses to give us any further information.' Her manner indicated it was not for a member of the public to decide what was and was not relevant in a case of this kind.

'So there's no real information for Pru and Verity Fry?' Darina summed up.

'As they have been told whenever they have rung.' Pat finished her wine.

'Perhaps they would feel more confident if someone contacted them every now and then to say so,' Darina suggested as mildly as she could, conscious nothing would be gained through rousing her guest's antagonism.

Pat regarded her with a steady eye. 'You could be right,' she said surprisingly. 'I'll make sure it happens in future.' She refused another glass of wine and stood up. 'I have to go, I'm afraid, can't keep men waiting, can we? Thanks for the drink, you must come over and have one with me. Perhaps when William gets back, it'd be nice to see the two of you together.'

Was it her way of declaring pax, of proclaiming she no longer had any personal interest in the sergeant?

Slightly startled, Darina thanked the policewoman and saw her out thinking that mutual respect between them was a possibility even if friendship seemed more problematic.

Then she refilled her glass and returned to the terrace to worry away at the details buried amongst the official non-information Pat James had given her.

First off, the police had discovered nothing that could suggest the accident was the result of anything but a hit-and-run driver. A driver who had knocked Constance Fry off her bicycle with no malice aforethought but who for some reason, probably because of a character deficiency, had been unable to remain on the scene and deal with the results of his or her carelessness.

Second, their routine investigation had so far eliminated the family and many neighbouring cars. Or had they? There was that bit about evidence being needed before they could be subjected to forensic examination.

What was it William had said once? That there was always contamination when two objects came into contact, be they humans or machines. Minute traces of material would be transferred from one to the other. Sometimes the quantities were large enough to be immediately visible and sometimes the traces were so minute it took forensic techniques to identify them. In this case a patch of paint from Constance's bike transferred to the car that had hit her could identify the driver but only, it seemed, if the paint could be seen with the naked eye or if there was other evidence that could provide sufficient grounds for the police to bring in the car for detailed examination.

What if no car was found with betraying paint marks? What if no driver came forward as a result of the appeal and no other evidence was forthcoming? Would the case just be marked down as another unidentified hit-and-run accident? And wasn't it, after all, more likely that that was what had happened?

Darina tried to identify her feelings of unease, why she felt so sure that was not the case.

The most obvious cause was the telephone call that Constance had reacted so powerfully to and Natasha Quantrell refused to explain. But second thoughts suggested a direct connection with the accident had to be unlikely. After all, it wasn't what Constance had said that was out of the ordinary, it had been her emotional state that had made such an impression. No, the call's significance was surely that each person in the kitchen had known Constance would be cycling to the Bailey that afternoon, that she was to arrive there at three thirty p.m. Darina herself had no idea how long that journey would take but everybody else would have done.

All of them, it would seem, had had the opportunity to drive along that road at that time. Verity said she had been working in her room and Pru had been alone in the shop. Even Simon had been absent from his restaurant around the right time and Darina only had his word that his car was causing trouble.

It was at this point Darina wondered whether her recent involvement in murder inquiries was making her look for mysteries where there were none. Surely common sense said the accident was no more than that, a dreadful accident. What reason would any member of her family have for eliminating Mrs Fry?

The only motive that could be identified was Simon's financial problem. Constance Fry was standing in the way of possible backing of his restaurant. With her gone would money be found from the farm to enable him to continue? Whether it would or not, that did not seem to Darina reason enough for Pru or Verity to run down their mother, their grief at her death seemed genuine enough. But Simon? He was resentful of Constance's interference in his marriage to Pru and had little love for his mother-in-law. Darina wondered how much money was involved. And just what were Pru's feelings towards him? Simon had said he wanted a reconciliation, what did she want? With her mother's disapproval removed from the scene, was there a chance Pru would return to her husband? Was the possibility of getting her back and of tapping into the farm's capital for his restaurant sufficient motive to drive him to murder?

Darina had little trouble divorcing her personal liking for the chef from consideration of his possible role in Constance Fry's death. This ability, she had found, was a strong asset when it came to exercising what Pat had referred to as her 'detecting instinct'. However much she liked someone, it never blinded her to the possibility that that person could be swayed by unexpected impulses or that there could be layers of emotion as yet unexcavated by herself.

But after considering the question for some time, she decided that in this case both motive and opportunity for Simon Chapman to run down his mother-in-law were weak. True, he'd known she would be cycling to the Bailey and when. True, he'd been out of his restaurant around the relevant time. But she really couldn't see straightforward Simon sneaking out to knock his mother-in-law off her bicycle in the hope of killing her.

After all, according to what Pat James had told her, Constance had actually been killed by hitting her head on a stone. Without that piece of bad luck, it seemed she might have survived.

If this was murder, the method seemed clumsy in the extreme. It had to have been an accident and Darina decided she must take herself in hand before she found suspicious circumstances surrounding every death she came across. She would do much better concentrating on the cookery book she was trying to write than seeing herself as some hot-shot version of Miss Marple.

In the Fry kitchen, Darina checked a last detail and hoped that now the funeral had taken place, even though the hit-and-run driver had not been found, Pru and Verity would be able to put their mother's death behind them. There were signs that the older girl was coming to terms with the probability that the culprit responsible for her mother's death would not be found. But Verity had been behaving very oddly, an air of suppressed excitement making her veer between laughter and tears, as though she had some secret she could hardly contain. And Darina didn't think it was anything to do with her engagement. Perhaps, though,

Oliver's reappearance the previous night would do something to calm her down.

'Here they come now,' said Jackie, moving with unexpected speed into the kitchen. She and June checked the large kettles on the Aga and Darina started opening wine bottles as the first cars swept down the drive.

# Chapter Eleven

Throughout the funeral, Verity felt split in two. One part of her was the new Verity, the girl still absorbing the extraordinary secret she had only just learned. Still assessing its implications, still trying to adjust to the way it changed her outlook on life. She felt like a landscape artist who had just discovered perspective and now found he had to redraw all his works. And, like the painter, she knew the balance when she had finished would make each view so much more satisfactory, so much more natural.

That was one part of her. The other was the ordinary Verity pretending on the surface that everything, though so tragically altered, was more or less the same. Who didn't want to tell Pru yet what she had learned and who performed her part at the funeral the way she knew Constance would have wanted.

She handed round glasses of wine and cups of tea and allowed herself to receive condolences from women she remembered from her childhood years. Women in whose kitchens she had sat with Constance, eating home-made biscuits and sponge cakes, idly kicking her legs and listening to the grown-ups talk, wondering how they could make so much of such boring things. When she grew up, she would go to London, do something exciting with her life.

These were the women who had been pessimistic about Constance's chances for success at running the farm after her husband died. Verity thought she had been splendid then. Young as she was, Verity had been excited at the growing reputation of Fry's Farm. It had given her something to boast about at school, that the animals raised on their farm were sold for more than ordinary cattle and lambs. She didn't mind that her mother had a reputation for eccentricity. It was being the same as everybody else that Verity feared.

Once she had moved to London, first to do her Cordon Bleu training, Pru grumbling at the cost but agreeing that the investment would be worth while because Verity was so good at cooking and so interested in food, then to join a small catering company, she hadn't been in Somerset much. And hadn't Pru been cross at that; she had expected her little sister to come home and help in the business. But Verity had had enough of the Young Farmers, there had to be more interesting men around than she found locally. And Constance had not objected; on the contrary, she had excused her to Pru and positively pushed her into leaving home. Iron teeth clamped themselves together in Verity's guts as she thought of how supportive Constance had always been to her.

Iron teeth that felt even sharper when she remembered the one time she had attempted to work near home. It had seemed such a good idea, working for Simon when Pru's second pregnancy meant she couldn't help with the new restaurant. Not, thought Verity sadly, that Pru had ever appeared particularly enthusiastic about the venture. She seemed to have welcomed the opportunity to return home and spend the time preparing the bacon, hams and sausages whose reputation spread so quickly.

Simon had been so proud when Alastair was born. Had looked forward so much to having his wife and two sons living above the restaurant with him. Couldn't understand why it was taking so long for Pru to feel strong enough to return.

Was that why they had drifted into that brief, disastrous affair? Yes, he was attractive. Yes, he was enormous fun, especially since there was no one else around. And, yes, they had so much in common, enjoyed talking together, planning the restaurant's development. But surely they should have seen the danger? They hadn't even been seriously in love. Bed had just seemed an extension of their winding-down drink at the close of the working day, a day that ended after midnight. She should have foreseen the risk of her living in. Come to that, Pru should have foreseen it. But sweet, silly Pru had trusted her sister.

Who wasn't her sister at all.

Well, everyone knew Constance and Tom had adopted her as a little baby and it had never been hidden from her.

Had it been something Pru had said that made Verity think, when she was quite little, that Constance was, after all, her mother, though Tom not her father?

To young Verity it made a certain sense. She knew Tom was fond of her but not in the way he was of Pru. His elder daughter he loved with a deep, silent passion. Neither felt any necessity to talk of that love or to show it in any way other than a simple pleasure in each other's company, a complete understanding of the other's needs.

With Constance it was the other way around. She seemed to love Verity and accept Pru. Verity knew she was being brought up very differently from her elder sister. With her, Constance laughed and had fun. They would go shopping together, make little trips to London on cheap-day return tickets. She would always find the extra money for a new dress when Verity wanted one. Pru would never ask.

Verity sometimes wondered if Pru resented her special relationship with Constance, particularly after her father died. Verity was ten then, Pru twenty and already helping on the farm; had never, in fact, wanted to do anything else. And with Tom gone, the two women had come closer together. Respect had grown between them. A closer understanding.

Until Simon came along.

Verity could remember his first visit to the farm. He'd just been appointed head chef at the nearby very chic, very expensive hotel. So chic and expensive the Fry family had never even thought of going there. And to get the chef turning up to discuss the possible supply of meat was a matter of considerable excitement. Even Pru, who was always awkward and monosyllabic with young men, grew talkative, took him round the farm and explained proudly how they reared their meat. He had left the farm with a box of produce promising to come back as soon as he'd had a chance to try it.

Verity had giggled to see the gradual transformation in her taciturn sister as Simon returned again and again, then asked her out on his one free evening a week. But Constance had not laughed. Verity had never been able to work out whether she didn't like Simon for himself, distrusting the easy charm, whether she hated the idea of Pru leaving the farm, or whether she was simply convinced her elder daughter would not be happy with the chef.

Verity looked across the room at Simon standing with the vicar's wife. All his attention appeared to be focused on the chatty woman, but Verity noticed his eyes continually checking for Pru's presence. Would they get together again? Or did that light that came into his eyes when Darina Lisle offered a plate of sandwiches mean Pru had missed her chance?

Verity didn't know how they would have managed without Darina since Constance's death. Even though they'd only just met her, Darina had appeared whenever they needed her, helping in the shop and making the charcuterie with unassuming skill. She had fitted in so easily. Seemed to know instinctively when Verity wanted to talk and when conversation would be an intolerable burden. And Pru felt the same about her. The competition judge had become a real friend, it was as though they had known her for ever. Verity would be really sorry if she turned out to be an impediment to her sister's chances of rediscovering happiness and hoped it was just a case of Simon flexing his macho muscles.

As Verity moved on to refill a couple of teacups, a hand fell heavily on to her shoulder.

'Well, it's beauty herself deigning to favour us with her presence!'

She instinctively backed away. She had forgotten how much she disliked Daniel Quantrell. Had forgotten him completely, in fact. In all the drama since she had come down to Somerset, she had not once thought of Natasha's cousin.

His lean, stooping figure, fine blond hair, ridiculously brushing his coat collar, and watery blue eyes added up to a poor showing of a man. But he had had the reputation of being attractive in his younger days. How had the dashing bachelor become lost inside that crumbling shell?

'I apologise for not having written to say how ineffably desolated I was at the demise of your dear mother.' The blue eyes were so watery Verity feared actual tears were about to drop.

'That's all right,' she muttered, having trouble in that direction herself. Why should it be the ridiculous phrases of this stupid man rather than the sincere words of Constance's friends that made it difficult for her to keep her equanimity?

'A veritable tragedy, cut off in the prime of life. The provider of such a cornucopia of provender to be reduced to dust!' He brought out a large spotted handkerchief and delicately applied it to his nose.

'Now, Daniel, stop wittering at the girl. Don't pay any attention, my dear. It's the writer in him.'

'Hello, Erica, how's things?'

At least Daniel had a minder these days. Not like the time he drove her up to London after the debacle with Simon. He'd known all the gossip, of course. Had insinuated she was now anyone's and then made a sordid grab for her. Verity blocked out the disgusting memory of his slack mouth desperately sucking at her face and the awkward fight she had had to get out of his car.

'Things is well, my dear. Daniel's chickens are getting quite a reputation, the herbs are roaring ahead and, have you heard, I'm on to organic mushrooms now?'

'No? Have you told Pru? I'm sure she'd be interested, she's talking of starting to make pâté and is looking for a source of organic mushrooms.'

'Not ready, yet. Consistency of supply is a problem. But I'll beat it in the end, nothing defeats me, does it, Dan?'

Daniel gave a weak smile, his gaze slid round the room, studying who else was there.

How could Erica stand him? Not only tolerate but work with him and, if gossip was to be believed, even look for a closer union? She was as tall as her partner and, thanks to his stoop, appeared taller, her lean body tough and wiry. She had appeared in Lamington several years ago and latched on to Daniel and his struggling herb business like a stray barnacle finding an unoccupied rock. Just as well for Daniel, in fact, he'd never have kept the herbs going without her efficiency and drive. She'd turned an amateurish concern into a thriving business. Quantrell herbs were posted to an impressive number of chefs in London and other parts of the country. Released from the day-to-day cares of that business, her partner had recently started raising quality chickens, apparently impressed by the prices the Fry birds commanded.

'Shocking business your mother's death, quite shocking.' Erica appeared genuinely distressed. 'I was with the herbs all day, didn't hear a thing. Not that I do in that walled garden. Cuts out all noise, you know, and of course the accident was some little way away. Curious, though, that nobody seems to have seen anything. Daniel was out all afternoon and it was all over by the time he got back, wasn't it, my dear?'

Another touch of the handkerchief to his nose. 'Could hardly get home, the police blocking the road, cars all over the place, such discombobulation. I think, my sweet, we must be off, just wanted to present our condolences.' He nodded to Verity, gripped Erica's arm above the elbow with surprising strength and steered her through the crowded room towards the door.

'What gall, showing his face here,' said Pru, appearing at Verity's side.

'But he knew Mother for ever!'

'You mean you don't know about their row?'

Verity shook her head, unable to find much interest in the matter. There were always violent arguments blowing up amongst the farming community; those who thought country people were placid and easy-going had never lived in a village. She resigned herself to hearing the tedious details of this particular cause of dissension but was spared by the county Chairman of the National Farmer's Union claiming Pru's attention.

'Need relieving of that teapot, darling?' Oliver was at her elbow. She smiled, explained she was just going to get a fresh pot and introduced him to a retired couple who had been among Constance's first customers, never buying great quantities but always regularly.

'You wouldn't prefer a glass of wine?' Oliver asked them, holding up the bottle he was carrying. 'Well, I'm sure you're wise. I do think it's remarkable, though, how many guests have preferred tea.'

Verity gave him a look that said he was doing perfectly and she was grateful, then left him exchanging smooth small-talk and went through to the kitchen feeling that special warmth that always came from any contact with Oliver.

Meeting him had been like finding the other half of herself; it was as though she had always known him even when they had only just met. In one way he was like a comfortable pair of shoes, slipped on easily and hardly noticed but essential for efficient movement through life. But in another he was like a bracing cold shower, stimulating all her faculties, opening her eyes to so many new experiences.

How was Oliver going to react to her news? Would he understand what a feeling of peace it gave her? Well, perhaps not peace quite yet, but it would when she got used to it, Verity was quite sure of that.

'Just wanted to say goodbye, sweetie. Come down to the

restaurant when you've got a moment, won't you, so we can have a chat?'

Without thinking, she held up her face for Simon's kiss and clung to him briefly. His body was warm with comfort and he knew even better than Oliver what Constance's death meant to her. Then she saw with weary resignation that Pru stood in the kitchen doorway gazing at them both, her face a thundercloud. Verity held her gaze, remained in Simon's arms and said nothing. Pru disappeared. A moment or two later, Simon, oblivious to the wordless exchange between his wife and sister-in-law, left by the kitchen door.

Verity wished everyone would go, she was tired of listening to people talking about Constance. Tired of filling teacups, of responding to sympathy. She wanted to be alone. The cathartic effect of funerals was amazing. An hour ago, this assembly had been choking back tears listening to the rector give his eulogy, now bright chatter and laughter filled the rooms; almost there was a party atmosphere. It was a rite of passage. The dead had been buried, now we can get on with life. Verity shivered.

At long last they were able to see off the last of the mourners. Then she, Pru and Oliver stood in the hall like mariners without a compass. Darina Lisle was restoring the living rooms to their usual state and Jackie and June were washing up in the kitchen.

'You look exhausted,' Verity said to her sister. 'Go to bed, we can see to the clearing up. When did you say you'd collect the boys?'

'They're staying overnight, they'll come home after school tomorrow. It seems as though they've hardly lived here at all this last week.' Pru drew a hand across her forehead. Her eyes were sunk deep in their sockets. 'I don't feel I've slept since it happened. Wake me at five if I haven't appeared, the stock will have to be fed.'

She moved towards the staircase, stumbling slightly as though blind with weariness. Then she stopped. 'What's that damn hat doing there?'

It sat on the newel post, fine straw with a cream silk chiffon scarf tied round the crown and dangling down the back.

Verity picked it up and stroked the supple weave. 'It's Natasha's.'

'I know it's Natasha's, why hasn't it gone back to her?'

'The police only returned it yesterday and I thought she would be coming here after the funeral so I left it there for her to pick up.'

'Well, she didn't come,' snapped Pru.

'She was at the church,' Verity said, 'I saw her sitting at the back, but she'd slipped out by the end of the service. I suppose she couldn't face all those people. Pity, I know she wants it, she told me she feels naked without it.' She held the hat up, remembering how it shaded Natasha's scarred face. 'I'll take it round later this afternoon.'

The hat was removed from her hand. 'No, darling,' said Oliver, 'not this afternoon. I've seen hardly anything of you, Miss Quantrell can wait another day.'

Verity was going to protest it need only take a moment then saw his face and gave him a quick kiss instead.

'I'll drop it in if you like on my way home.' Darina Lisle emerged from the living room. The hat was handed over to her.

'When did she leave it here?' Darina asked.

'She lent it to me after I spent the day at the Bailey, just before the accident. She said it was far too hot for me to walk back without one and that I could return it the next day. But in the morning she cancelled my visit, said she was too busy. So Mother said she would wear it to cycle over that afternoon.' Verity took a deep breath and quelled the sudden tears that again threatened to spill over. She remembered, fresh as spring showers, the excitement she had felt as she walked back along the baking-hot road, the sun still strong even though it was late afternoon. She'd held her head high, face shaded by the straw brim, imagining she looked like Natalie Duke, whose hat it had been, Natasha said. The stories she'd been told about the great cookery writer reverberated in her head, ideas for books of her own had danced along with them, she had dreamed of success and the future. Even if she had known then what she had been told later, she could not have felt greater sympathy with the hat's original owner.

She looked at the straw Darina now held and all at once her secret wanted to bubble out, to be in the open. 'Yes, please take it back,' she said to Darina and steered her towards the kitchen. 'And ask her,' she whispered quickly, 'to tell you what she told me the other day, the day after Mother died.'

Then she went back to Oliver. She'd tell him tonight, when they were alone together.

# Chapter Twelve

'Are you sure she said that?' Natasha sat in the Bailey's cool, shady living room. The hat had been tossed on the sofa.

'I'm not sure I'll ever be able to wear it again,' she'd said when it had been produced at the door of the Bailey, then had invited her visitor in.

Darina had been torn between a feeling of intrusion and a strong desire to take advantage of this opportunity to talk to someone who had been so close to Natalie Duke.

'I was just about to have a cup of tea. I know I should have gone back to the house after the funeral but it – it was too much.' Her restraint was austere in its refusal to plead but her need for company was quite obvious. So Darina accepted the invitation with a clear conscience.

She had followed Natasha into the kitchen at the back of the house. While the kettle boiled she leant against a dresser, still holding the straw hat with its chiffon scarf, and described the gathering at Fry's Farm.

Natasha moved quietly round the kitchen, assembling the tea, listening carefully. Just as the tray was ready, there had come a knock at the back door.

Darina recognised one of the funeral mourners. She had changed into faded dungarees and a short-sleeved shirt which curiously seemed much more stylish than the limp silk dress she had been wearing earlier. But the red hair streaked with grey and the direct eyes of a green not unlike orchid petals were instantly recognisable.

'Brought up some fresh herbs for the landlady.' She held out a newspaper-wrapped packet, then noticed Darina. 'Hello, Erica Strangeways.' She placed the packet on the table and came forward, wiping her hand on the back of her dungarees. 'Don't think we've met. Know who you are, of course.' She pumped the tall girl's hand enthusiastically. 'I'm a follower of your recipes in the *Recorder*, you always produce such interesting vegetarian ones. I'm trying to get Daniel off meat but there's a long way to go before conversion is achieved, I'm afraid.' Her laugh mixed amusement with a certain disgust, though whether that was directed against her partner or herself was difficult to decide. 'Ah, you've brought back the Hat. Told Natasha we could hardly recognise her without it. See the Hat anywhere and you know who's underneath it. Safeway's, Lamington High Street, down the lane, unmistakable!'

'A cup of tea, Erica?' asked Natasha Quantrell without warmth.

The woman gave a longing glance at the tray. 'Sorry, can't stop, got a whole load of packing to do before the delivery service collects, just thought you'd like these.' She nodded at the packet on the table.

'Very kind.' Natasha unwrapped it as the other woman disappeared out of the back door. A quick waft of basil reached Darina. It looked as though there were marjoram, chervil and dill as well in the deliciously fresh bundle. 'I have to say of that woman, she does know how to grow plants. And I suppose it's good of her to swallow her chagrin and bring me fresh supplies every few days.'

'Chagrin?'

Natasha gave an unexpected grin that transformed her scarred countenance. For a brief moment mischief and humour lit her face and Darina realised just how much the terrible experience she had been through must have affected her. 'If it weren't for me, Daniel would have inherited this house when Grandfather died. All the time we've been away, I think he's been looking on it as his, convinced Grandfather was going to disinherit me. He was so angry when I went out with Natalie to Greece. And when we settled in France, he said he washed his hands of me. Even though he used to write from time to time, it was quite a surprise to find when he died a few months ago that he hadn't changed his will after all. Daniel will have to wait. Most distressing for him. But I think Erica minds even more. Every time she comes in here it's as though she's counting the silver spoons.'

'Are they *together*?' It was so difficult to identify relationships these days, Darina thought. Had she and William been *together*?

Would they ever be again? She had had a postcard from him that morning, postmarked Washington, DC. It mentioned the White House, the Lincoln and Washington Memorials and the Smithsonian Museum, that was all. She pushed away a sudden sharp ache and waited with interest to hear just how connected Daniel Quantrell and Erica Strangeways were.

'Oh, they don't live together. Erica is in that modern house on the right as you go into Lamington, she was left it by an aunt. The story is she came down to see if she wanted to live here, I think her partner in some garden nursery business had died. She met Daniel, took one look at his set-up, sold her business and took over his.'

'A determined lady?'

'As you say.' Natasha was dry to the point of drought. 'No doubt the story has gained in the telling but she's certainly too comfortable in that little box to want to move into Daniel's damp cottage. The Bailey, though, would suit her ideas very well.' She looked at the bunch of herbs in her hand, buried her nose in them and inhaled deeply. When she raised her face, it bore a curious expression compounded of resignation and dismay.

'Since the fire,' she said, placing the greenery in a small pottery jug and filling it with water, 'my sense of smell, and with it my taste, has almost completely disappeared. Food used to be such a joy and now I eat only to keep body and soul alive. And sometimes I wonder why I do that; it must be to keep the Bailey out of Erica's clutches.'

'Did you do much cooking with your cousin?' asked Darina, following her through to the front of the house and into a room that was dark and cool with walnut panelling and chintz-covered seating, bowls of fresh flowers glowing on top of well-polished chests and tables.

Natasha handed her a cup of thin bone china in which fragrant Lapsang Souchong glowed like ripe barley, its smoky aroma oddly refreshing. 'Natalie was the creative talent, Natasha the technician. A good team.' The phrase sounded well honed.

'Did neither of you marry?' Darina hoped the question would not be considered too intrusive.

'No. When we were young, there were times both of us came close but it never quite came off for some reason or other. I don't think we missed much, life has been very fulfilling. Tell me, was that Verity's fiancé I saw with her in the church?'

'Oliver Knatchbull,' Darina nodded, then remembered Verity's whispered instruction to ask Natasha to tell her some secret or other.

After her initial surprise, her hostess sat looking for a moment at an array of photographs on a marquetry chest. Then she rose and picked up one in a silver frame. 'That was Natalie Duke at Verity's age,' she said, handing it to Darina.

It was a studio portrait, the light flattering and no doubt the print retouched. But no focus could be soft enough to disguise the strong planes of the face and the large nose that didn't quite manage to remove the charm of the impudent smile and frank eyes. Natalie Duke looked quite a character.

Darina studied it appreciatively then handed the photo back to the waiting woman with a questioning look.

Natasha stood staring at it. 'She gave it to Grandfather for a Christmas present. Not that he was ever keen on her, even then he thought she was a bad influence on me. I think it amused her to give him something so personal, especially in such a costly frame. I was very surprised to find it in a drawer when I got back, I thought he would have got rid of it. Maybe he hoped until the end we would return.' She looked at the face in silence then said, 'But you haven't noticed the resemblance?' She offered the photograph to Darina again.

The girl gave it a second scrutiny.

'You mean, the nose? Are you saying . . .?'

'That Verity is her daughter, yes.'

Even after all the clues, it came as a shock. Darina absorbed the information for a little, thinking what a bad detective she really was.

'Pru thinks Verity is actually her half-sister,' she offered.

Natasha looked genuinely startled. 'Her half-sister? She thinks Verity is Tom's child?'

'No, her mother's.'

'Ah.' The photograph was replaced carefully on the chest and Natasha went back to her tea. 'I can see how that might have come about but it's unfortunate.'

'What happened?'

Natasha poured more tea. 'I think I need to explain about

Natalie and myself. Our mothers were identical twins and we were very close. It's hard to realise now but, when we were young, we were considered very alike.' She touched her scars unselfconsciously. Trying not to stare, Darina studied Natasha's face and decided that, yes, despite the passing of years and the scar depredation, the bone structure was very similar to that of the girl in the photograph.

'Natalie's father was an explorer, the type that went off on long journeys into the wild then came back and wrote quite bewitching books about his trips. Her mother usually accompanied him. So Natalie spent a lot of time with me and my family. We lived here, with my grandfather. The Quantrells have owned the Bailey since Elizabethan times and it was my grandfather's great sorrow that I wasn't a boy and that there were no more children after me. At one stage he wanted me to marry Daniel, he's my second cousin and it would have made things very neat. That was when Daniel first came to live in the cottage. He was really quite good-looking in those days. Tall and blond, dashing in a slightly Hollywood way. Even I thought it might be a good idea, for a little.' She laughed briefly without much humour. 'That was before I got to know him. Natalie saw through him right from the start. "A poseur," she said. "You won't be able to stand him for more than a week, my dear." And she was quite right. But he got into my grandfather's good books by writing a history of the Bailey and getting him to pay for its publication. There is still a pile of copies around somewhere. And Daniel made sure he remained on good terms with his great-uncle Adam. Such good terms that, as I told you earlier, he had hopes of the Bailey coming straight to him.' Natasha glanced around the room.

'Both Natalie and I loved this house. We knew every corner, used to fantasise about earlier owners. "You are so lucky," she used to say to me. "One day it will all be yours." After my grandfather died we planned to return here. We were making the arrangements when the fire occurred.' There was an involuntary sigh.

'But to get back to Verity. Natalie was a journalist; she started on the *Bristol Evening Post* then got taken on by Fleet Street. Without actually being a foreign correspondent, she managed to get sent abroad quite often; she had a modern languages degree from Durham, spoke French and German fluently, quite good

Italian and Spanish and a bit of Greek. So we didn't see her down here much after she moved to London. I was working locally as a secretary, not a very interesting job, and quite often I went up to spend a weekend with her. It was never less than frenetic. People coming and going, always a crowd of us; we'd go off on a pub crawl or to a concert or the theatre, then back to someone's place for spaghetti afterwards. No one had much money but it was such great fun.

'Natalie was doing very well but one day, when she was in her early thirties, she came down here for a weekend and told me she had thrown up her job and was off to sit on a beach in Greece and write a cookery book.' Natasha sat silently for a moment.

'You'd had no warning she might have been thinking about doing something like that?'

There was a brief shake of the head. 'She was very restless, I knew that. And I knew she was interested in cookery. She was always bringing back recipes from her trips abroad. But this was out of the blue and after a bit of pressure I got the truth. She was pregnant; she didn't want to marry the father, we're both Catholics so abortion was out of the question, and she thought the best thing was to take herself out of the way until it was all over.' Natasha looked at Darina. 'People talk about the swinging sixties now as though anything went but unmarried mothers were not generally acceptable. Permissiveness was still struggling to gain acceptance and parents did not like to admit their young were even living with someone of the opposite sex, let alone becoming a single parent, that phrase itself was only just being invented. And Natalie and I weren't so young we had the urge to be shocking. I could understand her wish to arrange things so that she could take a sabbatical and then return to her professional life without a lot of gossip. If her stay in Greece produced a book, no one would question her time abroad.'

'And you decided to go with her?'

'Yes. I was fed up with my job and my life and I thought Natalie would need someone with her. She thought she could handle it all herself, tried to dissuade me, but I insisted. Greece does not offer the most up-to-date medical facilities even now and then it was something of a nightmare.'

'I suppose you had some private income?' Darina hazarded.

'We both lost our parents quite young. Natalie's father died abroad when she was nineteen and I think her mother just lost interest in life afterwards. Cancer took her two years later. My parents were killed in a car crash about the same time, we mourned together. It's curious how much of life we have shared, we really were closer than most sisters. So, we both had a modest competence and, apart from my grandfather, there was nothing really to keep us in England.'

'Where did Constance come in?'

'Ah, Constance. She was the daughter of a local farmer and we were great friends from early on. She is, was, a remarkable woman. Very strong. But she made a great mistake marrying Thomas Fry. Dark and masterful but monosyllabic. At first meeting he seemed the essence of romance, then you realised he didn't have a great deal of intelligence and was extremely obstinate. He wasn't a great one for the girls, which I suppose could have increased his attraction. Apart from his looks, he had his own farm and was considered quite a local catch; girl after girl went after him with very little success. By the time he was approaching forty, people had more or less given up expecting him to marry.

'Then he met Constance at a Young Farmers' dance. She was on the rebound from an unfortunate affair with a medical student and got quite carried away. As for him, he acted as though he'd met the love of his life. I think, though, that Constance would have realised she was only infatuated if she hadn't found herself pregnant. So they got married and almost immediately she realised she had made a terrible mistake.'

Darina imagined a male version of Pru with less intelligence and education. She thought of the difficulties Pru had with relationships. Life could not have been easy for Constance married to such a man, especially when he was so much older than herself.

'Apart from the appalling Thomas, she had to look after his dotty mother, who was in the early stages of senile dementia, and try and do something with a farmhouse that still had a pump in the kitchen, one very basic bathroom and an outside loo, a house her husband considered was quite adequate the way it was. It was a wonder to us that she stuck it. But she said she had chosen her situation and had no choice but to make the best of it.'

'I gather an alternative did come along a little later?'

'Ah, you know about Andrew? It was that affair that led to

her Greek visit. Prunella was about nine, I suppose, I don't know what she remembers.'

'Quite a lot, I think, it was she who told me about him.'

'Does she blame her mother?'

Darina thought about that. 'I'm not sure. I think she was resentful on her father's behalf.'

'When Tom found out he went berserk. It was the old story, he came back unexpectedly one day and found them in one of the barns, amongst the hay. He just went at the chap as though he wanted to kill him. Probably did. He knocked Andrew unconscious and would have beaten him to death if Constance hadn't held him back and screamed at him to stop. Finally he flung her off, walked out of the barn and disappeared. She didn't see him again until the next day, he spent the night in jail, arrested for being drunk and disorderly.'

'And Andrew?'

'He came to and appeared shaken but not seriously hurt. He and Constance decided that she would have to leave Tom and start life again with him. They knew it would be difficult for him to find another job and that Pru might be forced to stay with her father but Constance couldn't face living with Tom any longer and she said her farming skills could always provide them with a living. She'd taken over most of the stock management by then, she said she couldn't stand the way her husband treated the animals.'

'So what made her stay after all?'

'Andrew died. He collapsed a day or so after his fight with Tom. He was taken into hospital but it was too late. Tom could easily have been taken to court on a charge of manslaughter. But Andrew didn't have any close relatives, nobody except Constance seemed to care, and she said what was the point? Andrew had gone and there was Pru to think of. But the strain was all too much for her and she had a nervous breakdown. She sent us a letter asking if she could come and visit us in Greece. She said she had to get away and couldn't think of anywhere else.'

'Had Natalie had her baby by then?'

Natasha smiled. 'It was a few weeks old. Such a dear little girl, the image of Natalie.'

'And nobody else knew of her birth?'

'How could they? No one even suspected Natalie was pregnant and we'd discouraged any visitors. But we knew we could trust

Constance and she was obviously in great distress. We met her off the boat from the mainland. She looked dreadful. She'd lost a lot of weight and her eyes belonged to the living dead. We got the story out of her gradually over the next few days. I think it was Verity that saved her sanity. She could see neither of us knew anything about babies and the sight of the old Greek woman who came to help us look after the child appalled her. We thought Eleni was wonderful, she'd raised some dozen of her own, not to mention countless grandchildren, and we had complete confidence in her. But Constance took over the day she arrived. She just adored Verity. It was she who named her, we were still arguing about whether she should be given one.'

'You must have called her something.' Darina was listening in appalled fascination.

'Of course, Baby! Natalie was determined she should be taken back to England for adoption, she had all the papers ready, and she said as long as Baby didn't have a name, her identity was waiting to be given to her by her new parents. Constance said it was just like not giving a name to stock you were going to kill for the table. She said Verity had been Andrew's favourite name for a girl and couldn't we call her that? I think she had desperately wanted Andrew's child. She told us that after Prunella she had made sure she wasn't going to have another by Tom. She was really very maternal but I think she always resented the child for forcing her into marriage. With Verity she could love unreservedly.'

'Poor Pru, no wonder she's grown up into a difficult woman.'

'Has she?' The question was perfunctory and Natasha didn't wait for an answer. 'After three months Constance realised she really had to return to England. By that time she was more or less back to her old self, all her dutiful instincts had returned and she felt Pru needed her. But she couldn't bear to leave Verity and she begged us to let her adopt her.'

'What about her husband?'

'That's what we asked. Finally she agreed to return and talk to Tom. I don't know what she said but we were finally told it had all been arranged. We attended to the formalities and Verity was taken to London and handed over. I suppose Prunella could have thought Constance gave birth in Greece, maybe even Constance herself sometimes thought that, she was in such a screwed-up state when she first arrived.'

'And she never told Verity who her real mother was?'

'That was a condition of adoption. Natalie wanted to erase the whole episode from her life.'

'And the father?'

'The birth certificate said "father unknown" and Natalie never told me – nor, I think, anybody else – who he was. Certainly not Constance.'

'You didn't suspect who he might be?'

Natasha shook her head. 'She had lots of boyfriends, I knew of at least two serious affairs but both those had been over for some time before Verity appeared. Under the circumstances, it didn't seem particularly important. But from the odd hint she let drop over the years, I think he was a married man, rather older than her.'

'What decided you to tell Verity about her mother now?'

Natasha picked up the hat and played with the scarf ends. 'She was going to have to know sometime. Natalie left her estate to me with the understanding it would then go to Verity. Constance sent us a photograph of the child every Christmas with a little report on her progress. As Natalie began to realise how like her her daughter was, so she gradually developed a real interest in her. She was really looking forward to meeting her when we came back.'

'Similar to her in loving food and cookery?'

'That and other things. And Natalie never forgot how her private income, small though it was, had meant she could take a year out in Greece to write her first book.'

'It was a great success, wasn't it?'

Natasha smiled. 'It was, and by then Natalie was working hard on the second, on Provençal food. She realised she had found her métier in life. And I was happy, too. We made a good team. But it was all made possible by our private incomes, the books didn't start producing respectable sums for several years.'

Darina thought how lucky she, too, had been. Left a house and money by her cousin, she could now afford to work at writing her articles and books without worrying about a mortgage or how to finance recipe testing; it would take some time for her writing to produce a reasonable income. Twenty years ago she would perhaps have looked to marriage to bring her the same security; today she prized her independence and ability to pursue a career without distraction. Marriage, when it came, would be a commitment made for reasons other than the need for a meal ticket.

'When I met Verity,' Natasha continued, 'and found how like her mother she was, it seemed only natural to tell her the truth. Particularly after Constance's death. I told her the day after the accident and said that when I died her mother's money would come to her. And I've told her if she needs help in the meantime, to ask me.'

'Do you think she'll need any, now she's marrying Oliver? I understand he is extremely successful.'

'Well, that's another thing. She's too young to get married yet. And her fiancé is so much older than she is. It seems to me a terrible mistake. I've told her if she agrees not to see him for a year, I will support her while she makes her mark.'

Darina was taken aback. 'How did she react to that?'

'As you might expect; she's young and in love. But when she comes to think about it, I hope she may see sense.'

Sense in Natasha's book being to give up Oliver Knatchbull. Darina looked curiously at the quiet woman; she appeared to be wanting to take over Verity's life entirely. 'What about Constance, had you discussed your decision with her?'

Natasha's facial scars made reading her expression difficult. There was a quick movement of her eyes that could have been interpreted as embarrassment but it was impossible to be sure. 'That's what she was coming to discuss with me the afternoon she was killed.' So that was what Constance had reacted to so strongly on the telephone.

'And she was against it.' It was a statement, not a question.

'She wasn't receptive to the idea, no. But I'm sure once I'd had a chance to talk to her, to explain matters, she would have agreed it was best for Verity.'

Would she? wondered Darina.

'It must have been a terrible shock to hear of her accident.'

Natasha seemed to shrink and age ten years. The frailty of her hold on life was suddenly exposed. She didn't speak, merely twisted the hat round and round in her hands. Then she looked across at Darina, her eyes pleading.

'I had to ask her to come, I had to,' she whispered. 'I didn't have any alternative.'

'You can't blame yourself,' Darina said sympathetically. 'It wasn't your fault she met a hit-and-run driver.'

'No.' The woman sounded unconvinced. 'It's just, one can't help thinking, if I hadn't suggested she come over here that afternoon, she would still be alive.'

'A fatalist would say it was all predestined.'

'I am not a fatalist.' The voice was stronger, the back straighter.

'Neither am I,' acknowledged Darina. 'I think we make our own lives. And Constance's fate was as much in her hands as in anyone else's. It was bad luck, nothing more, that caused that motorist to come along at that particular time.' Was she, she wondered, as confident about that as she sounded?

'You're right, of course, one mustn't be stupid about these things.' Natasha's voice was matter of fact, she seemed to have recovered her composure. But lines deeper than the puckering of scar tissue pinched her skin by nose and eyes.

There was another question that bothered Darina. 'Why didn't you tell the police why you had asked Constance here?'

Natasha's shoulders hunched again with tiredness. 'Because it wasn't only my secret any more. I'd told Verity by then and she didn't want anyone to know, not until she'd got used to the idea. I was surprised when you said she wanted you to know. I can only suppose that now she's ready to tell everyone.'

Darina got up. It was time for her to go.

# Chapter Thirteen

Darina and Verity were packing orders in the back of the shop. Pru was killing chickens.

'I'm sorry,' Darina had said, 'it's the one job I won't do. Look at them, those bright eyes and lovely soft, fluffy feathers.'

'You don't mind cooking or eating them as long as someone else does the dirty work?' Pru grabbed a couple of chickens out of a cage containing a batch of some two dozen. There was an initial squawking and flapping of feathers but, curiously, the birds did not seem distressed at being carried upside down into the poultry preparation barn.

'Don't they mind?' Darina asked, looking on queasily.

'Not so long as they can't see the actual process. You're making the common mistake of anthropomorphising. Birds and animals don't have our feelings. They want to be comfortable, to be fed and watered. That's the limit of their ability to judge life.'

'Don't forget sex, that looms pretty large.' Verity came into the barn. 'There are four more orders for chickens, seven birds altogether.'

'I suppose if you live on a farm you get used to the life and death cycle?'

'The way I look at it is they can't be killed if they haven't had life and the life they have here is enjoyable. They are fed the best food, are free to roam around and have every care. And when the end comes, it is as stress-free as possible.'

Darina tucked her long hair into a mob cap and gave her hands a good scrub with a germicidal wash.

'Oh, these cards have to go with the new sausages.' Verity handed Darina a packet of postcard-sized paper slips.

Darina looked at one. This is a new recipe, we hope you enjoy it and would be most interested in any comments you may have it read, and was signed: Pru Fry. At the top was the farm's logo, with its name and address.

Pru stuck her head round the door. 'Forgot to say, that crook, Daniel, phoned last night, he's coming round sometime this morning, wants a couple of pounds of the new sausages so you'd better keep some on one side for him.'

'Natasha wants some as well.' Verity started on a new box. 'I suggested she came over for them around twelve thirty and had a glass of wine with us.'

Pru looked at her watch. 'Hope we'll have time for that.' She stumped off back to the barn.

It was almost a week after the funeral. Darina had spent three days helping them out, then she had had to apologise and say she must spend time on her book and her next article. Yesterday evening she had rung Pru, said the article had been dispatched and asked if they could do with a bit more help.

'I'll say we can,' Pru had sighed. 'I just don't have enough hands. Verity keeps popping down to see Natasha, Oliver is trying to sort out Constance's papers, and though he tries to help feed the stock he hardly knows one end of an animal from the other, and as for the boys, they're behaving so badly I wish I could export them to some penal colony for brats. I've advertised for help but the only applicant so far is a half-witted boy who let out all the pigs.'

Darina looked again at the slip of paper. 'How often does Pru produce new lines?'

'Not very often. Mother was a great one for sticking to proven successes. Pru only gradually got her to introduce ham and bacon, then sausages and recently the faggots and pies but it makes a lot of sense. It maximises the profit element, gives you a much better marketing story and makes the business more interesting. Once Pru started, Mother began to realise just how successful it could be. But Pru has still had to fight for every new idea of hers.'

'They seemed to get on so well, I thought.' Darina began slicing up braising steak for the first order.

'Oh, they did. On the surface. But' – Verity finished her box-making activities and stood up, stretching her back – 'if they hadn't been mother and daughter, they'd never have been in business together, they were like oil and water. Whatever one suggested, the other disagreed with, they threw ideas around like two terriers with a rat. By the time they finished, there was fur and entrails all over the place.'

'Perhaps, though,' said Darina slowly, 'if they hadn't been mother and daughter they might have got on much better.'

After a moment's thought, this idea seemed to appeal to Verity. 'You may be right. There was something very personal about their arguments, it was as if they had to get under each other's skin. It was far worse, though, when father was alive. The arguments were dreadful then.'

'Pru was closer to her father?'

'Much. It was terrible when he died. Pru didn't say anything for days. And one time when Mother tried to cheer her up, get her to eat, saying the stupid things people do say, like, life must go on and all that, I thought Pru would hit her. "You never loved him," she shouted at her. "I'll never forgive you for that and I'll always hate you." She was quite demented.'

'What happened?'

'Nothing. Mother just stood there, stock-still. Pru looked at her then ran off. She took her bicycle and disappeared, came back several hours later and started feeding the cows as though everything was all right. But it wasn't, not for weeks and weeks.'

'How did Thomas Fry die?' Even though Verity still called Constance her mother, Darina felt she couldn't refer to him as 'your father'.

'Tractor accident. It overturned with him inside and without the roller bar on. He was crushed. He didn't die immediately, though, he lingered in the hospital for several weeks. Didn't know anyone, the doctors said he'd suffered brain damage and would always be a vegetable. But Pru visited him every day. I'd go with Mother, I suppose it was two or three times a week. I hated it, she was always so bad tempered, there were these horrible smells and Dad looked so, strange, lying there in the bed and not looking like Dad at all. We'd just stand at the end of his bed and look at him for what seemed for ever then go away again. But Pru would hold his hand and talk, tell him what was going on on the farm, what the weather was like, anything that had happened in the village. She said she did it every afternoon. She was convinced she could get through to him. But no one could. It was a real blessing when he died. I'm all for euthanasia myself.

Uh-oh!' She put down the order sheets she had been studying with a groan.

'What's up?' Darina put away the rest of the beef and brought out some pork. She began to cut escalopes.

'I've just remembered I never sliced and vacuum-packed the ham yesterday. I promised Pru I'd do it when I got back from visiting Natasha but Oliver said he hadn't seen me alone for days and took me off for a drink at the local. Then we decided to go out to dinner and I forgot all about the ham. Oh well, it's hardly a tragedy.' She scrubbed her hands then fetched a cooked ham from the chill-room and placed it on the big slicer. She adjusted the thickness and started peeling off the pink layers of meat, arranging them on a tray lined with paper. 'But Pru does get really cross if one doesn't do what one says.'

'How long is your fiancé staying?'

'He says as long as I need him. But apparently Mother's affairs are reasonably straightforward, the will is very simple, Pru gets two thirds of the business and the house. I get one third of the business and we split her estate between us. Not that there's much money, I doubt I'll end up with more than a few hundred pounds, if that. But at least we're not burdened by heavy mortgages. Not like so many of the farmers around here.'

'It sounds as though your mother was a pretty good manager.'

'Oh, she was. But she inherited some money from her father, just after Dad died, and I think all that went into the farm.'

Darina looked round the well-equipped work-room. 'So you're part-owner now of a thriving concern.'

Verity made a small face. 'You could say that but I'd rather have cash.'

'You mean, sell out to your sister?'

'Well, it would be better for her, give her complete control.'

'Do you need the money?' Darina thought of Oliver, his Rolls-Royce, his aura of success.

'One always needs money.'

There was such feeling behind the words, Darina couldn't help smiling. 'Surely Oliver has enough?' she suggested.

'But it's dreadful to be dependent on a husband, have to beg for an allowance! Now I've given up my job, I have nothing coming in. There are lots of possibilities but nothing actually producing filthy lucre. It's too degrading to have to run to him for every little thing. And he certainly wouldn't give me more than a few hundred without wanting to know what it's for and he gets very funny about people who run up credit-card debts and things.'

From which Darina gathered that Verity's financial affairs were in trouble.

'Have you talked to Pru about buying you out?'

Verity gave a funny little sigh. 'It's no go, she wants to save Simon's restaurant for him so she's raising all the money she can for that.' She continued slicing meat in silence for a few moments. 'It's not that I grudge him her backing, it's just all such bad timing. Why did his bloody partner have to go bankrupt just at this moment?' The meat-slicer gained a vicious edge to its whine as another slice of ham fell off the cutting blade.

Darina went on preparing meat for the mail orders.

At noon Natasha rode up slowly but steadily on a bicycle that looked as old as Constance's. Verity's face lit up and Darina watched her greet the older woman with warm affection. 'Come and have a drink,' Verity suggested. 'We've just about finished here and I'm dying for a glass of cool white wine. How about it, Pru?' Her sister had appeared behind Natasha.

'What a good idea.' She dragged the mob cap off her dark curls in a weary gesture. 'I put some muscadet in the fridge this morning.'

A shadowy figure darkened the doorway and a male voice said 'How very kind.' Daniel Quantrell moved inside and picked up two packets of sausages. 'Can I keep these in your fridge for a few minutes? I certainly can't resist such an invitation.'

Pru took the sausages from him and put them in one of the big fridges at the back of the shop with an air of resentment. Darina was amused at the way lack of enthusiasm for Daniel's company was combined with a reluctance to tell him he had not been invited to join them for wine. But he was enrolled to help with the general stacking of the sealed packages in the chill-room to await the delivery company's van before Verity led the way through the house to the conservatory outside the sitting-room.

There, shaded from the sun's brilliance by carefully drawn blinds, Oliver was going through a stack of files. He stood up as the small party entered.

Darina watched the tall man greet Natasha and Daniel with

grave courtesy and unhurriedly fetch wine, ice and mineral water.

Pru had paused in the kitchen and appeared behind him carrying a tray loaded with a large chunk of pâté, a basket of French bread, plates and knives.

'I'm thinking of adding another new line,' she announced, setting it all on a convenient table. 'Have a taste and tell me what you think.'

Daniel reached greedily for a plate and helped himself to a generous portion. Natasha had seated herself in a chair beside a flowering oleander bush in a huge terracotta pot; too late she discovered Daniel had chosen the chair next to her. She looked at his loaded plate with distaste.

'Can I offer you a little?' Oliver held out a plate with a more modest portion. Natasha took it without comment. She sat hunched in her chair and held the plate, making no effort to try the pâté.

Darina helped herself and sampled reflectively.

Daniel wiped his mouth with the back of his hand then took a slurp of the wine Oliver had passed round. 'That's going to win no prizes,' he said with a certain satisfaction.

Pru flushed slightly but said nothing.

Verity shot him a look of dislike. 'It's only Pru's first attempt. I can't see you doing any better and at least this is made of wholly organic ingredients, including the mushrooms.'

'You sound as bad as your mother. Organic doesn't offer anything more special than conservation. And at least I'm not denying my poultry the benefits of modern medicine. With all your high-faluting ideals of animal welfare, you won't give them a good worming when they need it. And what's so special about your organic feed? Don't you allow it to contain up to ten per cent non-organic material?'

'By dry weight, because it's impossible to get hold of sufficient organic high protein material such as soya and luçerne for winter feed,' Pru sounded exasperated. 'And we do not make our animals suffer if medication can help them. You know nothing about organic farming, you just like getting up objections to a system you could never aspire to. Mother had your measure. And if she hadn't died, she would have told everyone just how you feed your precious chickens.'

Verity tried to stop her angry sister. 'There's no point, Pru, what does it matter now?'

'What does it matter? It matters that thanks to what he goes round telling them, people are getting conned into buying chickens they think are fed without additives and more or less raised organically, and it's just not true.'

Daniel's face had whitened, the only colour a slash of red on each cheek. It was hard to decide whether he was angry or afraid. But what could he be afraid of?

'Your mother knew nothing!' he spat out.

'Nothing, eh?' sneered Pru. 'What about the feed you had stacked in your back barn? That wasn't for the chickens, I suppose?'

'Snooping, that's what your mother was doing. She had no right to be in that barn. I could have had her for trespass.'

'She was going to have you for misleading statements.'

'What misleading statements? I've never claimed my chickens were organic.'

'No.' Pru was as white with suppressed anger now as Daniel. 'What you say is "Poultry raised with care to conservation standards, tasting like chickens used to taste". Nothing about the additives in the feed.'

'Daniel, is this true?' Natasha was looking at him with astonishment.

'True? What do you mean, is it true? What does it matter? My birds *are* raised with care, they *do* taste like birds used to taste. What I feed them on is my business and there's no law to say I shouldn't. Most of the chickens in this country thrive on that feed.'

'But I understood your birds were as near to organic as made no difference, that's what you gave me to understand.'

Daniel stood up and thrust his shaking hands deep into the pockets of his trousers.

'Gave you to understand? Oh, yes, you know all about that, don't you? You know all about living lies, don't pretend that you don't. But you didn't realise just how close your cousin and I were, did you? There were some secrets she didn't share with you. And I bet everyone in this room has their own little secret, is pretending something is something that it isn't.' It was as if he had regained control, had the upper hand now on them all.

Nobody spoke. He gave a cold little smile. 'I'll take my sausages, you can put them on my account. And I'll certainly have a go at producing a pâté for you, Pru, it couldn't be any duller than that one.' He gave a contemptuous flick towards his empty plate. 'In fact,' he gave another tight little smile at them all, 'I'm willing to bet nobody here could make as interesting a pâté. I understand about taste, you see, that's why my herbs and chickens are so successful.'

He sauntered slowly from the terrace, round the side of the house, perfectly happy with himself once again.

'Oh, that man!' Verity burst out in disgust.

'What on earth has been going on here?'

Pru swung round. 'Simon! When did you arrive?'

The chef stepped down from the living-room door. 'A few minutes ago, when you were in the middle of your attack on Daniel's rearing methods. Is it really true your mother was going to expose him, did she really go snooping around?'

'You bet! She reckoned he didn't have the tenacity or the commitment to raise his birds properly, that he would have to rely on feed that contained growth promoters and other artificial additives.'

'Why does he bother to make it sound otherwise?' asked Darina.

'Because he can charge more if people think his birds are free of additives, raised naturally. He wants the cash benefit without the hard work. He started raising chickens when he realised how well Mother was doing with hers. He made a great song and dance about how his would be every bit as good but of course it was much too much bother to conform to the standards needed for any of the recognised organic labels so he latched on to "Conservation Standard". There are a number of farmers who produce under a system they call "Conservation" that's almost organic and who do a good job but Daniel Quantrell isn't one of them.'

'I always thought the man was a charlatan. And what's this about a competition for pâté-making?'

Pru explained to Simon about her idea for a new line. The chef tried some of the pâté she had produced and made a small face. 'Needs much more flavouring. Would you like me to have a go?'

She regarded him doubtfully. 'Would it be something I could produce easily?'

He grinned at her. 'Don't worry, I know your production limitations.'

'Why don't we all have a go?' suggested Verity. 'We could make it into a real competition. You could do one, couldn't you, Darina? And how about you, Natasha?'

The older woman smiled painfully at her. 'I might be able to remember something Natalie once did but I have so little taste now I couldn't rely on it being edible.'

'Of course it would be.' Verity looked lovingly at her.

'You're on,' Pru said decisively. 'Winner to be awarded a joint of his or her choice?'

'Irresistible,' said Simon.

'I'll give Daniel time to get home then ring and announce what you've offered as a prize for the best pâté, that'll get him all excited. Then I'll add he hasn't got a chance of winning,' said Verity with satisfaction.

'How about everyone getting down to it tomorrow? The sooner I can add the line the better.'

Verity glanced guiltily at Natasha. 'I'm sorry, Pru, I forgot to tell you, we're going up to London, Natasha has made an appointment for me to meet Natalie's agent.'

The girl could hardly contain her excitement at the prospect. Darina remembered her own sense of wonder at acquiring an agent. It had seemed a seal of professionalism, a badge that guaranteed her authenticity. And so many things had become so much easier: contact with publishers, the sifting of possible book ideas, discovering what was marketable and what was not, not to mention the joy of having an expert to take financial negotiation off her shoulders. And Verity could have no better start to her career than to be represented by Natalie Duke's agent. Lucky girl to have such an introduction.

Pru's forehead creased with annoyance. 'But tomorrow's the day I take the van to Dorset, to the market. I was relying on you to be here, there are several orders that are going to be called for and the boys need picking up from school.'

Verity's face fell. 'Oh, Pru, I'm sorry, I didn't think.'

'You never do,' her sister said roughly.

Verity turned to Darina. 'You couldn't help out, could you?'

'I'm sorry, I have to go to London tomorrow myself for a few days. I could give you a lift up, in fact, if you'd like one, though I expect it would be quicker by train.'

Verity looked at Natasha, who nodded. 'That'd be great,' the girl said.

'But you refused my offer to drive you there and back,' Oliver said quietly.

There was the tiniest of pauses, then: 'It would have put you to so much trouble and you know you want to finish going through Mother's papers,' Verity said in a rush. She went and hugged his arm. 'It's different with Darina going up anyway.'

He dropped a kiss on the top of her head. 'I shall try not to feel too rejected,' he said in a light voice and looked across at Pru. 'I can deal with callers as long as what they have to collect is clearly marked and I might even manage collecting the boys.'

'I can do that,' said Simon unexpectedly, giving the tall man a look of dislike.

It all seemed to fall smoothly into place. Darina would pick up Natasha and Verity first thing in the morning, Oliver would collect them at the station in the evening. And Simon would meet the boys from school and look after them until Pru returned from Dorset. The chef then asked for his order and left.

'You couldn't have arranged that so easily if Mother had still been alive,' said Verity, watching his battered car drive away.

'If Mother had still been alive, I wouldn't have needed to,' Pru retorted crossly.

'What about Daniel Quantrell?' asked Darina as they returned to packing up sausages. 'Are you going to take on your mother's crusade against his practices?'

'I haven't the time.' Pru packed half a pound of ham, two chickens and three pounds of rump steak into a box. 'And, anyway, I lack the same urge. Mother couldn't bear people to be conned in any way. I can't be bothered now, I've too much else on my plate, it's up to the public to make sure they are actually getting what they think they are. But Mother was a fanatic. If she'd lived, I wouldn't have cared to be Daniel.'

# Chapter Fourteen

Darina spent three days in London and didn't hear about the second tragedy until she returned to Somerset. She had a frustrating afternoon discovering the number of her instructions that had been either ignored or altered by the decorators. Then the next two days were packed as she tried to ensure the house would be finished to her satisfaction and caught up with several of her London friends. She knew she ought to remain in town, that the decorators could not be trusted on their own, but the weather was scorchingly hot, the friends seemed to be involved in lives that had little to do with her own and she longed for the calmer atmosphere of the country.

She refused to admit that part of her restlessness came from a chance meeting in the King's Road with William's aunt, who had greeted her with great warmth and insisted on carrying her off home for a drink.

'It's too long since we've seen you,' Lady Doubleday had said once the Pimm's had been organised on the shady terrace of their house just off Eaton Square. 'Do tell me exactly what William is up to in New York. We've had one postcard which told us little more than he'd been up the Empire State Building and sailed round Manhattan. Sounded more like a tourist than a policeman getting on with an investigation.'

Darina said she knew little more.

Honor Doubleday regarded her thoughtfully.

'My dear, tell me if I'm a stupid old lady who should mind her own business but would it help to talk about it? We're so fond of you both.'

Part of Darina wanted to pour out the whole story, hear what her sympathetic and wise friend would advise. Instead she had looked across at the bright geraniums spilling out of their pots and shaken her head, unable to trust herself to speak for a moment. If only she understood herself. If only William hadn't found somebody else. She blinked determinedly and turned to her hostess with a wide smile. 'It's just one of those things,' she said. 'There are some compromises that are too difficult to make.'

'Ah,' Honor Doubleday murmured. 'Sometimes what is today's unacceptable compromise becomes tomorrow's willing capitulation. From both sides.'

'I think it's gone beyond that.'

'I would hate to think you are right. Have faith.'

'But if I'm happy with the way things are?'

'And are you?'

There was no answer to that.

With practised ease Lady Doubleday moved the conversation on and they enjoyed each other's company for half an hour or so before Darina took her leave, pleading another engagement and promising to invite Honor and her husband to supper when she was next in London.

She started back to Somerset very early the next morning, before the sun could get too hot. It was typical, she thought, driving under a grey sky, that the weather should change without warning. But the chill matched her mood. What she needed, one of her friends had said, was a new man. Easy to say, the only men she seemed attracted to these days were unavailable. Simon Chapman, for instance. If it hadn't been for Pru, perhaps . . . But if there was any chance at all that Pru and Simon's marriage could be resurrected, Darina would not interfere. Oliver Knatchbull was also someone else's property. And, despite the gap in ages, Verity was deeply committed to him. That fact had become very clear during the drive up to London.

Darina had collected Natasha first then had continued on to Fry's Farm. Even at six thirty in the morning Oliver was up and dressed to see his fiancée off. Waiting for Verity to appear, Darina had commented on the early hour. Oliver smiled. 'No hardship in this weather, it's a privilege to see the sun come up. Just look at that light.' Darina had admired with him the pearly dawn shining with translucent splendour through the orchard trees, converting their green to a shimmering silvery grey, then Verity had dashed out.

She exchanged a lingering kiss with Oliver then got in the back of Darina's car, giving Natasha a quick peck on her scarred cheek before turning in her seat to wave goodbye to the tall man standing outside the kitchen door.

As Darina manoeuvred the car, taking care to steer very clear of Oliver's resplendent Rolls-Royce, Natasha said to Verity, 'I hope you don't mind too much not having your fiancé drive us to London?'

'No, I told you, it's all right,' Verity said quietly. 'The last thing I wanted was for him to spend the whole day chauffeuring us around.' There was a small pause then she added, 'But I wish you could tell me why you dislike him so.'

Natasha shifted in the seat beside Darina. 'I don't dislike him, darling, please don't think that.'

'Then why are you so against my engagement?'

'I just think you are too young. You have an exciting career before you, it's too soon to get yourself tied down. If you marry you'll find your life will no longer be your own. There'll be children, the demands of running a home, looking after your husband's interests. You've got the chance now of doing so much, so many things are breaking for you.'

For miles as Darina drove towards London she listened awkwardly to the ding-dong battle between the woman and the girl. She refused to be drawn into the discussion, she knew too little of Verity, didn't understand Natasha's antagonism. But she was full of admiration for the way Verity handled the querulous objections to her engagement, steadfastly reiterating Oliver's commitment to her career.

'There's so much I could do for you,' Natasha said at last. The scars on her face flared angrily. 'But if you insist on this insane course of action, I don't think I can continue in the same way.'

There was silence from the back of the car. Then Verity said in a quiet, cold voice, 'What do you mean by that?'

'The arrangement between Natalie and myself regarding her money was very informal, you know. I don't have to leave you anything. Or help you in any way.'

For one moment Darina thought Verity was going to fly at the woman and braced herself for what might happen.

But the girl suddenly leant forward over the back of the seat and hugged the woman. 'Silly you, you're just worried I'm going to disappear out of your life. I won't, I promise. I'm not going to give either of you up. Make up your mind to that.' Beneath the soft voice was implacable resolution. There was no doubt Verity knew her mind and that she intended to get exactly what she wanted in every way.

Beside her in the front seat Darina sensed Natasha Quantrell accept the finality of this, heard a long sigh escape her. 'I don't think you realise just how determined I can be,' she said and asked Darina to pull into the service station they were approaching. Here she made a telephone call then announced that she had cancelled the appointment with the agent.

For a moment Verity looked nonplussed. And not only nonplussed but angry. 'For heaven's sake,' she started but then stopped and looked rather like a parent confronted with an obstinate child. She swallowed hard and gave a curt laugh. 'You win, for the moment, Natasha. And what do we do now? Catch the first train back when we get to London? It'll be a difficult journey, there isn't a direct train until the afternoon.'

The woman and the girl stood facing each other, both with iron determination etched in their faces. Then Verity's dissolved into a sweet smile. 'Let's take a day off, shall we? Not worry about any fiancé or career or my mother or anything else? Let's have a day out in London, go for a good meal somewhere, perhaps see if there's a matinée. How about it?' Her voice was cajoling.

Natasha looked very tired, a tic pulsed at the corner of one eye. 'How like,' she said, 'how very like you are.'

Verity beamed. 'I love it when you say things like that. Perhaps I won't stop you talking about my mother after all. Come on, let's get back in the car, Darina has to get to London, she's got a time schedule even if we haven't.'

The rest of the journey had been accomplished in an atmosphere of great good humour, generated and nourished by Verity.

Just what were her motives, Darina wondered as she listened to her teasing Natasha. Did she hope to woo her into accepting Oliver? Or was she really resigned to the dashing of any financial hopes she had had of Natasha helping her in her career or even, maybe, of paying off her debts? It was impossible to judge.

Just what had happened during their day in London, she wondered with some curiosity as she drove back to Somerset.

* * *

She drew up outside the cottage and sat for a moment, gearing herself up to face the mess she knew was inside. If time had been short for working on her book, it had been non-existent for housework. The kitchen looked even worse than she remembered. She cleared up the sink then started to defrost the refrigerator, discarding several items unidentifiable beneath the fur. Why did she find it impossible not to hang on to bits of food until any hope of use was long past?

With the kitchen table loaded with usable items and a bowl of hot water speeding up the defrosting process, she made herself a cup of tea and tried to decide on her next task. It should be cleaning the floor but there was no point in doing that until the fridge had been done. She ought to get back to her book but the break in her working routine had left her too restless to settle yet to the word processor. She ought to ring her mother but felt she couldn't face a renewal of the campaign to persuade her to make it up with William.

Then she remembered the pâté she had made in London and brought down with her. Working out the recipe had taken her mind off other things while she had been in town. It had had a day or so to mature now and should be ready for sampling.

She went inside and rang Fry's Farm.

Pru answered. Her voice was strained and in the background Darina could hear a child crying. The other girl broke off to shout at him to shut up; louder cries came in response. Pru apologised over the racket.

'Don't worry,' Darina said, 'it's obviously not a good time, I'll call again later.'

'No, don't go.' There was an urgent quality now to Pru's voice. 'We're in the most terrible state here, you couldn't come over, could you? I'm desperate for some help and I badly need to talk to someone.'

'What's the matter?'

'You haven't heard?'

'Heard what? I've only just got back from London.'

'Natasha's dead.' The bald statement was followed by a crash as of some falling furniture and then by even louder wailing. 'Look, I can't talk on the phone, can't you come over?'

No sooner had she agreed than Darina found her connection had been cut.

When she arrived at the farm she found Pru making sausages. 'What,' she demanded, 'happened to Natasha? She seemed fine on Tuesday. And where's Verity, why isn't she helping you?'

'She's giving a statement to the police, Oliver took her to the station after breakfast.'

'The police! Pru, for heaven's sake, what exactly has happened?'

The other girl pushed cubed pork into the mincer. 'Natasha died the day after you all went up to London. The police appear to think she was poisoned.'

Darina's stomach gave a nasty lurch. 'Poisoned?'

Pru finished mincing and began seasoning the meat with salt and pepper and dried herbs. 'Daniel's dog has died as well.'

'Dog?' Darina seemed unable to produce sentences of more than one word.

'It was a dreadful mutt, but Daniel rescued it when it was a puppy from some boys trying to discover how long it took to drown an animal, and he was devoted to it. He's been round here flinging all sorts of accusations at us.' Pru finished seasoning the meat and wiped her forehead wearily.

'He thinks *you* poisoned it? But why?'

'I don't understand it any more than you, Darina. I think Daniel is off his rocker. He keeps harking back to the argument he had with Constance. I can't believe anyone could have poisoned Natasha deliberately and why the police think Verity had anything to do with it, I can't imagine. I mean, she and Oliver did everything they could to help.'

Darina pleaded with her to start the story at the beginning.

Pru started filling a casing, the long sinuous sausage began to circle the tray positioned to catch it as it bulged, glistening, from the nozzle of the machine. 'Sorry, didn't I explain? She rang Verity that night and said she was dying.'

# Chapter Fifteen

Detective Constable Pat James collected Verity and Oliver from the front hall of the police station and escorted them to the interview room where Detective Inspector Grant was waiting.

The investigation into the death of Natasha Quantrell was still in its infancy.

'Suspicious death,' the hospital had said, which meant there were circumstances that needed looking into.

First off had been a brief examination of the deceased's home to check for the presence of digitalis tablets. The local doctor had denied supplying her with any. 'The only prescription I've given her was for pain-killers after she came to see me on her return from France,' he'd said. 'I suggested she try to manage without as much as possible but she'd been through a hell of a time and who was I to deny her some surcease? No digitalis in those. But I have no idea what those French doctors could have prescribed.'

All that had been found in the Bailey were the prescribed pain-killers in a bathroom cabinet and a supply of Panadol beside Natasha Quantrell's bed.

'That would have been the easy explanation,' said Grant. 'Perhaps too easy.'

'Then there's the dog,' said Pat.

'Ah, yes, the dog.'

It had been Pat who had had to deal with a Daniel Quantrell almost beside himself with grief and anger when he rang in to the station the day before, demanding to speak to a detective about the murder of his dog.

Pat had driven out to his cottage.

'It's those damned Frys,' was the first thing he had said to her.

She opened her notebook and sat primly on the small settee that managed to find room for itself in the cottage's living-room amidst a clutter of broken-down chairs and dusty tables bearing an assortment of bronze figures and pottery mugs. There was a nastily pervasive smell of damp and rotting wood.

Daniel Quantrell was pacing backwards and forwards, somehow finding a free path amongst the furniture.

'How do you know the dog was poisoned, sir?'

He'd stopped in his stalking of the floor and bit back the accusations that had been freely flowing ever since her arrival.

'How?'

'Yes, presumably you found the dog dead; how do you know it was poisoned?'

He flung himself into an armchair that sagged on one side and had stuffing erupting from the other.

'I got the vet to do an autopsy.'

'What made you think there was something suspicious about the death?'

'I just wanted to know why Rupert died, damn it,' he roared at her, bringing a hand down hard on his knee. 'It was my dog. Perfectly healthy one day, dead the next. It wasn't natural, of course I was suspicious. Vet said it was unnecessary, probably a heart attack. Heart attack? The dog was only five years old! I insisted on an autopsy. Of course I did.'

'And the result?'

'The vet said he wouldn't know exactly until he'd had the results of some tests but that it was a heart attack probably brought on by some sort of digitalis poisoning. Asked if the dog could have got hold of some heart pills. Ridiculous! I've never had heart pills. Erica's never had heart pills.'

'Is Erica your wife?'

He glared at her. 'Wife? Of course not, she's my partner, runs the market garden side of things, lives in the village. Rupert and I were often over there.' His voice had dropped to a mumble and Pat had to strain to catch the words.

'Rupert, the dog?'

'Named him after Prince Rupert, most of him was cavalier spaniel, you see.'

Pat was not sure that she did. 'And the vet felt the dog could not have ingested the digitalis' – she glanced at her notebook to check she had the word correct – 'that is, that the digitalis could not have been picked up naturally?'

Daniel laughed, a raw sound totally devoid of humour. 'Unless he'd had a yen for a field of foxgloves, no. And when was the last time you saw more than the odd foxglove around here anyway?'

Wild-flower spotting had never been one of Pat James's hobbies and she was willing to take Daniel Quantrell's word on the prevalence of foxgloves. For a brief moment she wondered about heart pills. Were there fields of foxgloves grown for medicinal purposes, like fields of poppies for opium? But Pat James was not given to flights of fancy and she quickly dismissed the idea as ridiculous.

'And you have no idea how the dog could have ingested the digitalis?'

She was treated to another diatribe against the Frys.

'I'm sorry, sir,' she said as he paused to take breath. 'I am afraid I still don't understand why you suspect either of the Miss Frys of poisoning your dog.'

He gaped at her. 'I don't mean Pru or Verity. It was their mother, Constance. She was the one who had a grudge against me and she knew how much Rupert meant to me.'

Pat wondered if the sun was getting to her, it was like playing one of those space invader games where figures rushed at you from all directions and only the fastest of responses won you the game.

'But Constance Fry is dead,' she managed after swallowing hard.

'Doesn't mean a thing,' the man insisted.

Pat dismissed a vision of Constance Fry coming back from the grave to wreak vengeance. After all, why should she want to wreak vengeance?

'She could have planted the stuff weeks ago. Who knows, she could have been returning from planting some poison or other when she was run over. And it would have served her right.'

'Our investigations into Mrs Fry's death suggest she was cycling towards the Bailey when she was killed, not back from it,' said Pat.

Daniel Quantrell was not one of those who let facts stand in the way of a good theory. Nor could he see that his insistence on Constance Fry's vendetta against him was producing a reluctance on the part of Detective Constable James to consider seriously his charges of dog poisoning. She had taken some more details then extricated herself from his cottage as gracefully as she could, promising to contact him if anything could be discovered relevant to the dog's death. And had driven back to the police station convinced it was the last she need bother with what she found herself referring to as the Case of the Poisoned Dog.

Only to find the case of Natasha Quantrell's death from suspected poisoning by an excess of digitalis had been opened. It was far too pat to be coincidence.

As was the constant reappearance of the name of Fry. For it had been Verity Fry and her fiancé who had summoned the ambulance for Natasha Quantrell the night she collapsed.

Which was why Inspector Grant had requested them to attend for interviewing. He took Verity Fry first and asked Oliver Knatchbull to wait in another room. He'd wanted his fiancée to have a solicitor in attendance but she had refused. She had nothing to hide, she said; she'd prefer to get the interview over with as quickly as possible, not wait for a solicitor to be summoned,

She sat perched uneasily on a chair while Grant explained the procedure of taping the interview. Pat never ceased to be grateful to the machine for releasing her from the necessity of taking notes. It meant she could concentrate on the witness, not only on what was being said but how it was said. The tape could record the words; what it left out were the body movements that went with those words, sometimes movements that were at variance with what was being said. There was talk of video recording now and it couldn't come soon enough for Pat.

She looked at Verity Fry. The girl was making little effort to disguise her nervousness. A small, pink tongue moistened her lips constantly. One slim leg was crossed over the other, then recrossed the other way. She leant forward in her chair, then leant back. Her eyes were raised to Grant's only to fall as soon as they met his quiet, assessing gaze.

Pat had noticed how very different Verity Fry and her sister were at the time she interviewed them after their mother's death. There had been a stolid dependability about Pru Fry that had escaped her sister completely. And the younger girl seemed much more sophisticated than the farmer, with a delicate bone structure that now seemed even more noticeable. There were dark shadows under the blue eyes, a pinched look to the too-large nose. At the previous interview, the mop of fair hair had been glossy with cleanliness, now it had lost some of its shine, needed washing. Then the face had shone with health and wore a minimum of make-up, now it was drawn and a couple of spots failed to be disguised by the hastily applied foundation.

'Please tell me exactly what happened the night you went over to see Miss Quantrell.' Grant had recorded the preliminaries, now he was ready to start the interview. He sat with elbows resting on the little table between himself and his witness. Formal as always, he retained his suit jacket in the small airless room, his shirt as buttoned down as his manner.

Verity Fry gave another lick to her lips. 'It was about three in the morning,' she started in a small voice, then cleared her throat and spoke a little more confidently. 'We, that is, I was woken by the phone, got up and went downstairs to answer it. At first,' she swallowed nervously, 'at first I couldn't recognise who it was, thought it must be a wrong number.' Her eyes closed for a moment. 'Then it was as though a bad line had cleared and I recognised Natasha's voice. She said, quite clearly, "Verity, help me." Then her voice went all indistinct again, as though she was having trouble speaking. I asked her what was the matter, was she ill? She said, and again it was quite distinct, "Yes, ill, dying." Then she tried to say something else but her voice had gone all funny again. I could only pick up the odd word. It sounded like, mishtake, then something else, and shouldn't have, another slurred jumble, and finally I thought I heard poison.' Tears splashed on to the table and Verity Fry fumbled in the pocket of her jeans for a handkerchief. A large white one was passed across to her.

'And then?' asked Grant, making a note on his pad.

The girl scrubbed the tears from her eyes. 'There was a noise that could have been her falling and then nothing. I dressed as quickly as I could, and so did Oliver, my fiancé, and we rushed round to the Bailey, where we found her collapsed on the floor by the telephone. Then—'

'Just a minute, Miss Fry,' Grant interrupted. 'How did you get into the house, did you have a key?'

'No.' Verity looked if anything even more nervous. 'Natasha never kept the door locked.'

'She didn't lock her door at all?'

'She said there was no need.' Verity's eyes switched their gaze between Grant and Pat James. 'We often leave our door open, people round here do.'

'They are learning not to,' Grant said grimly. 'And the burglary rate climbs higher and higher even when all the doors are locked.'

'Well, then,' said Verity with a tiny triumphant note in her voice, 'if you are going to get burgled anyway, what does it matter?'

Pat James waited for the inspector to start on his standard speech, the one itemising crime statistics showing the high percentage of break-ins that were crimes of opportunity, mostly by youngsters. Stop those and you cut out the main chance of losing your possessions. But instead he gave a slight shake to his head and returned to the night Natasha Quantrell had made her last phone call.

'So, you entered the house by the open door and found Miss Quantrell collapsed on the floor by the telephone. Where was that, in the hall, her bedroom, or somewhere else?'

'In the hall, she didn't have an extension.'

'And then?'

'I rang for an ambulance.'

'And while you waited, what happened?'

Verity looked mystified. 'Nothing happened, we just waited.'

'You stayed by Miss Quantrell? Didn't move into another room at all?'

'Oh, I see what you mean. Well, I remained in the hall, sitting by Natasha. She looked dreadful, her face was all distorted and her tongue was poking from her mouth, it looked swollen, perhaps that's why she couldn't speak properly. I couldn't find her pulse but she was still breathing. Oliver had got a cushion and a rug from the morning room and we'd made her as comfortable as we could. I sat on the floor and held her hand. And then Oliver brought me a cup of tea.' Grant made another note.

Pat thought that Oliver Knatchbull looked the sort of man who could be relied on to produce a cup of tea when it was needed. Bit like William Pigram with those tall, well-cut looks and diamond-bright educated accent but, like William, with no side about him. The sort who would go to the heart of a matter, not worry about social protocol or class barriers.

'So your fiancé went into the kitchen?'

'We both came in through the back door that way.'

'Do you remember anything in particular about the room?'

Verity thought for a moment then shook her head. 'I was worried about Natasha, I just dashed straight through.'

'And when the ambulance arrived?'

'I told the driver she thought she'd been poisoned and then we, that is, Oliver and I, followed it to the hospital.'

'How long did you stay there?'

Verity thought for a little. 'I suppose it was about a couple of hours. We waited in casualty for what seemed for ever and then finally a doctor came and told us she was in a coma and we might as well go home and call the hospital in the morning. I wanted to stay but Oliver said there was no point. We rang at about nine that morning and were told she hadn't come out of the coma, then a little later someone called and told us Natasha had died. I went straight there and the doctor told me she had never regained consciousness and started asking me about heart tablets.'

Tears were flowing freely and Grant waited patiently until Verity had them under control. Then he asked, 'You seem to have shown enormous concern for someone who was no relation of yours and can only have been a recent acquaintance. I understand Miss Quantrell had spent most of the last twenty years or so abroad.'

Verity bit her lip. 'She was a relation,' she said at last in her small voice. 'Her cousin, Natalie Duke, was my real mother. I was adopted by the Frys. Natasha Quantrell has been as kind to me as if she had been my mother herself. We had a very close relationship.'

This was news to Pat and, she thought, to Grant as well. She looked at Verity curiously. 'When did you find out exactly who your mother was?' she asked.

'Natasha told me the day after Mother, that is, Constance Fry, died.'

'Mrs Fry had not told you herself?'

'No.'

Pat and Grant waited.

'I think my mother, Natalie Duke, that is, wanted to keep it a secret but then she died a few months ago and after Natasha had met me, she decided I should know.' She fiddled with the handkerchief again then burst out: 'How did she die? You must know something!'

Grant looked at her coolly. 'The admissions doctor recognised signs of acute digitalis poisoning. He thought Miss Quantrell probably had a history of heart disease and had overdosed on tablets given her against an attack. But there is no sign of Miss Quantrell having had digitalis in her possession and we are conducting further inquiries.'

'Surely you don't think she could have been deliberately poisoned?' Verity's eyes were now as scared as a rabbit's who has seen the farmer with his gun.

'Why are you surprised, you stated you thought Miss Quantrell had said she'd been poisoned?'

'I know but I thought that meant she had food poisoning or something. We'd had lunch together in London that day, I thought she might have been checking to see whether I felt ill as well. She ate very little, though, hardly anything in fact. It was such a pity because it was a superb meal.'

That meant an investigation into where they had had lunch and the reason for their trip. Once again Verity seemed increasingly nervous. Pat was certain that a day out was not the main reason they had gone to the capital but Grant did not press the point. 'You went on a cheap day-ticket, no doubt?'

Verity explained they had been given a lift up by Darina Lisle. Pat James heard Grant give a small sigh and she knew exactly what he was thinking. Even with William Pigram out of the country, it seemed impossible to keep his girlfriend out of a murder case. 'And Oliver met us on our return. We dropped Natasha off at the Bailey and went straight back to Fry's Farm.'

'Is there anyone who can confirm that?'

Verity gave him a startled look. 'No, my sister was out. Why, does it matter?'

Pat James interjected, 'Your sister has two small boys, was nobody baby-sitting?'

'Both my sister and the boys were with her husband, Simon Chapman,' said Verity with a certain dignity. 'They spent the night with him and returned the next day.'

'And, as far as you know, Miss Quantrell spent the rest of the evening alone?'

'Yes.'

There was little else the witness could contribute.

When her place had been taken by her fiancé, Grant took

him through the same procedure. And received the same information until the point when the call to the ambulance had been made.

'And after that?' Grant asked again.

Oliver Knatchbull paused for a moment. 'That must have been when I made us a cup of tea,' he said.

'And you went back into the kitchen to do so?'

'I believe it's where tea is usually made.' The voice was pleasant but this was a witness who was not going to allow police procedure to get him down.

'And what do you remember about the kitchen, sir?' Grant asked impassively.

Another pause for thought. 'It looked as though Miss Quantrell had had a light supper. There was a tray with a plate and knife and a wine glass which could have contained white wine. Apart from that, the kitchen was tidy, no food out on the table or on the work surfaces. I found some milk in the fridge, there seemed very little else in it as I remember.'

'And there was just the one glass on the tray? Any others around the kitchen?'

Oliver Knatchbull gave careful thought to the question. 'No, I only saw the one glass.'

'And you left them where they were, sir?'

For the first time Oliver Knatchbull looked, not precisely nervous, but a little less than his cool self. He adjusted the knot on his tie and cleared his throat. 'Actually, Inspector, I washed them up while waiting for the kettle to boil. There seemed no reason not to.'

Grant watched him closely. 'Not when poison had been mentioned?'

There was no further sign Oliver Knatchbull was anything but in full control now. 'I believe my fiancée did tell me something of the sort as we were driving over but her account of what Natasha Quantrell had tried to say was so disjointed, I'm afraid it didn't register. Even if it had, I have to say I probably wouldn't have given the washing-up of a plate and glass a second thought. I can see now, though, I was mistaken and I apologise.' It was handsomely done.

Grant made another note.

* * *

No sooner had the interview ended and the witnesses been seen off the premises than Grant told Pat they were to return to the Bailey. 'I've arranged for the daily woman to be brought there for questioning,' he explained as she drove the Ford out of the police station. 'And I want a word with the owner of that dog which was poisoned.'

Pat sighed, she'd known it would come but she would prefer not to have to deal with Mr Quantrell again.

'What did you think of Miss Fry?' asked Grant as they drove towards Lamington.

Pat marshalled her impressions. 'Very nervous, sir,' she said finally. 'Of course,' she added, 'she was in a police station, being recorded but, even so.'

'Yes, a touch too much of the trembling lip and tearful eye, I thought. But the two stories tallied exactly.'

'And why not? They've had enough time to perfect them.'

'If they needed to, eh?'

'Yet it all rang true, I thought.'

Grant mused for a moment then said, 'I thought Knatchbull was just a touch specious about his washing-up activities. Fine way to remove evidence. We'll give any possible motive on his part close attention.'

Mrs Boult, small and spry, about sixty years old, was waiting in the Bailey's kitchen, attended by a uniformed constable. She was sitting on a chair and looking at the floor as though she wished she were scrubbing it.

'It's very good of you to come here,' Grant said after he'd introduced both himself and Pat.

'It's not my morning, I have to say that.' Mrs Boult tucked the corners of her mouth firmly away. 'And the washing's waiting at home so if you wouldn't mind getting round to exactly what you want, I can be off back to my work.' Mrs Boult's hands clutched her large black bag a little tighter and clamped it more firmly on her lap.

'It's about the morning after Miss Quantrell was taken to hospital,' said Grant without further ado.

Pat found a convenient chair and pulled out her notebook and pencil.

'And what about it?' Mrs Boult bristled as though her competence had been called into question.

Grant explained he wanted her to tell him exactly what she had found on her arrival. Mrs Boult sucked her teeth and looked at him steadily. Pat compared Grant's interview techniques with William Pigram's. The sergeant would have set the woman at her ease, made a friend of her. The inspector preferred a more direct approach. But Mrs Boult decided it was one she could handle.

They heard how she had found a note on the kitchen table. 'From Miss Verity it was, saying Miss Quantrell had been taken to hospital and she would let me know later that morning how she was. Can't say it surprised me, ever since she came back from France Miss Quantrell's not looked good at all. Gave me quite a turn, and I'm not talking about those scars, poor lady, what a mess her face was.' For a moment it seemed as though she would add something else, then her mouth snapped shut.

Patient questioning by Grant slowly elicited the information that there had been a tray with two teacups and a teapot sitting on the kitchen table when she arrived.

'No other dirty crockery anywhere?'

'No, just what I said.'

'And how was the rest of the house?'

Mrs Boult blinked rapidly, showing distress for the first time. 'The only room as wasn't as it should've been was the bathroom. Terrible mess that was in, poor soul. No wonder she'd been took to hospital. But I got it cleaned up.'

'It looked beautifully clean when we were here yesterday,' put in Pat.

Her only reward was a sharp glance from nearly black eyes that said she could try that with some but Mrs Boult wasn't falling for it. 'And what were you doing here, may I ask?'

'We are investigating Miss Quantrell's death,' explained Grant. 'Anything you can tell us about her last days could be of great help.' The inspector got another old-fashioned look and Mrs Boult said nothing.

'Were you here the day before she died?'

'Nah, that's the day I go to Mrs Beamish. I comes here Mondays, Wednesdays and Thursdays. That was a Tuesday.'

'Was there anyone Miss Quantrell did not get on with?'

Mrs Boult cocked her head on one side, her eyes bright as a magpie's. 'Miss Quantrell's private life is her private life. No business of mine.'

'Then there was someone she quarrelled with?' Grant pounced swiftly.

Mrs Boult continued to regard him beadily. 'Now that's not what I said and no amount of you putting down my words is going to make me say it neither.' She looked pointedly towards Pat's notebook.

Grant stood up and asked his witness if she would take them through the food in the kitchen and tell them if there was anything that hadn't been there when she'd left on the Monday.

Mrs Boult rose readily enough. 'Don't mind doing that. Mind you, I'm not saying I'll know for sure but Miss Quantrell never had too much food about. Hardly ate enough to keep body and soul together. Said she'd lost her appetite when she lost her taste.'

The fridge door was opened and its meagre contents inspected. 'Nothing was here that wasn't there Monday. She's eaten the soup she made, intended for her supper that was. There was some nice brown bread, that's gone, probably had that with the soup I dare say. Most of the herbs seem to have gone, there was quite a bunch here on Monday. Can't think what she would have used those for, Miss Strangeways brings her a new bunch every few days and normally not more 'n half ever get used.'

Then the larder was gone through. Old fashioned, opening off the kitchen, it was stacked with tinned goods, stored kitchen equipment, the harvest of several years' empty jam bottles, old thermos flasks, a fish kettle and some very large, very dusty saucepans. There was generous space for the storage of fresh food on two thick stone shelves that stood scrubbed and ready for the provender of more ample days when the house had held a larger family than one frail spinster.

Mrs Boult took her task seriously. She peered along the shelves of tins and dry goods, moved bags of flour and sugar, officiously checked under the stone shelves where large pottery crocks stood, no doubt waiting for a consignment of pickled eggs or meats. Grant watched her patiently. If he thought she was taking an inordinately long time over her task, nothing in his demeanour suggested it.

And he was rewarded by Mrs Boult swooping into a dark corner of the larder and drawing out a loaf tin. 'This was never here when I left Monday, I'm sure of that. I scrubbed down the shelves that day. That's why I looked so careful 'cause I'd had everything out, knew exactly where it went back. And this was never here.'

'If you'd just put it down on the shelf, Mrs Boult,' said Grant colourlessly.

Mrs Boult shot him one of her sharp looks then carefully placed the tin in the centre of the stone shelf and stepped slowly away from it as though it might explode.

Grant and Pat James drew closer.

The tin held what to Pat looked like meat loaf, only not quite. More like the coarse pâtés she saw in delicatessens, that she had sometimes bought until she had discovered just how much fat most of them contained. About an inch was missing from one end, as though a thick slice had been lifted out.

'Pork, would you say?' asked Grant.

'Probably,' she said doubtfully, thinking pork was what those pâtés had mainly seemed composed of.

'Pâté de campagne,' said Mrs Boult, making quite an accurate stab at the pronunciation. She gave a laugh that was more of a cackle at their surprise. 'My sister works in a deli, she's always bringing it home. Goes right tasty with a cobber. And Miss Quantrell told me she was going to make one, brought some meat back specially from Fry's Farm on Monday, said there was some sort of competition. Said . . . ' Once again Mrs Boult's jaw clamped tightly shut.

Grant tried several approaches: oblique, direct, cajoling, threatening, nothing would move Mrs Boult. There had been nothing else she was going to say and even if she had, it was no business of the police. The only other relevant piece of information they gleaned was that the meat Natasha Quantrell had come back with on Monday could not be found. It was not in the fridge, the larder or the deep-freeze. Finally Grant let the cleaning woman go.

'You can have another try later,' he said to Pat as Mrs Boult was driven off in the police car, back to her washing, highly delighted to be chauffeured around. 'Maybe the woman-to-woman approach will work better.'

Pat thought of Mrs Boult's firmly compressed lips and doubted it.

# Chapter Sixteen

Natasha Quantrell dead! Darina found it difficult to take in. It had only been a few days ago that she had sat listening to the quarrel between her and Verity, then had dropped them in the West End seemingly reconciled with each other if not with their respective attitudes towards Oliver Knatchbull. Well, at least Verity didn't have to cope with Natasha's hostility to her fiancé now. Any more than Pru had to cope with her mother's towards Simon.

She helped Pru make sausages and listened to the story of what had happened since she last saw Verity and Natasha, noting along the way that Pru had stayed Tuesday night with her estranged husband. Estranged no longer?

'They were having such a good time when I went over to collect the boys after getting back from Dorset, Simon said couldn't I stay, they could eat in the restaurant, I could help and, well, it all seemed to follow on from there.' Pru gave a shy smile that lit her dark face but seemed to apologise for something she had had little control over. Darina thought what a pity it was she didn't smile more often. It made her look so much more attractive than the scowl she usually wore.

'Was the restaurant full?'

'Not bad for a Tuesday, mostly tourists. We had two tables that came in on spec. Simon was awfully pleased. He says the weekends are really busy now.'

'And are you going to back him?'

Pru twisted a last sausage into its separate lengths and straightened her back. Her smile had vanished but she no longer looked sulky. Purposeful was more the word. She nodded. 'We're going to have another go at our marriage. Simon is terribly fond of the boys and they adore him.'

'What about you?'

Pru stood looking at the neat piles of sausages. 'I could never really believe he loved me,' she said slowly. 'Simon is so attractive, such fun, could have had anybody. And I've never had any illusions about my looks. I thought I had to help Mother, that it was my duty to keep things going here but I think, actually, I was making sure I had something of my own for when things went wrong between us. I couldn't believe he wouldn't get tired of me. I suppose I made it into a self-fulfilling prophecy by never giving him enough time, never involving myself in his career, just expecting him to understand my need for my own.' She was bitter with self-recrimination. 'I can't even blame Mother, I merely allowed her to reinforce my own stupidity.'

'And the affair with Verity?' Darina thought if Pru was bringing herself to face unpalatable facts, she might as well face them all.

'I was as much to blame for that as they were. Looking back, I can't believe how stupid I was. I practically forced them into bed.'

'You hardly pointed a gun at their heads,' Darina commented drily.

'No, but leaving them alone like that, making Simon think I'd lost interest in him and his ambitions, that I was only interested in my own concerns . . . And Verity was very young. She's always had everything she wanted, almost as soon as she's realised she wanted it. Things have just fallen her way.' There was only simple acceptance of a fact of life in Pru's voice, no bitterness or envy of her little sister. It was a remarkable turnaround from her previous attitude.

Darina remembered Verity cajoling Natasha into a better temper after their argument over Oliver and wondered how much work she had done mending bridges with her sister. It wasn't all luck that brought Verity what she wanted.

There was the sound of a vehicle pulling up in the yard. Pru glanced out of the window. 'Heavens, it's Erica Strangeways. I hope she hasn't got Daniel with her. I'm not in the mood for any more of his accusations.'

'Anybody home?' Erica Strangeways entered the shop and insinuated her way past the counter towards the back where Pru and Darina were working.

Pru greeted her without enthusiasm.

'Brought you your herbs.' A basket brimming with various

bunches was placed on the counter. Darina sniffed appreciatively at the cleanly aromatic scent of basil.

'Met you at Natasha's, didn't I? Day of the funeral?' Erica Strangeways studied Darina. 'Yes, of course, you're the cookery writer.'

'And you're the herb expert,' said Darina.

Erica Strangeways cheerfully admitted she was. 'But I didn't come here to talk about my herbs,' she said to Pru. 'I wanted to say Daniel's really sorry he made such a scene the other day.'

'He'll be round to apologise, then?'

'Oh, dear, you know Daniel. That dog meant all the world to him, he's just lost without Rupert. But how he could have suggested your mother poisoned him I don't know. They didn't get on, of course, but, quite apart from the fact she's dead, I know Constance would never have done a thing like that. Vindictive she was not.'

Pru finished wrapping the last batch of sausages in clingfilm and carried the tray into the chill-room. 'Time for a spot of lunch. Will you join us, Erica? It's pâté but there's some cheese as well if you'd like to stay.'

'That's really civil of you, Pru, I'd like to.'

Darina went and rescued her tin of pâté from the cool-box in the back of her car. She unmoulded it on to one of Pru's oval plates, turned out the one Pru had told her Verity had made on Monday evening, garnished both with some parsley and carried them through to the conservatory, where Pru was arranging a hunk of farmhouse Cheddar, a loaf of brown bread and a jar of home-made pickles.

'This is nice,' said Erica appreciatively, taking in the blazing colours of potted plants arranged round the glazed area. Though the wind outside was blowing rags of cloud across the sky and threatening rain, inside it was a summer's day. She wandered along the display, automatically taking off dead geranium heads and moving round plants that had developed a habit of growing towards the light. She admired various specimens, some of which it became clear she had given to Constance as cuttings.

Then she reached the flowering oleander, particularly resplendent with many deep pink frilly-edged flowers in full bloom. Erica frowned at it. 'What with your children and all those animals, I'm surprised at Constance keeping this,' she said. She had her hands on her hips and was standing well back from the plant.

'But it's grown so well and is so beautiful,' exclaimed Pru.

'It's highly toxic,' said Erica. 'You didn't know? I told Constance when she first got it, said it was most unwise to have anything so poisonous, you never know what small children are going to put in their mouths.' She turned to the two boys who'd run in from the garden in response to Pru's ringing of a handbell. 'You haven't touched this ever, have you?'

They stared at her then Alastair said, 'Gwan said we weren't to come in here. She said this was for gwown-ups, not us.'

'Fighting brats, she said,' offered Mark, then he hooted with laughter and pummelled his small brother on the back. In a moment the two of them were on the tiled floor, rolling over and over.

Pru gave a deep sigh and grabbed one son with each strong arm. In a moment they were standing in front of her. 'That's better. Now, here's a sandwich each. And a Coca-cola. If you can't sit nicely in here, you'll have to take them outside to eat.' She thrust a hastily made cheese sandwich into one hand of each boy and an opened can of cola into the other. The brothers looked at each other for a brief moment then gave high-pitched hoots and disappeared out of the conservatory.

'It's not that they don't miss their grandmother, they don't really understand that she has actually gone,' Pru said. For a moment she blinked hard then she looked again at the oleander and said in a very different tone, 'If it's true what you say, I'd better get rid of it. Would you like to take it?'

Erica looked at the bush more closely. 'If you really mean it, I'd be delighted, it's a handsome specimen. Though it seems to have suffered a slight accident.' She bent down one of the main stems so that Pru and Darina could see where its top had been roughly broken off. 'But I'll soon tidy that up. I'll put it in the back of the van now, then I won't forget it.' She bent down, embraced the heavy pot and lifted it with ease, refusing the help offered by both girls.

Pru watched her stride off with it round the side of the house. 'She really jumped at that, didn't she? Do you think that was just a story, about it being poisonous?'

'Unlikely, don't you think? It's easy enough to check up on.'

'Doesn't your pâté look good!' Pru had caught sight of it on the table. 'I'm not sure I could handle lining the tin with bacon though, too time-consuming.'

'I should have thought of that.' Darina was apologetic. 'I'm afraid I just did it automatically but of course it isn't necessary.'

Erica reappeared from the house, drying wet hands on a hanky. 'Thanks, Pru, it'll look really great in the flowering greenhouse and it's much better out of the boys' reach.' She sat down and helped herself to bread and cheese.

Pru took a helping of Darina's pâté. 'It's great,' she said after a couple of mouthfuls. 'Really tasty. What's in it?'

'Just belly of pork, back fat, pig's liver and some smoked bacon, plus various herbs and spices. Oh, yes, and some reduced cider. All things I thought you would have available and wouldn't be expensive.'

'I haven't tried the one Verity made on Monday evening yet, with all the drama we've forgotten about it.' She picked up the plate. 'That's odd, someone's had a slice.' She looked at the meat in a puzzled way then took a chunk and tasted it. 'Not as good as yours, Darina, not nearly so tasty. Did you use organic meat?'

'I'm afraid I couldn't get hold of any but that's the next best thing, a good conservation grade.'

'Don't start any arguments about conservation grades, please,' said Erica. 'I have enough of that from Daniel. Oh, and by the way, he really appreciated the slice of pâté you left for him the other night.'

Pru looked up in surprise. 'Pâté? What do you mean?'

'The slice you asked him to taste, wasn't it as part of a competition or something? I think Verity told him you were all going to have a go. Dan said it was a great improvement on your first effort, I think he said he was going to have a tougher challenge than he thought. But the next day there was all that fuss about the dog and I never heard anything more.'

'Erica, I can't think what you are talking about. The only pâté I've given Daniel was when he was here at lunch-time last Monday when his behaviour was almost as disgraceful as it was yesterday.'

'But I was there when he found it,' persisted Erica, her bushy eyebrows coming together in a puzzled frown. 'Under the milk cover outside the cottage door. A slice of pâté with a card from you saying you hoped he would enjoy it.'

'A card? Was it printed or written?' asked Darina.

'Printed I think but I hardly looked at it. Daniel ate the meat for supper, I had an omelette *fines herbes*. Don't like anything too heavy late at night, particularly after a strenuous day.'

'What had you been up to?' asked Pru, still frowning over the mystery of the pâté.

'Went up to Norfolk to look at a rival establishment. Like to see what the opposition is up to. Long drive there and long drive back. Had a good lunch though, find that keeps me going on these long trips.'

'Daniel didn't share the driving?'

Erica smiled sardonically. 'Didn't come along. He seems to have handed the herb side over to me completely these days, just involves himself with his chickens. He's talking of erecting another shed, heaven knows where he's going to get the money from, I think he's hoping the bank will cough up, though with interest rates the way they still are, I think it'd be most unwise. But as long as he keeps it apart from the herb business, it's nothing to do with me. I just went over when I got back to fill him in on my trip and found him standing on the step, looking at the slice of pâté I told you about.'

'The note sounds like one of those cards we were putting with the sausages the other day,' said Darina.

'I wonder if it could have been Verity and that's where the missing slice from that tin went.'

'She wouldn't have had time, surely,' said Darina. 'Tuesday was the day she and Natasha went up to London with me.'

'That's right, they didn't get back until just after nine.'

'Dan found the slice about nine thirty,' said Erica.

'She must have dropped it off when they took Natasha back,' Pru decided.

'Here she is now,' Erica said as Verity and Oliver came into the conservatory from the house.

Darina thought how tired they both looked.

Verity collapsed into a chair. 'Get us both a proper drink, please, darling,' she said to Oliver. 'I need something stronger than white wine.'

'Did you take a slice of that pâté you cooked to Daniel on Tuesday evening?' Pru asked as Oliver disappeared into the house again.

It took Verity a little time to understand what was being asked. 'Of course not,' she said at last. 'By the time we got back pâté was the last thing on my mind. Anyway, it needed at least another day to mature properly.'

'Ah,' said Oliver bringing out a whisky decanter, ice, water and glasses on a silver tray. 'If you're talking about that pâté, I had a slice for lunch on Tuesday.'

Pru's face cleared. 'Of course, I'd forgotten you were here.'

Verity looked resigned. 'I'm not going to ask what you thought of it. It was made in much too much of a hurry.'

'It was fine,' he assured her.

'How did the interview with the police go?' asked Pru.

Verity gave a small groan. 'Interviews, you mean, we were each dealt with separately. It's quite incredible, they seem to think Natasha was deliberately poisoned.'

Oliver offered whisky round but the only taker was Verity. 'I wouldn't say precisely that,' he said. 'They just mentioned something about possible digitalis poisoning, I got the impression it could have been accidental.'

'They asked if she'd ever had any heart trouble and been prescribed digitalis,' interjected Verity. 'As if I'd have any idea.'

Out of the corner of her eye, Darina saw Erica Strangeways' mouth open, then close, as if she had changed her mind over some utterance.

'I just told them exactly what happened on Tuesday night after Natasha rang here,' went on Verity, then had to repeat her story for Darina and Erica, who hadn't heard the details before. She ran through them rapidly then turned her attention to the pâté again. 'Do try some, darling, this is really good, much better than mine.' She offered some of Darina's to Oliver.

He shook his head. 'I'm sure it's excellent.' He gave Darina an apologetic smile. 'But I don't seem very hungry, the events of the last few days appear to have removed my appetite. I'll just have a sliver of cheese.'

Erica was studying the plates of meat. 'Funny,' she said. 'Pâté seems to be turning up all over the place. I found a whole hunk on the compost heap at the herb garden yesterday. At least, it looked as though it had been a whole hunk before a fox had been at it. Can't think how it got there, neither Dan nor I ever put anything like that on the compost, could attract all sorts of undesirable vermin.'

'What did you do with it?' Darina asked her quietly, while the two boys rushed in to greet Verity and Oliver.

'Put it in the dustbin, of course.'

'Did you ask Daniel if he knew anything about it?'

'Absolutely. But he said he had no idea, his only suggestion was that Natasha might have put it there, she used to add her kitchen debris to the heap every now and then but I'd told her animal waste should always go in the dustbin.'

'She did say she was going to do a pâté,' Darina said slowly. 'And I think she took some pork home with her from here on Monday.'

For a moment she and Erica sat looking at each other then the other woman got up. 'Goodness, look at the time,' she said. 'Thanks a million for the bite to eat, Pru. I'll see you around and don't forget, Daniel really is contrite, even though you'll never get him to say it.' She vanished out of the door.

Darina quietly followed her, catching up with the market gardener as she was getting into her van.

'Miss Strangeways.' Darina held on to the driver's door.

'Erica, please.'

'Erica, then, I'm wondering if you are thinking along the same lines that I am.'

The weather-beaten face with its shrewd eyes regarded her thoughtfully. 'If you mean am I going home to fish out that hunk of pâté from the dustbin and take it to the police, yes, I am.'

'I suggest you also take them that oleander bush.'

'That thought had also occurred. But I don't think it would be wise to say anything to anybody else for the moment.' A steely glance was flashed at Darina.

'I agree,' she said and allowed the van door to be slammed shut. She watched the vehicle accelerate up the lane before turning back towards the conservatory. At the back of her mind's eye was the picture of Natasha and Daniel Quantrell sitting either side of the oleander bush the previous Monday.

# Chapter Seventeen

'What a funny old stick she is,' Verity was saying as Darina re-entered the conservatory.

'Daniel wouldn't be anywhere without her,' said Pru.

'How is it he's living in that cottage, anyway?' asked Oliver.

'His great-uncle, old Colonel Quantrell, made it available years ago, I think Daniel was fired from the advertising firm he was working for. I was only about five at the time but I remember how he went around when he first arrived saying he was going to make his name writing books but, apart from a history of the Bailey, nothing ever appeared. Mother said he had great charm and could talk up a storm. I think he sold the odd article from time to time, then the Colonel gave him the walled garden when he dreamed up the herb-growing scheme but until Erica came along it was the feeblest of enterprises. She'd run a market garden and really knows her stuff.'

'I don't suppose Daniel could believe his luck,' said Verity. 'Erica with her independent means, her know-how and efficiency actually interested enough to go into partnership with him.'

'She smartened him up then practically took over the herb company. It all meant he could spread his wings a bit,' continued Pru. 'Before we knew it, he was in the chicken business. Mother couldn't believe it!'

'He's doing well, then?' asked Darina.

'Well enough,' said Pru. 'He's got a contract with a chain of supermarkets that takes off birds in their thousands every seven or eight weeks. I wonder, though, how long it will be before he's tired of the effort.'

'I wonder if he'll sell the Bailey and try and retire on the proceeds,' thought Verity.

'You mean Natasha has left him her house?' Darina was

amazed, there had been little love lost between them the previous Monday.

'It wasn't hers to leave anybody,' said Verity sadly. 'She explained it to me. It is the Quantrell family seat and, as such, her grandfather left it to Daniel, his male heir, with the proviso that it was Natasha's during her lifetime. The Bailey and all its contents are now his but Natasha was doubtful he'd have the income to keep it up and she said she was damned if she was going to leave him any money. At least, that's what she said last week,' she finished.

'Selling some of those pictures would probably raise enough to finance living there,' suggested Pru. 'But he and Erica will probably marry now, it's only the thought of that dreadful cottage that's been holding her back, and she should be able to contribute towards the running costs if not take them over altogether. Her aunt's house will raise a tidy sun.'

'How can she stand him!' Verity gave a comical grimace. 'The man's a leech. A disgusting lech.'

'Why hasn't he moved in with Erica?' Darina wanted to know.

Pru shrugged her shoulders. 'Who knows? Perhaps he hasn't been too keen on marriage. I don't think she got on too well with the Colonel and perhaps he thought he would be jeopardising his heritage. Or maybe he just didn't like her modern house any more than she liked his run-down cottage. One thing I do know, Erica won't let the Bailey slip through her fingers. She's been dying to get her hands on that garden ever since she met Daniel.'

'Oh, Darina.' Verity remembered something. 'I think the police will be wanting to talk to you about taking Natasha and me up to London.'

'Really?'

'Well, I can't imagine why, it's not as though our journey could have anything to do with Natasha's death,' Verity hurried on. 'But they did seem interested when I said you'd driven us up there. They wanted to know everything about her day.'

Verity was looking at her with something like desperation in her eyes. She didn't say it but Darina knew she didn't want her to tell the police about the way she and Natasha had argued.

'I shouldn't think they'll be all that interested,' she said to Verity, unable to manage anything more by way of reassurance.

'Well, I hope they've finished with me.' Oliver reached for the whisky decanter and refilled his and Verity's glasses. 'I shall have to return to London at the end of the weekend,' he said to Pru. 'I've finished sorting out your mother's affairs, they seem in good order and I really must get back to my own business.'

'With all the telephoning you've been doing, I should have thought you were running it very successfully from here,' said Verity. But she said it cheerfully, it was obviously something they had already discussed.

'I really am most grateful, Oliver, for all your help,' said Pru.

'I hope Verity can manage to rejoin me in London quite soon,' he said, smiling at both sisters. It was a loving smile but there was a hint of steel there as well. If Verity spent much more time on the Fry farm, he would want to know exactly why.

'I'll be back as soon as Natasha's affairs are cleared up,' Verity assured him.

'What do you mean?' asked her sister.

'Verity is expecting Natasha to have left her the money she inherited from Natalie Duke,' said Oliver, a trifle drily.

'Well, that's what she said she'd do,' burst out Verity, she obviously found it no joking matter. 'After all, I am Natalie's daughter. I can't see why she wouldn't have left it to me.'

'People are funny about money,' murmured Oliver. 'Just don't pin all your hopes on it, that's all. It's not as though I haven't more than enough for both of us.'

'When are you planning to get married?' asked Darina diplomatically.

'As soon as Verity sets the day,' Oliver said promptly, so promptly they all laughed and the atmosphere lifted.

Verity shot him a dancing look. 'Don't worry, I'm not going to keep you hanging around ready for anyone else to get her paws on, I shall make you mine quite soon.'

Was she genuinely that mercurial, or had she the ability to change her mood to whatever the situation called for, so that life remained pleasant and those around her saw the person she wanted them to see?

'Can you manage for this afternoon?' Darina asked Pru. 'I must get back to my book.'

'Of course, I feel guilty at having dragged you over here, the whole situation was just getting on top of me. But the girl who serves in the shop is back now and I think I've organised someone to help with the stock so things should be well under control, even when Verity goes back to town. Thanks for coming over.'

Darina gave her a quick kiss, promised more help if it was needed, then held out her hand to Oliver. 'In case I don't see you again, I'll say goodbye, I've really enjoyed meeting you.'

The charismatic blue eyes looked back at her as he grasped her hand. 'It's not goodbye, we shall see you again, soon I hope. Perhaps you can find an evening to dine with us in town?'

Darina said that would be fun, kissed Verity and made her escape, promising to send Pru the recipe for the pâté.

She was certain, though, that if Simon came up with a version that wasn't either complicated or expensive, Pru would use that – and quite right too.

As Darina drove back to the cottage, she told herself firmly that she was delighted that Pru and Simon had got back together. One good thing had emerged from the recent tragedies. Then she found herself thinking about the details she had heard that day regarding Natasha's death.

It had been a definite shock, no doubt of that, but the real shock lay not in the death itself. Somehow the Grim Reaper had seemed only a step behind that poor scarred woman's shoulder ever since Darina had met her. No, the shock had been in the possibility she had been poisoned by person or persons unknown. In, not to put too fine a point on it, murder.

But did Natasha's death *have* to be murder? The fact that Detective Inspector Grant was involved in investigating the death need not necessarily mean an unlawful killing, surely?

Natasha had collapsed murmuring the word 'poisoned'. This could, as Verity had suggested, merely mean she thought she was the victim of some food poisoning. But the police were apparently investigating not a food bug but, what was it Oliver had said, the symptoms of digitalis poisoning? Something like that. It seemed the police had ruled out the possibility of Natasha overdosing, accidentally or deliberately, on medicine prescribed by her doctor. Which had to mean that the poison had been introduced into something Natasha had consumed that night, since Verity said they had both eaten the same meal for lunch.

Which brought one inescapably to the inordinate number of different pâtés there seemed to have been knocking around. A delicatessen would have been pushed to produce more. Nothing so far to suggest pâté had been the murder weapon but if the hunk Erica had found on the compost heap did prove poisonous, the picture, far from clearing, was going to look very confused. And the odds seemed high that it had been poisoned. It looked as though it had been gnawed at by some animal, Erica had said, and Daniel's dog had died. Apparently poisoned. And he had accused Constance Fry, who had died a fortnight earlier.

Darina changed down gears as she came to a particularly nasty bend, then realised she was coming to the stretch of road where Constance had been killed. Constance cycling innocently along towards the Bailey in Natasha's hat.

Natasha's hat! Erica's words after Constance's funeral came back to her. Natasha was known by that hat, people recognised first her headgear, then her. And she was a cyclist. Had Constance been, after all, deliberately knocked over but by someone who thought the cyclist was Natasha? Could it have been a first, failed attempt on her life?

But who could want Natasha killed?

There were two immediately obvious candidates: Daniel Quantrell and Verity.

Daniel stood to inherit the Bailey. With Natasha dead there was nothing to stand in his way of either gaining possession of the lovely and valuable old house with its equally valuable contents or of marrying Erica Strangeways. Which could mean he needn't bother with raising chickens or herbs any more. He could have made the poisonous pâté, given Natasha a slice, dumped the rest on the compost heap, then made another and put the slice where he could find it when Erica was there as a witness, to provide himself with some sort of alibi.

But he and Erica seemed to have achieved an admirable modus vivendi that had worked for a number of years and his chickens and the herbs appeared to be doing well. Was he that desperate for the Bailey?

Darina left consideration of Daniel as murderer on one side and turned to Verity. Now there could be someone with a more urgent reason to help Natasha from this world. She had told Darina herself that she wanted money, had suggested in fact that she needed money. Oliver might be rich but he would certainly not prove a ready source of cash, however much in love he was.

'He gets funny about people who run up large credit-card debts,' Verity had said. She looked like a girl who constantly overspent, Darina never saw her wearing the same clothes twice and the little Metro was a recent model. Verity was looking at a career that was unlikely to produce great cash returns in the short term, and she wanted her sister to buy her out of the family business.

Natasha had threatened Verity with disinheritance the morning they'd all gone to London. Darina remembered Verity's passionate anger and the way she had swallowed it, managing to sweet-talk Natasha round. Well, almost around, they hadn't been to see Natalie Duke's agent, though.

And Verity had cooked pâté on Monday night. Certainly the one they were eating at lunch-time, that Oliver had tried on Tuesday, couldn't have been poisoned. Could she have prepared another one? And given Natasha a slice after they got back from London? Dropped off an innocent slice on Daniel at the same time and discarded the rest of the poisoned meat on the compost heap? It sounded possible but didn't quite fit. Verity had had no reason to think she might be disinherited on Monday evening. She might well have decided, though, that Natasha's inheritance was needed immediately.

Of course, pâté might have had nothing to do with Natasha's death, some other way of feeding her poison may have been used.

Had the oleander played any part? Any at all? Erica Strangeways had certainly seemed convinced it was highly poisonous and there it had been that Monday lunch-time, Natasha sitting on one side of it, Daniel the other.

But any of them could have helped themselves to a deadly branch from the bush.

Pru, for instance. Pru, who, like a deep river, looked quiet on the surface but was undoubtedly passionate and quick-running underneath. She certainly had the means. She could have cooked a poisoned pâté on Monday evening and delivered any number of deadly or innocent slices on her return from Dorset before conveniently removing herself from the scene overnight. Except, what would be the motive? Merely to get Verity out of her hair? It seemed unlikely at best.

There was Simon. Again, no shortage of opportunity but where was the motive? Well, if he thought Verity might go into partnership with him if she came into money, that might do it. But Pru had already told him she was going to back his restaurant. Or had she? She had certainly told Darina but was that the same as telling Simon? Something to be checked.

Oliver? Again, lots of opportunity, indeed, more than the others since he had been in the house alone most of Tuesday, plenty of time to cook quantities of pâté. But he seemed even more motiveless than Pru. It couldn't be in his interest, surely, to see Verity made independent of himself? And somehow Darina couldn't see the polished businessman gliding down to the Bailey in his Rolls-Royce with two slices of pâté on the front seat beside him.

Of course, Darina thought suddenly, opportunity was by no means confined to those who were present that Monday lunchtime. Take Erica, for instance. Daniel might well have shown her the slip of paper that had accompanied the sausages he'd taken back that day. She could have found some excuse to call round on the Tuesday and snatch part of the oleander, they only had her word she'd spent the day driving to Norfolk. If anyone had seen her, she need only have said she was bringing herbs to Pru. She wanted to be married to Daniel and châtelaine of the Bailey, according to Pru. But, in that case, why draw attention to the pâté found on the compost heap and the poisonous nature of the oleander? Unless it was a double bluff? And had she, in fact, been going to give the meat to the police if Darina had not run after her? Maybe mentioning both pâté and shrub had been merely to lay some sort of false trail if the murder weapon came to light.

After a little more thought, Darina concluded that none of it added up to give motive, opportunity and means in a convincing package.

The nearer she got to the cottage, the more she wished she could discuss the whole affair with William. His cool mind, so used to sifting evidence, so skilled at disentangling motive and seeing behind the surface appearance of things, was just what was needed here. She was good on the instinctive approach, he provided the analytical, professional method. Well, this was one time she would have to do without Detective Sergeant William Pigram. He was involved with matters the other side of the ocean and no doubt discussing pertinent details of his case with the fascinating Elaine.

Darina pressed her foot a little harder on the accelerator, conscious she was now very tired. She had spent a busy time in London, driven down very early that morning, helped Pru and absorbed the shock of hearing what had happened to Natasha. What she needed was a nice cup of Earl Grey tea. It might even be warm enough to sit in that sheltered spot outside the kitchen, some of the clouds that had threatened earlier seemed to have disappeared. But there were the contents of the fridge to restore to the defrosted machine and the kitchen floor to wash first.

As soon as she arrived at the cottage, though, Darina knew something was wrong. She had left all the windows closed; one was now open. She remembered William saying that the first thing a burglar does is to prepare an escape route in case his entry route is blocked. But about to turn her car round, drive to the village and phone for the police, Darina had second thoughts.

The burglar would undoubtedly have heard her car and be off the moment she drove away. She couldn't let William's cottage be burgled and make no attempt to catch the thief, or thieves.

She wished she had a car phone, then thought: they don't know I don't have one. I could tell them the police are on their way.

She put the car into neutral, applied the hand brake and left the engine running. She got quietly out of the driver's seat and ran silently across to the garage, picked up an old gate-post of heavy metal that had been leaning against the wall for months waiting for William to get around to replacing it, then made her way to the front door. Carefully she slipped her key into the lock, opened it and entered.

She stood in the little hallway, listening. No sound but she could swear there was someone in the house.

Quietly Darina opened the door into the dining room. No one there and William's silver golfing trophies that he'd won at university were still on the alcove shelves. She opened the door to the sitting-room on the other side of the hall. No one there either and the television and video were both untouched.

She crept towards the kitchen. The door was ajar. She pushed it open. By the stove, against the light and reaching for the Georgian tea caddy, stood a dark figure. Darina raised her heavy bar. Then found herself unable to strike a man without warning. 'Put your hands up,' she croaked, 'I have telephoned for the police on my car phone, they will be here any minute now.'

The figure turned. 'Let's hope they can manage to recognise a member of their force.'

It was William.

# Chapter Eighteen

Inspector Grant and Pat James were going through the contents of Natasha Quantrell's desk when the constable on duty outside the Bailey told them a Miss Strangeways wanted a word with the inspector.

Grant told the constable to bring her in, then motioned the red-headed woman to take a seat.

Erica Strangeways looked at the open desk without comment and remained standing. She was holding a plastic carrier bag.

'How can I help?' asked Grant.

She held out the bag. 'I found this pork pâté on my compost heap. It looked as though a fox or something had been at it and I put it in the dustbin. But it has just occurred to me that perhaps Rupert, Mr Quantrell's dog, may have eaten some of it. If so, you could possibly be interested. Sorry about the smell, it seems to have gone off.'

Grant took the bag, opened and looked inside it. Apart from a distasteful wrinkling of his nose, his expression gave nothing away. He placed the bag with its fetid contents on the table in front of the sofa and sat down, motioning Erica Strangeways to do the same.

She chose an upright armchair and sat leaning slightly forward, her face intelligent and questioning. Pat decided that here they were likely to have found a co-operative and informative witness. She found a chair and got out her notebook and pencil.

'Perhaps you can tell us a little more about this compost heap, Miss Strangeways.'

Speaking in short, concise sentences, Erica Strangeways explained the location of the Bailey Herb Garden and its fertilising arrangements.

'Have you any idea how long this – ' Grant gestured towards the bag – 'had been there?'

Erica leaned further forward. 'I've been thinking about that. I can't say for certain except it wasn't there on Monday.'

'You are sure about that?'

His witness was not the slightest bit disturbed by the sharp question. 'Oh yes, Miss Quantrell's gardener was here that day mowing and he dumped all the clippings on the heap. I always have to make sure it is well aerated after that, grass clippings pack together, you see, don't allow in the air with all its useful bacteria. It's the bacteria that break down the material into humus.' She glanced from inspector to constable, decided they had taken in enough compost culture for their purposes and continued. 'I gave it a good forking, made sure the grass was mixed with other vegetable matter, then added some potato peelings from Mr Quantrell's cottage, where I'd prepared a meal earlier that day. There was definitely no pork pâté there then. But I didn't add anything else to the heap until yesterday, when I found that.' She waved a well-shaped hand with dirt-engrained fingernails towards the plastic bag.

'And Mr Quantrell's dog died when?' As if he didn't know the answer to that question, Pat thought, after she'd had to report back on the investigation into his complaint.

'Sometime between midnight Tuesday, when he came in from a late run, and six thirty in the morning when Daniel found him in the back pantry. He rang the vet immediately but the dog was quite dead.'

'And what makes you think that piece of pâté may have been responsible?' No hint, Pat noted, that it was what might have killed Natasha Quantrell as well but surely that was what they were all thinking?

Erica Strangeways looked straight at the inspector. 'Sometimes people bait pieces of meat to rid themselves of vermin – foxes, rats, that sort of thing. I thought at first it might have been something like that. But Daniel swears it was nothing to do with him and I don't know who else would place something like that on my compost heap, except—' She paused.

'Yes, Miss Strangeways, except for whom?' Grant was at his most intimidating.

'Well, except for Natasha Quantrell. She used the heap for her kitchen refuse, said she liked to help us along. We need all the organic compost we can get hold of, I don't use anything else on the herbs.'

'So you think Natasha Quantrell might have placed a poisoned piece of meat on your heap? Not very organic, wouldn't you say?'

'It could well have been completely organic. And Natasha several times discarded animal refuse there, I spoke to her about it but I'm not sure she really took in what I was saying. She hasn't been a well woman, you know.' She paused. 'There was also a rather curious little matter of a slice of pâté being delivered to Daniel on Tuesday evening. It was accompanied by a Fry's Farm card but nobody seems to know who actually sent it.'

Grant asked for more details and Erica Strangeways related a conversation with Pru Fry and Darina Lisle that lunch-time. Pat saw Grant raise a resigned eyebrow at the mention of Darina Lisle's name but he allowed the reference to pass without comment. 'What did this pâté Mr Quantrell received on Tuesday look like?'

Erica hesitated then said slowly, 'I have to say it looked very like the one I found on the compost heap. Same sort of texture, no bacon wrapped around the outside and . . . ' She gave a slight pause before saying: 'The same greenish flecks, which I took to be some sort of herb.'

Then the plant expert asked if they would accompany her outside, to where her van was parked. Grant rose immediately and allowed the woman to lead the way to a smart dark green vehicle with THE BAILEY HERB FARM painted on its side.

Erica opened the back. 'That, Inspector, is an oleander. It's highly poisonous. Constance Fry had it in her conservatory. I pointed out to Pru Fry this morning that it was not a good plant to have around where there are children and animals and she suggested I take it. It's recently had a small branch broken off it.' She reached into the van and swivelled the heavy plant round so they could see the damaged stalk.

Grant thought for a moment. 'Who have you told about this?'

Erica straightened herself thinking carefully. 'Pru Fry and Darina Lisle were present when I explained that the plant was poisonous. Verity Fry and her fiancé arrived a little later before I mentioned finding the piece of pâté.'

'Did you tell them you were going to bring either the meat or the plant to us?'

'I didn't mention my suspicions at all. It was only during the lunch that the possible implications of all this occurred to me. But Darina Lisle followed me to my van, she had obviously had the same thoughts. She suggested I show you the oleander as well as the meat.'

'Most helpful Miss Lisle, always has been,' Grant said without inflection.

The inspector took another look at the oleander bush. 'If you don't mind,' he said, which meant there was little she could do about it if she did, 'we'll have that down to the lab for an examination.' Then he went back inside the Bailey, picked up the pâté she had brought and took it through to the kitchen. There he carefully tipped it out of its bag on to a plate, waving away the unappetising taint that rose from the meat.

Pat held her breath and looked at the hunk carefully. It had probably started life as a loaf shape, like the pâté found in Natasha Quantrell's larder. But something had chewed or gulped away a large part leaving an odd shape with one more or less right angled corner.

'Rupert was probably disturbed, perhaps Daniel called him, otherwise I can't understand why he didn't finish it, the greed of that dog!' Then Miss Strangeways remembered that the animal in question was dead and left his reputation free from further attack.

'Perhaps he realised it was poisoning him?' Pat James suggested.

'I don't think so. Very little affects even a smallish animal that quickly,' said Erica. 'Most poisons have to enter the bloodstream and get carried round the body before the victim starts feeling the effects.'

'Bring that into the larder,' ordered Grant. 'Let's compare it with the one waiting for the forensic boys.'

Pat picked up the plate with the misshapen lump.

Grant switched on the light, the constable placed the plate beside the tin and all three of them studied the two specimens.

'If you were asking me and, in a way, I suppose you are,' commented Erica, 'I would say they looked identical.'

'Hmm,' muttered Grant. 'And would you say your friend Mr Quantrell's slice of pâté looked exactly like these as well?'

She shook her head. 'It looked roughly the same but I didn't study it closely, I'm a vegetarian.' The logic of the remark escaped Pat.

'You seem to know a certain amount about toxic effects, Miss Strangeways. What can you tell us about oleander poisoning?'

She looked the inspector straight in the eye. 'I am a herbalist, not a toxicologist. However, before coming to see you I consulted some books.' She paused for a moment and Pat wondered if she was deliberately heightening the tension or if the effect she was creating was unconscious. 'The toxic properties of oleander are caused by glycosides which produce the same effect as acute digitalis poisoning.'

# Chapter Nineteen

Darina dropped the iron bar she was holding. It fell and cracked one of the kitchen clay tiles. Her initial feeling of overwhelming joy was immediately replaced with a strong sense of grievance.

'William! What are you doing back?'

He picked up the bar and placed it carefully outside the kitchen door. 'No word of welcome for the returning hero?' He looked very tired and far from someone home in triumph.

'Why didn't you tell me you were coming back?' Darina tried to conceal her chagrin. Not only had all her elaborate attempts to foil a burglar ended in anticlimax but, with the contents of the fridge spread over the table, the kitchen looked even worse than it had done that morning. She wished she had cleared it up properly, that things didn't look such a mess, and she wished she could roll back the tape, come into the cottage normally and give him the welcome he so clearly needed.

'I thought I had but it appears you don't open your mail.' He gestured towards the pile of letters she had picked up from the doormat that morning and left on the table with everything else when she answered Pru's cry for help. She hadn't even glanced through them, so completely had she given up expecting to see one with an American stamp.

'I didn't think you were due back for weeks yet,' she said, wishing she could come out with something a bit warmer.

'In the end the investigation got wrapped up in a rush. All very successfully, I may say, and there was nothing to justify my spending any more of the credit company's money so here I am. I didn't really hope you would meet me but I must say I hadn't expected to be attacked as an intruder in my own house.' As an attempt at banter it was lame and Darina looked at him more closely.

The curly hair had lost its usual shine and the dark-flecked grey eyes held more than tiredness. 'I'm sorry,' she said, 'I've been in London. If I'd known, of course I would have met you.' She took a grip on herself. 'Let me make you a cup of tea, you look as though jet lag has hit in a big way. How did you get back?'

'Got a taxi, the credit company will pick up the bill.' He sat wearily at the table and watched her fill the kettle. Then she stood holding the tray.

'Have you enough energy to move outside or would you prefer to have it in the sitting-room?'

He rose and made to take the tray from her. She firmly removed it from his reach. 'Use your energy to open the door and make it to the terrace. I'll bring this.'

She followed him to their sheltered corner. He sat with a cup in front of him, long legs stretched out, hands behind his head, looking at the orchard. Darina sipped her tea and said nothing.

'It's all so incredibly, beautifully *green*,' he said finally. 'New York assaults you. Everything is sharp corners, hard surfaces. Everything reflects back, the sun on the pavement, light on the windows, those buildings that look like mirrors, everybody's dark glasses, shades. It's as though everything has something to hide. And talk is always in code. Have a nice day, there you go, you're welcome. None of it means anything. And the noise! Even in the dead of night New York pulsates with sound. Screeching cars, police sirens, construction work. People shouting at each other. It's a jungle and you need every instinct honed to its sharpest to steer a safe course through.'

'Could you get outside the city much? Thank you for your card from Washington.'

William shifted his position, handed over his cup for a refill and avoided catching her gaze. 'Yes, we, that is, I got driven round quite a bit in Pennsylvania. It was beautiful there, I admit. Huge gracious trees, lots of green. But somehow it was so different from – this . . . ' He gestured towards the trees with their burden of ripening fruit, the long grass leading down to the little river, the cattle grazing in the meadow beyond, the bees buzzing around the rosemary growing on the edge of the terrace, all the sights and sounds of a Somerset scene.

'How did the job go?' Darina asked while wondering just what had happened to that promising relationship.

'Oh, that went fine.' For a moment he seemed to recover some of his energy. 'I tell you, the New York scene makes our Somerset policing a job in paradise. I've never seen so many crimes of violence, it's impossible to keep up with them all. But, you know, you get a charge there, it's like working plugged into electricity. Every instinct blazes away not only on solving whatever it is you are working on but also to keep you alive.'

Darina heard renewed appetite break through the tired voice. 'Would you like to go back?'

He shook his head. 'Too easy either to lose that edge or become so hardened you forget so much of the humanity involved in that terrifying city is in a desperate state. Too many bad sights, too many sad cases, too many unsolved crimes. But one thing I've decided . . . ' He paused.

'Yes?' Darina prompted gently.

'I'm applying to move to the metropolitan force. Hopefully as an inspector. As you know, I've passed my boards, it's just a case of waiting for the right opening. Somerset is going to seem far too quiet after New York, that's for certain.' For the first time since they had sat down, he looked directly at her. 'So what's been going on with you, finished that book?'

'Not yet, still working hard on it.' She didn't want to tell him about Constance Fry's and Natasha Quantrell's deaths before he'd had time to recover a little.

'Still producing delicious little dishes to be tested?'

'Not to mention the disasters you also have to eat your way through. Have you enough energy for supper tonight?'

He stretched his arms. 'Wild horses wouldn't keep me from one of your meals. I'm tired of fast food, hamburgers and Caesar salads.'

'You're not trying to tell me that's all you ate over there?'

He gave her one of his old grins. 'No, I have to admit we had some really good meals at a fantastic range of restaurants but home-cooked food seems to have vanished from the New York scene. There were many times I hankered for your food.' There was an awkward little pause. He'd said both too much and too little. Hankered for her food but not for her? Should she be grateful he'd thought of her at all? Did she want him to have thought of her?

'Why don't you have a nice long soak in a bath and I'll see what I can sort out,' she suggested.

'What a wonderful thought,' he stretched again, luxuriously. 'But don't let me fall asleep in the bath, I may never wake up.'

He must already have taken his suitcase upstairs, thought Darina, there had been no sign of it in the hallway. Had he noticed she had moved all her things out of the double-bedded room and into the tiny one at the back? But that was not the sort of thing he would overlook, even at a cursory glance. He had said nothing, did that mean he was too tired to tackle the situation? That he preferred to take things one step at a time? Or that he was happy with this arrangement? Darina wished she knew, just as she wished she knew whether she herself wanted to keep the arrangement as it was or not. She had moved out because she had been unable to bear that big bed without him. Had no longer wanted to be reminded of him every time she opened her eyes on the familiar room.

And what was he going to say when he heard she'd managed to find yet another murder case on his patch? He'd never been able to accept with any great equanimity the way she had of not only becoming involved in cases but managing to contribute to their solution.

'Have you rung Grant to say you are back?' she asked once the supper plates had been stacked in the dishwasher and they were relaxing with coffee in the sitting-room, a Mozart piano concerto on the CD player.

'I called him from New York last week as soon as I realised the investigation was winding itself up more quickly than I'd expected. He said I could have a few days off. If I ring him now, he'll only find some excuse to pull me in.'

'He may at that.' Darina told him about the investigation that was going on into Natasha Quantrell's death.

'Not another murder case you've got yourself involved in!' It was a groan but teasingly good humoured.

'I don't think it's officially classed as murder, yet.'

'Well, I'm sure he can handle it without me, particularly if he's got you on the team as well.'

She gave a small giggle of relief. 'I think he's got to interview me on the lift I gave Natasha up to London with Verity the day she was poisoned. I don't suppose he's looking forward to that.'

She would have said more if it hadn't been for a tiny snore from the other chair. 'Time for bed,' she said instead and switched off the record.

William woke with a jerk and levered himself out of the chair. At the door he stopped. She returned his look steadily and after a moment he sketched her a brief wave and went upstairs.

The telephone rang at nine the next morning. William, who'd been up since six, answered. It was the inspector. Five minutes later the sergeant had agreed to drive Darina in to give a statement.

'Don't let them bully you,' she said as he drove his old Bentley out of the garage. 'You've earned your time off, you take it.'

He gave her a quick glance. 'I've some ideas on that, remind me to tell you about them later.'

At the station, Grant was at his most urbane and Pat James openly glad to see William. But Darina knew immediately that, whatever the constable might have felt for him a year ago, it was plain comradeship now. She wondered she could ever have been jealous of the neat policewoman. Not at all William's type, however well he got on with her.

The sergeant sat in on her statement.

'So,' said Grant when she had finished. 'You say they had a serious argument?' He looked at some notes he had made. 'And that Miss Quantrell had threatened to disinherit Miss Fry if she didn't break her engagement?'

Darina nodded.

'Did she say why she disapproved of Miss Fry's fiancé?'

'No.'

'Can you think of any reason for this disapproval? I take it you have met him?'

'Yes and I can't see why she objected to him, he is a successful businessman, well connected and attractive. His only drawback could be said to be that he is rather older than Verity. But from what Natasha Quantrell said, I felt it wasn't so much Oliver she objected to as Verity getting engaged at all. She seemed to feel she should get on with her career and leave marriage until later.' She was conscious of William's keen attention.

'But Miss Fry was adamant she wanted to settle down and get married?'

Darina moved irritably on her chair. 'She was convinced she

wanted to marry Oliver Knatchbull and that she could continue to pursue her career in exactly the same way as she would have if she was single. Miss Quantrell said Verity didn't understand how demanding marriage would prove. She claimed her cousin, Natalie Duke, owed her success to the fact that she remained single.'

Grant left that and moved on to the atmosphere prevailing between Natasha and Verity when Darina left them in London. 'Although Miss Quantrell had cancelled the appointment she had made to introduce Miss Fry to her cousin's agent, you thought they were back on good terms?'

Darina hesitated. 'Miss Fry had been very sweet to Miss Quantrell. She seemed to feel the real objection to the engagement was that Natasha would lose her, Verity's, affection. That they wouldn't see as much of each other as they might otherwise do. She appeared to want to reassure her that their relationship would survive intact.'

'And just what was this relationship?'

'Verity Fry was Natalie Duke's daughter. Until her return to England a few weeks ago, Natasha Quantrell hadn't seen her since she was a baby. They appeared to hit if off immediately and Natasha told her the truth about her mother, after which their relationship deepened and they became very close.'

'Hmm.' Grant thought some more, made some more notes. Then he sat back and looked at her for a few moments in silence. 'You are a cook, Miss Lisle, let's have some of your expertise. Tell me about all this pâté that's been floating around.'

'Pâté?'

'A hunk on Miss Strangeways' compost heap, a slice on Mr Quantrell's doorstep, a tin in Natasha Quantrell's larder and more at Fry's Farm. And do I understand there was some sort of competition?'

Darina explained about the tasting on the Monday and Daniel's challenge. As she spoke, she heard again his bitter voice.

'Would it have been possible for Miss Quantrell to have made pâté after that lunch-time party? We've been told she took meat back with her from the Frys'.'

'Yes, of course it would. It doesn't take all that long. It's a good idea to let it stand for a few hours before cooking, to let the flavours develop, but it isn't essential and she would have had time for that anyway. She didn't mention she'd made any, though.'

'But she did say she would be entering the competition?'

'It wasn't really a competition, just a friendly challenge to find a good recipe for Pru Fry. I got the impression that Natasha had lost her interest in cooking after her sense of taste was badly damaged in the fire that killed her cousin. It's very difficult to take an interest in food when you can't taste it properly. You mentioned finding a tin of pâté in her larder, do you think *she* cooked the pâté that was found on the compost heap?'

'From a cursory examination,' said Grant with some reluctance, 'the pâté in her larder looked very like that found by Miss Strangeways, who said the slice delivered to Mr Quantrell was also similar.'

Curiouser and curiouser.

William broke in. 'Do you know yet if Miss Fry *has* inherited from Miss Quantrell?'

'We've found a simple will in Miss Quantrell's desk that says all her estate is to go to Verity Fry. It was dated two weeks ago and witnessed by her daily woman, Mrs Boult, and Miss Strangeways.'

'Do we have any idea how much money is involved?' William seemed to have slipped back into the team without effort.

'Her bank books reveal a hefty income and there seems to be some sort of property in France. Also what looks like quite valuable jewellery.'

'A sizeable inheritance then for Miss Fry?' suggested William.

'As is the Bailey and its contents for Daniel Quantrell,' said Grant.

# Chapter Twenty

'Do you mind if we call in at Fry's Farm on our way back?' asked Darina.

William had managed to remind Grant he had been given several days' leave and finally prised himself away from the police station.

'I want to get a chicken from Pru for tonight's supper.'

'I thought we might go out tonight, celebrate my return,' he said, changing gear smoothly on the old car.

Darina glanced at him. 'I was wondering if I wouldn't move to my mother's, now that you're back,' she said.

'No need for that,' he said easily. 'It's here we turn for Lamington, isn't it? That is, unless you particularly want to go to your mother's?' He gave a slightly wolfish grin. William knew exactly how well she got on with her mother: fine in short doses.

At Fry's Farm it seemed the whole family was in the kitchen. Pru was there, the boys, drawing at one end of the big table, Verity sitting beside Oliver, and a small woman with bright button black eyes. Darina was welcomed in and she introduced William very briefly as 'a friend'; no mention of his official status.

'You're just in time for coffee,' said Pru.

'Mrs Boult is telling me all about my mother,' Verity said excitedly. Oliver smiled at her patiently.

Mrs Boult was enjoying holding the floor. 'Over thirty years I've done at the Bailey,' she said to Darina. 'Knew them all. The Colonel, Miss Natasha's grandfather, he was a Tartar, he was. Mister John, her father, and her mother. She was twin to Miss Natalie's mother. Like as two peas in a pod they were. And so close. Never happier than when they were together. Tragedy all of them dying so young like that. Miss Natasha was all right with the Colonel though. Thought the world of her he did. Only trouble' – Mrs Boult helped herself to a chocolate biscuit – 'was when Miss Natalie came down. Every time she was with us there was trouble. Too much noise, too many undesirables visiting the house, that's what the Colonel said. She'd take off to go Heaven knew where and back Heaven knew when. Many's the time I'd arrive to find the two of them giggling in the kitchen. "Banished, Mrs Boult," they'd say. "He's banished us again, doesn't want to see us until we've reformed our ways." Reformed their ways indeed! They were only slips of girls. Just like your ma.' She turned to Pru. 'She was often with them.'

'What was she like then, Mrs Boult?'

'Lovely girl. Real pretty, blonde hair, quiet. She and Miss Natasha were real friends, don't think she got on so well with Miss Natalie, though. When she started going with your father, Miss Natalie told me there'd be trouble. I remember her now, standing in that kitchen while I was scrubbing out the larder saying, "Constance, you'll never be happy with that man. He may seem like an Heathcliff," least, I think that's what she said, "an Heathcliff, but you'll find yourselves bound together with nothing in common. What you talk about now, I can't think." Funny thing to say, I thought, what does it matter what one talks about? And your father was quite a catch. T.D.H., as we used to say in those days; fashion for tall, dark and handsome men seems to have gone now.' For a brief moment her gaze rested on William, who could certainly be said to fit that description. 'Everyone seems to go for these scruffy chaps with five o'clock shadows today, I like a man who looks something.' Her glance fell on Oliver, dressed with his usual quiet elegance, his fair hair smoothed back, not a shadow of a shadow on his square jaw.

'And what did my mother say?' Pru did not look at Mrs Boult but stirred the sugar in its bowl, her fingers white with tension.

Mrs Boult thought for a moment, her face settling into lines of concentration. 'She said Miss Natalie didn't understand, he was such a relief after, after somebody or other, couldn't catch the name. But she'd been going with a doctor's son over t'other side of Lamington and the story was he'd been into drink and then done a runner. Found someone else up at university, so they said. Couldn't understand that meself. Miss Constance was quite a catch. Father had that nice little farm and no sons, only her. 'Course, when you arrived so prompt,' she nodded at Pru, 'I reckon that's what she had been.' Mrs Boult gave a chortle, then realised no one had followed her joke. 'Caught, I mean, begging your pardon. But that's country ways for you.' Mrs Boult reached for another chocolate biscuit.

'Tell me more about my mother,' Verity insisted.

Mrs Boult settled herself even more comfortably in her chair.

'Well now. Of course, it was a shock to hear that she was your mother. Miss Natasha told me, must have been 'bout a week, ten days ago. Brought back the old days it did. I remember the time Miss Natalie came down and said she was going to Greece. What a to do there was about that. The Colonel was in a state for days, said he mightn't always have seen eye to eye with her but he felt in loco something or other, like a parent anyway. He was ever so angry, said she was a fool to throw up her job. It was a real good one, writing for one of them papers, always going abroad, all expenses paid, and ever such a good salary, you should have seen her clothes. But Miss Natalie was cool as you please. She'd made up her mind, she said, it was no business of his and she was not a child any longer. I'll say she wasn't, over thirty by then if she was a day. And then Miss Natasha ups and speaks and says she's going with her. I was polishing the hall at the time and there was no way a door could keep out their voices.' Mrs Boult dared them to accuse her of eavesdropping.

'I thought the Colonel would have a heart attack, I did straight. Finally he told Miss Natasha if she went, she needn't bother to come back, he'd done with her.'

'But she went?' Verity breathed.

'I could have told the Colonel that was no way to get Miss Natasha to do what you wanted. Soft as butter she could be but that obstinate once she'd made up her mind to something. "Nat," she said to her cousin' – Mrs Boult was in fine form now, acting out the whole scene for her audience's benefit – ' "Nat, I'm coming with you and if Grandfather doesn't like it, well, I'm sorry, but he'll have to live with it." "Tash," says Miss Natalie, "you know I'd love it if you came but don't do it just for me." But Miss Natasha said she was fed up with her job in Bristol and she didn't care if she never saw Somerset again. So off they went.'

'And you didn't know why Natalie Duke had thrown up her

job and decided to go to Greece?' Darina slipped in the question quietly.

'Not then, miss, no. 'Course when Miss Natasha told me the other week about the baby, young Verity here what was adopted by Constance, then I understood but at the time I just thought it was over some man or other. Miss Natalie was always in and out of love. You are when you're young, aren't you? I tell you, I had some times before I settled down with Ted.' For a moment it seemed as though Mrs Boult would favour them with an account of her love life. But after a reminiscent chuckle, she was back with her story. 'I remember saying one time to Miss Natasha she shouldn't let Miss Natalie put so many over on her, should stick up for herself a bit more. But she just said as long as Miss Natalie didn't pinch any of her men, she didn't mind what she got away with.

'Well, that wasn't very likely, was it? I mean, Miss Natalie always went for the arty types what would argue with her and Miss Natasha liked them quieter. The only time it looked as though there'd be difficulty was over Mr Daniel. Even though he was a good bit younger then either of them, he was a great one for the girls and he and Miss Natasha looked as though they might have a bit of a thing going, then Miss Natasha gets it into her head there's something between him and Miss Natalie. She was in tears in the hall one day as I was doing the stairs. Told Miss Natalie she didn't mind if she was really serious about him but if she was going to drop him like all her other boyfriends, to do it now, she couldn't bear to see him hurt. Miss Natalie tells her, all abrupt like, she didn't know what she was talking about, there was nothing between Mr Daniel and her and she wouldn't look twice at him anyway. That was the only time I ever saw Miss Natasha upset with Miss Natalie, apart from the row they had over the Colonel, just before they went to Greece.' Mrs Boult paused but for no longer than it took Verity to beg her to continue.

'They was in the garden and I was doing the little room, the one that gives on to the terrace. "Why don't you tell him about the baby?" Miss Natasha was asking, well, pleading more like. Miss Natalie says something about he'd never understand, it was the gap in their ages. And Miss Natasha says she ought to give him a chance and Miss Natalie says why couldn't she damn well let her alone and he could go to hell as well. Then Miss Natasha bursts into tears. Well, that was no way to talk about the Colonel even if he was too old to understand youngsters like her and Miss Natasha.

'Of course, now I know the whole story, I can see what she was getting at. He would never have gone along with a bastard, saving your presence, young Verity. It's all different these days, nobody has to worry. There's my Dottie's eldest, she's got two without fathers. And her middle one's living with a chap on the social security. But I don't reckon the Colonel would tolerate it even now. Sometimes I think he weren't ever young.'

'How old was he when he died?' asked William curiously.

'Ninety-nine,' said Mrs Boult as proudly as if she had been responsible for every year of his age. 'I said at the time, he'd be that angry at the Pearly Gates, he was really looking forward to his hundred, wanted the telegram from The Queen. Not that he ever said, of course, but I knew. Nearest he came to it was when he said to me one day, "Mrs Boult, we'll have a party for it," his birthday he meant, "and Miss Natasha will be the guest of honour." Only sign he ever gave he missed her.'

'What a shame she didn't return before he died,' said Verity, a curiously closed expression on her face.

'And what a shock it was to see her when she did get back.' Mrs Boult accepted another cup of coffee and helped herself to more chocolate biscuits. 'I suppose you forget people change, though I have to say my mirror shows me I'm not what I used to be.' Mrs Boult's bright black eyes gleamed at them, daring anyone to agree with her. 'And I'd heard about the accident in France. But it were still a shock.' She shook her head.

'Those scars were a bit unnerving the first time you met her,' said Darina suggestively. William had a resigned expression on his face. But she knew he would be able to give her an almost verbatim account of Mrs Boult's narrative afterwards. Notebooks for William were merely for other people to assure themselves his memory was as good as he claimed.

'It wasn't that so much.' Mrs Boult dunked a chocolate biscuit in her coffee reflectively. 'It was more her manner. She wasn't the Miss Natasha of old at all. Must have been the shock of Miss Natalie's terrible death.'

Alastair pulled at his mother's sleeve. He'd got down from the table and was standing on one leg, clamping the other one around it. 'Want to go,' he announced when he had her attention. With a sigh Pru swept him off.

Mrs Boult appeared oblivious to the loss of one of her audience. 'She seemed right pleased to see me, mind you. Asked me immediately if I would go on looking after the place for her, just as I'd looked after it for the Colonel. Told her I'd be delighted. And that it'd be far less work than when he was alive, what with his nurses and that housekeeper. What a household that was!' Mrs Boult was obviously surprised at herself for having managed to stick it.

'The thing with Miss Natasha, she just didn't seem to care any more. Didn't seem to want to hear anything about the Colonel's last years. And she'd always been so interested in what was happening in the village, what they were all doing, how my family was. Now it was as if she didn't care at all.'

'She'd been away a long time,' said Verity.

'And then there was Mr Daniel,' went on Mrs Boult as if there had been no interruption. 'He and Miss Natasha had always got on so well. As I told you, at one time the Colonel even thought . . . well, nothing came of that, but they still used to spend time together, especially when Miss Natalie wasn't around. That was after that time I just told you about. But after Miss Natasha came back from France, they just sort of got across each other. She accused him of wanting her out of the way, so he could have the Bailey. Said it must have been a real disappointment to him she hadn't died along with her cousin. But, then,' added Mrs Boult comfortably, 'Mr Daniel's always been a queer customer. And he's got queerer with the years. Can't say I blame Miss Natasha for not getting on with him now. Don't know how that Miss Strangeways manages to get along with him, really I don't. Reckon she's got her eye on the Bailey as well, she's always making some excuse to come round. Bunch of herbs, some new plant to show Miss Natasha, just dropping in for a bit of a chat. But her eyes are everywhere, just as though she's checking to see all the pictures are still there. Always polite enough to me, though,' Mrs Boult acknowledged fairly.

'Well,' she finished her coffee, 'I mustn't stay here all day, got to get on.'

'And what about coming here on the days you used to go to the Bailey?' Pru had returned to the kitchen, Alastair in her arms.

'That'll suit me fine,' Mrs Boult assured her. 'Reckon Mr Daniel will be moving in as soon as the police is out and I don't suppose that Miss Strangeways will be far behind. Can't say I reckon too much on working for them. Suit me much better here.'

'What are the police doing there?' asked Verity. She looked tired now. Tired and anxious.

'What aren't they doing?' Mrs Boult challenged her. 'That's what I'd like to know. Poking around in all the cupboards and larder, sorting through I don't know what. Asking people what have nothing to do with things to come down and answer their questions. Well, I wasn't going to tell them about Mr Daniel and Miss Natasha, not if they asked for a month of Sundays.' Her mouth snapped shut.

'But what was there to tell?' Verity asked.

'Nothing!' asserted Mrs Boult. 'There was nothing and that's what I told them.'

'Quite right,' said Pru. 'Thank you so much for coming and I'll really look forward to you starting on Monday. I need someone very badly.'

'I can see you do.' Mrs Boult looked pointedly around the disorderly room. 'Real sorry I was about your ma,' she said to Pru as she went out. 'Hadn't seen much of her, of course, since Miss Natasha left, but she was always friendly when we met. Makes a body feel real old, all these deaths.' She disappeared out of the door and in another moment they saw her riding past the window on her bicycle.

Pru came back into the kitchen and collapsed into a chair. 'Well,' she said somewhere between a giggle and despair, 'Do you think she'll ever get any work done or will it be all talk?'

'I'd love to hear more about my mother,' said Verity, 'but I'll make sure it's not on your time.'

'Anyway, you won't be here much longer,' stated Oliver quietly.

'Can't leave Pru completely in the lurch,' Verity said.

'I won't be,' her sister assured her calmly. 'I'm really getting organised now. As well as the chap to help with the stock, I've organised the butcher to spend all of Tuesdays here so he can do the sausages after he's finished the butchering and I'm interviewing three girls who sound promising to help with the charcuterie side. With Mrs Boult in the house, I should be fine.'

'There you are, darling, nothing to prevent you coming back to London, picking up your career and keeping your poor fiancé from going into an early decline.'

Verity laughed. 'Oh, you! Before you know it, you'll be complaining I'm around too much.'

He smiled.

Darina remembered the chicken she wanted to buy and Pru went to fetch her one from the cold store.

'You have the luck of the devil,' said William as they drove off.

'You mean?' asked Darina, straight-faced.

'You know what I mean. "Just pick up a chicken," she says, and walks into an audience with the biggest gossip in the county who just happens to have been working in the house of the murder victim.'

'I notice you weren't exactly parading your official status.'

'Don't have any at the moment, remember? I'm on holiday.'

'You can't tell me that even now your mind isn't sifting everything Mrs Boult said for some nugget that could help Grant.'

'And?' asked William. 'What about you?'

'You keeps your nuggets and I'll keeps mine,' was all Darina would answer.

# Chapter Twenty-one

They decided to dine out that night after all; the chicken could keep until tomorrow.

After scrambled eggs for lunch, Darina finished cleaning the kitchen, fitted in some work and then had a bath. There was something different about the police sergeant, she decided. For the first time since she'd known him, he was holding back, not pressing her for some decision.

She told herself it was because the decision had been made before he went away. But she knew that wasn't it. The old William would have insisted on having the situation out in the open, told her exactly what his feelings were and suggested she move out or make some commitment. Perhaps it was just jet-lag, maybe he didn't feel up to it yet. Or had he returned to England like Natasha Quantrell, with scars, only they were not quite so visible?

Darina dressed herself carefully and brushed out her shining cream-coloured hair, leaving it loose, the way he liked it, caught at the sides with two combs. Careful, she told herself as she applied eye make-up. Don't let yourself be caught in the same old mess. But would it be the same old mess? She didn't know about William but she was sure some of her certainties had lost their certainty. Priorities had shifted. There were compromises that no longer seemed so unacceptable.

Darina had phoned Chapman's for a reservation, only to be told they were full that night. She asked to speak to Simon then pleaded to be squeezed in somewhere no matter what time. He laughed and said he'd probably be able to find them a table around nine thirty.

When they arrived, the waitress took them to a quiet corner at the back of the restaurant where they had a good view of anything going on. Then, with a wide smile, she brought them both a Kir Royale. 'Compliments of the house,' she said and left them with their drinks and the menu.

'You seem to be a valued customer,' said William.

'The chef/patron is the one I wrote to you about, who was asking for help with his book. What I didn't know at that time was that he is married to Pru Fry!' Darina filled him in on Simon's place in the Fry family.

'So,' said the policeman, 'you could say his bacon has been saved by Constance Fry's death, his bacon being not only his restaurant but also his marriage?'

'You could say that, yes.'

'Interesting,' said William and he gave his attention to the choice of food.

It was as they were halfway through their main dish, cod seared on a hot stove and accompanied by a spicy julienne of vegetables, that William interrupted his account of his New York investigation and said, 'Isn't that part of the Fry family?'

Darina looked across the restaurant and saw Verity and Oliver.

'They look happy enough,' he said as Verity laughed at a comment from her fiancé then gave some sparkling retort. 'Attractive girl. He appears quite a powerful personality too.'

Darina admitted that she found him quite attractive.

William looked at the couple for a moment then said, 'Just take me through the circumstances leading up to Natasha's death as you know them once again.'

Amused at his interest and only too willing to enter into a discussion of the personalities involved, Darina ran through the whole story.

'So,' said William when she had finished. 'If you look at opportunity, the two with the most have to be Daniel Quantrell and Oliver Knatchbull. And of the two Daniel has the better motive.'

Darina agreed. 'Indeed,' she added, 'I can't see that Oliver has any at all.'

'Other than that Natasha objected to Verity marrying him and he is obviously devoted to his fiancée.'

'I think Verity could have handled that in time, she seemed to have established an extremely good relationship with Natasha. Anyway, I don't think Oliver was aware she objected to his engagement. And I can't see any other motive. It's not as though he needed Verity to inherit Natasha's money. He's an extremely successful businessman.'

'Just how successful, I wonder? I might make a telephone call to my uncle tomorrow. He'll know all about Knatchbull, you did say he was in the financial world, didn't you?' William's uncle, Lord Doubleday, was semi-retired but remained on the boards of several companies and maintained considerable influence in the City. Darina considered the possibility of an Oliver Knatchbull on the verge of bankruptcy, having to sell his Rolls-Royce and present himself to his bride-to-be as a pauper. It was an unlikely scenario. But unlikelier things had happened.

'Would you think either Daniel or Oliver knew enough about cooking to produce a pâté?'

'Certainly Daniel,' said Darina. 'It was he who suggested he make one and he's lived on his own for years. Cooking pâté isn't difficult; get hold of a good recipe and it's really just an assembly job. The tricky bit is getting it well flavoured.'

'And everyone knew that Natasha didn't have much taste anyway,' William mused.

'Don't you think it would be a bit hasty on Daniel's part to murder Natasha? She never looked as though she had a great hold on life.'

'Maybe there was some pressure on him, perhaps his chicken farm needs money, or his partner was threatening to decamp. It's amazing how little it takes to push someone into murder.'

'They certainly weren't on the best of terms. You heard what Mrs Boult said today and last Monday he made some very odd accusations to Natasha. She was quite shaken.'

'What sort of accusations?'

'I'm not sure I remember precisely,' Darina said slowly. 'But for a moment she looked really frightened. Like . . . ' She paused, bringing the scene into focus in her memory. 'Like a victim looks at a blackmailer.'

'Interesting thought,' observed William. 'Except it's usually the blackmailer who gets murdered, not the victim. Why don't we ask the engaged couple to join us for coffee. That is, unless you want pudding?'

'You know I'd love it but I'm not going to fall for one of Simon's calorie-loaded bits of seduction tonight.'

'And how many other times have you fallen?' William asked slyly, then moved quickly across to the other couple.

A few minutes later the four of them were seated round Darina and William's table.

'Oh, this is nice,' said Verity happily. 'We saw you but I said I was sure you wanted to be alone.'

'Not at all,' said William. 'How are your plans going, Darina tells me you are planning a cookery book?'

'I've been so lucky.' Verity glanced at her fiancé. 'Since I won that competition, all sorts of offers have come along. And a publisher is actually interested in an idea I've got for a book on party food. How to do dinners, buffets, suppers, with different themes. You know, all Indian, or Halloween with diabolical food, or an outdoor meal with everything green, that sort of thing. Food that makes everyone gasp when they see it but tastes good as well. The publisher wants lots of pictures. And I've been in touch with Natalie Duke's agent, explained she was my mother and I've got an appointment with her next week.'

'Let me tell you that living with a cook isn't always the fun it's made out to be,' observed William to Oliver with a heavy facetiousness that alerted Darina. 'People say how wonderful, you lucky dog, but you never get your favourite meals, you're always having to test yet another damned new dish, and often before it's quite right.'

'Oh, Oliver knows all about that,' Verity said seriously. 'He had to eat my competition meal hundreds of times. He's a great help with telling me what's needed.'

'You cook yourself?' asked Darina.

He smiled at her. 'I can't pretend to reach the sort of standard you and Verity achieve but I can manage something reasonably simple.'

'Don't be so modest, darling, you can turn out a superb meal. He said he got tired of eating in restaurants all the time.'

'If you're interested in food, as I am, preparing a meal is not too difficult,' said Oliver simply.

'The other downside,' continued William as though nothing else had been said, 'is that just as you're thinking it's time for a meal to come along, when you're really hungry and don't care what sort of mistake'll turn up this time, you hear the sound of the typewriter or word processor and groans of some deadline. Then you know you'd better start discovering what's in the cupboard that you can prepare. I warn you, old man, it's a hazardous business taking on a cook for a wife!' He blinked owlishly, the picture of a diner who'd drunk too well.

Oliver raised his glass of brandy to Verity. 'I can't wait for the day.'

His fiancée turned to William. 'You see, Oliver is so involved with business, he's usually late or abroad, so he's really grateful I've got something to keep me occupied. Not like his first wife.'

'Elizabeth wanted nothing more than to make a comfortable home for me and children. Unfortunately, there was some problem over our having children and I had to spend most of my time away from home, so . . . ' Oliver made an oddly final gesture of the hand, 'I'm afraid the marriage failed. Perhaps I expected too much, waited too long, I was over thirty when we married. I think I've learned to be more flexible now and I realise,' he said to William, 'there will be times when Verity has to work and I'll be free, when I'll wish she could drop everything and do what I want, but life always calls for compromises, doesn't it?'

'And why should wives deny their own ambitions and creative impulses just to be at the beck and call of us fellows? Is that what you're saying? I tell you, Oliver old chap, even these days I don't see many men falling into line on that one. Woman's place is in the home, say I.'

'We're all different, old boy.' Oliver gave a delicately sarcastic edge to the phrase. 'All I can say is, I'd rather suffer the inconvenience a wife of intelligence and ambition can bring with her than lose her because I held out for an outdated system of sharing; one where the man provides financially but takes in every other way while the woman allows herself to be kept but is otherwise the giver.'

'Hear, hear,' said Darina. 'And I'm sure,' she said to Verity, 'Natasha would have come to realise you were quite right about Oliver.'

Oliver looked blank.

Verity laughed ruefully. 'Darina means Natasha objected to our engagement, thought you would hold me back from my career.'

Her fiancé looked shocked. 'You never told me that, darling!'

She squeezed his arm. 'There didn't seem any point. I wasn't going to give you up and I didn't want you to become prejudiced against her. She'd have come round in the end, I'd have made sure of that.'

'Have you set the day yet?' Darina asked.

Verity looked at Oliver and shook her head. 'It'll be as soon as we can but Oliver has a lot of business to catch up with, he says he's spent too much time down here.'

'I have to visit Hong Kong and Japan next week,' he said.

'Financial consulting, isn't that your line?' William gave what looked uncommonly like a leer. 'Nearest thing to legal robbery these days, isn't it? I wouldn't mind a go at that sort of thing myself.'

Verity looked at him with something like incredulity.

Darina thought she saw where her companion was heading. 'William's *so* lucky, he doesn't need to worry about money,' she said in the sort of tone that explained a multitude of otherwise inexplicable circumstances and looked at him adoringly.

'The days of cowboy finance are over,' said Oliver repressively. 'We have so many regulations these days it's a job to get the most straightforward of deals through. It's certainly not worth trying to break the rules.'

'Glad to hear it, old boy. Well, I'm always in the market for a good deal, usually have a bit of cash floating around looking for a profitable home. Can you make any suggestions?'

'I don't deal in personal finance,' said Oliver shortly. 'My business is all corporate.'

'Will you go to France for your honeymoon? I just adore France.' Darina was playing along. 'Wouldn't it be romantic to spend it at your mother's house?'

Verity flushed. 'I don't know when I can get possession and we hadn't really discussed honeymoons.' She looked uncertainly at Oliver.

'The best honeymoons are kept a secret,' he said shortly.

'Where is this house?' asked William. 'Jolly good thing to have, I must say. I have lots of friends with places in France, often thought of getting one myself.'

'In Brittany.' Verity was valiantly trying to pretend everyone was still enjoying themselves. 'We were looking at it on the map the other day, it's about twenty-five miles south-west of Rennes. Not near the seaside at all,' she added regretfully.

'Doesn't sound like the best sort of place for a honeymoon.' Darina glanced coyly at William.

'The best place for a honeymoon,' said Verity, 'is where the two of you are together.' She looked firmly at both of them.

The waitress approached their table and spoke to Oliver. 'Your car has arrived, sir.'

'Ah, thanks. My bill please, and place everybody's after-dinner drinks here on it as well. No,' he waved away William's protests that the invitation had come from him, 'I insist.'

'Remarkably sensible of you to have a car,' observed William as Oliver gave a brief but careful look at the bill then pulled out a small pile of bank notes, placing a goodly portion on the saucer.

'Can't afford to lose a licence these days.'

'I takes my chances, it's always worked so far.' William gave a last silly-ass smile as the other couple left with the briefest of goodbyes.

'Well,' said Darina, 'at least they didn't ask what it was you did for a living.'

'Not having to worry about money,' he raised his glass to her, 'I expect they thought I didn't work at all.'

'Just as well, I can't think anyone would employ the sort of person you made yourself out to be this evening.'

'They exist, I assure you. He's very self-controlled, isn't he?'

'And can cook but he didn't know Natasha Quantrell objected to the engagement.'

'Unless they're both in it together and have agreed the line they're going to take.'

'If he is in financial difficulties, he gave no sign of it.'

'Nor did he fall for my easy-sucker line, there was no suggestion of a good bit of business he could put my way.'

'I may have lost a promising friendship there, I hope it was worth it.' Darina was a little plaintive.

'I think the chef's coming to pay us a visit,' said William.

Simon Chapman approached, asked if he could join them, dropped into the chair vacated by Oliver and grinned cheerfully. 'Hope you're enjoying yourselves. Didn't want to come over sooner, I always get the impression Oliver Knatchbull thinks I'm something the cat brought in.' He was cheerfully unconcerned. 'How was the meal?'

Darina declared it had all been delicious then added, 'I gather congratulations are in order, that you and Pru are getting together again.'

He grinned at her a trifle sheepishly. 'It looks that way. We're both a little wary but it seems worth giving it a go, especially considering the boys.'

'Plus the fact she's willing to back your restaurant?'

Simon was unabashed. 'There's that, too, of course. But that could all have been settled purely as a matter of finance.'

Darina wondered if Pru would have let such a bargaining chip slip so easily from her hands.

'Another career girl for a wife,' William remarked pointedly.

'Another? Oh, you mean Verity? Pru's not like her sister and at least I know exactly what she's involved with. Verity's like a firecracker, you never know in which direction she'll jump next. I'd say Oliver will have his hands full just keeping track of her doings. No, Pru's got a good solid business, one I may be able to help with as well. Daniel Quantrell going under can't do her anything but good, either.'

Darina looked at him in astonishment.

'Do you mean his chicken business?'

Simon nodded genially. 'Sure do. A chum of mine popped in to see me yesterday morning, runs a restaurant not far from here and buys his chickens from Quantrell. Thought I did too and wanted to warn me. He went round there the other day and found him standing in the middle of his bloody great chicken house, surrounded by cheeping birds, reading a letter. Beside himself with anger he was, said the supermarket he sells most of his birds to won't take any more. Not only that, they weren't going to pay him for the last lot they had. When my chum asks why, Daniel thrusts the letter at him, then snatches it back again but not before Brian had managed to read something about the firm acting on information received, analysis of chicken carcasses, finding unacceptable substances that voided their contract. Quantrell wasn't making a great deal of sense but my chum gathered the chicken business was up the spout. Says he was offered some cheap birds but preferred not to take them. He came to give me a friendly warning but I told him I have a safer source of supply and suggested he contact Pru himself.' He leant back smugly in his chair.

'When exactly was this?' William's hand gently played with his brandy glass and he looked the picture of relaxation but under the lazy lids the grey eyes were alert.

'I think it was Monday afternoon. It isn't general knowledge yet. Brian said Quantrell seemed to be in shock, if he hadn't come along at just that particular moment, he would no doubt have spun the story that's being pushed around now of low prices to expand the market. Apparently Quantrell's even talking of a second chicken house.'

'Natasha's death seems to have come just in time for him,' said Darina, wondering how much Erica Strangeways knew about the matter. 'Who do you think shopped him?'

'Bet it was Constance. Pru says she was all ready to say something about his activities and I reckon she wrote to the company. Takes some time for these things to work themselves through the pipe-line. Well, I can't say I ever got on well with my mother-in-law but I always admitted she had character. And her daughter's the same. Have another brandy?'

William accepted with thanks but Darina refused; it had been agreed that she was to drive them back that evening and she'd confined her drinking to one glass of wine.

Simon sighed. 'No wonder meal prices are having to rise, we don't make any money on the bar side. And the number of couples I've heard say they prefer to have a Marks and Spencer meal at home then they don't have to worry about the drive back! Which reminds me, Darina, have you thought any more about the offer I made you?'

'What offer would that be?' William eyed the chef cautiously.

'She hasn't told you about the cookery book I'm battling with? I want her to collaborate, put it all into cookeryese, as you might say, instead of a series of engineering instructions for fellow chefs. We'll go fifty-fifty, how about it? Come on, darling, I'm desperate.'

Darina was greatly tempted. She liked his recipes, knew she could help him; the only question was whether she had the time. She waited for William to remind her of her other commitments, then realised it was a decision he was leaving entirely up to her.

'Yes,' she said, 'but not fifty-fifty. Let my agent sort something out with yours, I expect there are established percentages for this sort of thing and all the creative work is yours, remember.'

He leant forward and gave her a smacking kiss. 'You're a doll.'

'Let me have your efforts and I'll see what I can do.'
Simon leapt up.
William looked after his vanishing back with speculative interest. 'Now, there's a chap who seems to have got his life sorted out for him,' he said.

# Chapter Twenty-two

William came downstairs early the next morning to find Darina already at her word processor, a cup of coffee at her right hand, her attention given exclusively to the screen in front of her. He shut the dining-room door as quietly as he had opened it and went to the kitchen to find some breakfast.

He'd first woken at four thirty, thought he was back in New York, lay bracing himself for the siren sounds, the noises of a violent city that never slept, slowly relaxing as he realised the only thing he could hear was a cow on heat, lowing for a mate. He'd put on the light, read for half an hour and fought the temptation to go next door and see if Darina was awake.

After all he knew she wouldn't be, her capacity for sleep could only be envied, particularly at that hour of the morning. And he knew if he went in there he would end by wakening her. He'd learned more than police procedure in New York.

He abandoned his book, turned out the light and lay thinking about the previous evening.

On the way home they had discussed Natasha's death. He knew Darina had been nervous of his reaction to her involvement in it. He hoped he had demonstrated that not only was his own interest caught but that he was perfectly happy to talk over aspects of it just as if she was another officer on the case. Pat James, for instance.

How the hell had she managed to become jealous of Pat? It could only be because of the camaraderie between them, the understanding that grew up between people who worked together, particularly as closely as they did in the CID. It was easy, he supposed, for others to consider themselves outsiders.

He had learned a lot from Elaine. Crisp, confident, intelligent, beautiful Elaine. Her quick lawyer's mind would have analysed motive, opportunity and means in this case, possibly reached conclusions more quickly than he or Darina though undoubtedly they would have been the same. But would she have made the intuitive leap Darina's mind had produced just before they arrived home?

'You know what you said about it being the blackmailer who usually gets murdered, not the victim?'

He'd nodded.

'Put the car away then I'll offer you a brand-new theory.'

In the kitchen, boiling up a kettle for a quick cup of tea before bed, she'd suggested: 'Suppose Natasha died by error? That she herself made the pâté, two sets of pâté, one with oleander and one without. Then somehow got the slices mixed and gave Daniel the innocent one and ate the poisoned one herself? Didn't Verity say she'd heard something over the phone that sounded like "mishtake".'

William thought about it. 'I can't see anyone being that careless about a piece of poisoned pâté.'

Darina sat at the table with the freshly made tea and poured out a cup each. 'It was the end of a long and very traumatic day for her. She'd had a most upsetting argument with Verity, eaten hardly anything for lunch, then she would have had to be polite to Oliver when he collected them at the station. It must have been a tremendous relief to get home and she may well have felt hungry by then. According to Grant, there wasn't anything else fresh for her to eat and I don't see Natasha as the sort of person who would be willing to open a tin of something. So there was the pâté. Perhaps she had already given Daniel his slice. No, that can't be right, she left early in the morning and he didn't find it under the milk cover until late evening. She probably took it over as soon as she returned. She could have been perfectly convinced she knew which pâté was which.'

'But if the evidence of the dead dog is to be believed, she discarded the poisoned pâté on the compost heap; are you suggesting she got them muddled again?'

'She looks so distrait most of the time I wouldn't put anything past her.'

'But what would Daniel be blackmailing her about?'

'I can think of a highly blackmailable situation,' she'd said slowly, looking at him over her cup of tea, her soft grey eyes enormous and the creamy hair slipping forward over her shoulder. She'd tossed it back with an impatient gesture then produced her possible scenario.

'Yes,' he'd said. 'That would indeed be eminently blackmailable.'

'It could also provide a motive for Constance Fry's death.'

'A first attempt to protect her position?'

'You have to admit it's a possibility.'

Yes, if you accepted the basis for blackmail, both deaths could have been murder by the same person for the same reason.

Finally Darina had said, 'The answer has to lie in France.'

Lying in bed in the early morning hours, he felt there could well be something to Darina's theory, more than he had been willing to concede at the time. Then he'd slept until seven.

Now he ground himself some coffee and placed it in the cafétière thinking of what he should do next. No, what they should do. In this at least they were to be a team.

He'd have to ring Grant. Even though it was Sunday, the inspector would probably be working on the case. But, before that, he would call his uncle and check out Oliver Knatchbull. Other possible scenarios should not be ignored.

'Dear boy.' John Doubleday was delighted to hear from him, asked if he couldn't come up to London for a few days to stay. Then listened with his usual unshockable sang-froid as his nephew outlined his request.

'Oliver Knatchbull? I'd have said, off the cuff, sound as a bell. But these days the oddest things do happen. You want me to make a few discreet inquiries? Of course, no trouble at all. As long as everyone's not on holiday, and who is these days, I should be able to get back to you quite soon. I take it you'd like to hear as soon as possible?'

Grateful thanks and messages to his aunt given, William rang off. He went and found a map of France. Some twenty-five miles south-west of Rennes, Verity Fry had said. He looked at south Brittany then consulted his address book and made another call. Finally he rang the police station.

Later he took Darina a cup of fresh coffee, finding her scowling over her notations on a recipe. 'I'll have to retest this,' she sighed, 'I can't make out if I used one or two tablespoons here. Both have been crossed out and I can't remember which I settled for. If only

I could be more efficient! Lucky it's chicken breasts, I can joint that one we brought back yesterday.'

'Have you got everything you need or do you want me to pop down to the village shop, they'll be open until twelve?'

Darina swung round from her word processor and inspected him closely, it was as though she had expected to find he had changed colour or grown wings. He'd only offered to go shopping, for heaven's sake!

'Could you pick some mangetout from the garden?' she asked doubtfully instead. 'It's come along beautifully, I thought you were going to miss it all.'

William said he thought he could manage that then inquired, 'How do you feel about a few days in France?'

She obviously felt delighted about a few days in France. 'You mean it?'

'I've had a word with Grant. He thinks the possibility should be checked out. He's applying for a Commission Rogatoire, that's the official permission for us to conduct inquiries there, they can't have us chaps crawling over their patch just any time we want. I told Grant we were planning a few days there ourselves and he's delighted for me to do the investigation. Only trouble is, the permission usually takes two to three weeks to come through. Can you wait that long?'

'It'll give me a chance to get some more of this sorted out so I can enjoy myself with a free conscience. Grant didn't quibble at my presence on the scene?'

'With the whole trip costing minimal expenses to the Avon and Somerset Police Force, what do you think?'

'Poor Pat.'

'Unworthy of you.'

She grinned but offered no further comment.

'I've also been in touch with a chum who has a *résidence secondaire* not far from Rennes. He says we can borrow it for as long as we want, he's not planning to use it until September but his sister may want it with her four children during August and he'd love to be able to say someone else's got it!'

'We can't stay that long!'

'We can't?'

Darina gave him a glance that said she was in no mood for stupid suggestions. 'You're retiring from the force? Pull the other one. Now, let me get on with this or lunch will never be ready.'

William hesitated for a moment. 'There's just one other thing, Grant wants me to follow up on some Actions. At the moment we have no evidence to support the blackmail theory and a multitude of other suspects to consider.'

Darina hunched her shoulders over her keyboard. 'Tell me something new! I never thought you'd stay away for more than a couple of days anyway. It'll be a miracle if we get time for a proper meal in France but I shall live in hopes.'

William half expected Darina to say she would return to London until their break abroad but whether it was that she didn't want to disrupt her work on the books – she'd started on Simon's as well as continuing on her own – or was too interested in the murder inquiry to move away, or had some other reason for wanting to remain in the cottage, he found it impossible to decide. He could, of course, ask her. He said nothing.

The days settled into a well-worn routine of detailed inquiry.

Autopsy reports on both dog and Natasha Quantrell stated stomach contents included traces of pork pâté which included fragments of oleander leaves. However, the piece of pâté Erica Strangeways had rescued from the compost heap proved to contain only the most innocent of ingredients. As did the pâté found in Natasha Quantrell's larder. The green flecks proved to be roughly chopped herbs, mainly tarragon.

'So we've got to look for yet more pâté,' reported William. 'I can hardly believe there could be any more around. But there seems no other explanation.'

'The oleander could have been concentrated in one end,' Darina suggested. 'It would be quite easy to mix chopped-up leaves with a little of the farce then add it to the rest in the tin. Didn't that photograph of the terrine found in Natasha's larder show that it had a little ring at one end of the loaf tin, for hanging up, and wasn't that the end the slice was taken from? The ring could have been used to identify which end was the poisoned one. And it could have meant that when Natasha threw the pâté on to the compost heap, she may have thought it was clear of poison. Unfortunately for Rupert, it wasn't.'

The theory was noted.

The inquest on Natasha Quantrell opened and was adjourned for police inquiries to be made.

A statement was taken from Mrs Boult, who made no bones about her feelings on policemen who didn't declare their official status when listening to private conversations.

William went to London and had interviews with the lawyer who dealt with both Natasha Quantrell's and Natalie Duke's affairs and with Natalie's agent. Both interviews were singularly unproductive but he eventually emerged from the lawyer with a statement which just might prove helpful.

A scouring of old medical records had not assisted in any way.

William had a long interview with Daniel Quantrell, who first of all blustered he had no idea what the sergeant was talking about but eventually was persuaded to make a statement of his suspicions regarding Natasha. Asked about his chicken business, he denied it was in real trouble, claimed he was able to replace his main customer without difficulty and produced what looked like promising inquiries from various sources. Plus a cash-flow projection for expanding the business.

Verity returned to London. Inquiries into her financial state revealed several thousand pounds outstanding on a number of credit cards and her bank had asked her to come in to discuss her overdraft with them. However, the manager felt the situation could be organised so the debts were consolidated and, if she could accept the discipline of their suggested repayment programme, everything should work itself out over a period of several years. She would, of course, have to curtail her spending considerably unless her income could be dramatically increased.

William's uncle reported that Oliver Knatchbull's financial credit was spotless. 'He is very highly thought of and his company seems to be flourishing. I've studied his last accounts and they are quite impressive.'

William checked into the investigation on Constance Fry's death, still quietly chugging along without new information coming to light. All the regular agricultural commercial travellers had been eliminated and few other leads had emerged. CID did not yet feel the case could be defined as a road accident and handed over to Traffic but it looked as though the file would soon become dormant unless new information came to light.

Darina continued to work on the two books. She complained that helping out at the Frys' had set her back more than she had realised on her own book and regretted taking on Simon's as well. But William watched her develop a routine, dividing her time between working on her book, both writing and recipe testing, and rewriting Simon's. When the work went well, she had a ready smile for him and was full of interest in the investigation. And there would be delicious dishes to taste. As long as he was prepared to be constructive, any criticism was welcome but she glowed with particular beauty when he was able to give wholehearted praise.

When the work was difficult, he learned not to expect more than the odd grunt on his return home. On those occasions he would search the fridge and prepare some sort of meal with what he found. He remembered his comments to Oliver with some irony, he hadn't realised just how true they had been. Nor had he realised quite how often Darina must have abandoned work to get his supper in the months they had lived together before he had gone to New York. How blind had he been to her requirements? And how willing was he to continue this sort of existence, he asked himself, as he ironed a couple of shirts and sorted out the linen basket to set the washing machine going.

It was not much more than two weeks before the Commission Rogatoire arrived from France. The Foreign Office, of course, still hadn't provided their paperwork but it wasn't strictly necessary. William contacted the travel agent for a ferry booking.

The first one they could get was on a lunch-time sailing from Portsmouth. Which meant they drove down the Cherbourg peninsula to Brittany in the last of the murky light and then had to search for his chum's house in the dark. The fine weather hadn't returned and there was drizzle, which did not help visibility or William's temper, frayed after a choppy boat ride which Darina had withstood better than himself. They had an argument over whether to stop for supper or not, until finally Darina brought the car to a halt outside a Routiers restaurant and insisted they had a meal.

After that it got better. Remarkable what a bit of food could do to put you feeling right with the world, William thought, then smiled at Darina and said it to her. He watched relief flow into her face and realised just what a bear he must have been. This was no part of his plan at all. He covered her hand with his. 'Sorry,' he said. 'Friends again?'

‘Friends,’ she replied with happy emphasis. And asked what the procedure would be the next day.

‘I have to present myself to the Chief Inspector of Rennes tomorrow morning and give him all the details of the case. He’ll take us to the Examining Magistrate’s clerk, who will go through exactly what we want and why. Our objectives are clear cut and obtainable and there shouldn’t be any problem in presenting them to the Magistrate himself, who may or may not ask us the odd question. If he’s satisfied, he takes our request to a Judge for permission to proceed.’

‘That seems a hell of a procedure,’ Darina gasped as he finished.

‘Doesn’t it! But it does cut out a lot of time-wasting by forcing us to have as much preparation work done as possible and makes sure we know exactly what we are after and why.’

‘How long is it all going to take?’

‘Not all that long. They’ve been warned to expect us.’

At last they wound their way down a lane to a stone farmhouse with two barking dogs beyond which lay three old barns converted into a spacious house of considerable charm, furnished sparsely but more than adequately in French Provincial style. Darina took their bags upstairs while William got a fire going to remove the chill of the evening. He wondered how she would sort out the accommodation. And, if he could find a bottle of wine, whether this would be a good time to tell her about New York.

She leant over the gallery above the living room. ‘I thought you’d like the room at that end,’ she pointed to her right. ‘It’s got an en suite bathroom. I’ve taken this one.’ She waved to her left and disappeared.

No, New York would have to wait.

# Chapter Twenty-three

The house that Natasha Quantrell had shared with Natalie Duke stood in a small hamlet deep in a rural area well away from major roads: an area studded with small forests and lakes and villages that looked as though all that had changed in the last fifty years was the plate-glass window installed in the local boulangerie or épicerie.

It was just after midday. Most of the morning had vanished in a welter of official procedure that had followed William's outline the previous evening. Eventually he had been given permission to go ahead.

They had found their way down the main Nantes road to the turn off that eventually brought them to this small manoir with its little turrets and windows that looked on to a tiny lake fringed with green trees. It was out of a fairy-tale until you looked at what remained of the outbuildings, still ugly with blackened stones, charred beams and the collapsed roof of a devastating fire.

William fished out the key-ring Grant had found in Natasha Quantrell's desk and opened the heavy iron gates into the courtyard.

It seemed inevitable to Darina that she should look first at the ruined part of the building. Amidst the rubble, seemingly untouched since the fire, she could see the blackened and distorted remains of a portable gas fire. Signs of shelves could be made out on two of the walls and underneath all the debris could be discerned layers of ruined paper, half-consumed books and notes. Darina thought of her own study back in Chelsea, the shelves of carefully collected cookery books, many from previous ages, some valuable. The files of recipes, fully worked out or just notes. Ideas jotted down in notebooks alongside accounts of meals eaten in restaurants or with friends, of visits to food producers, conversations with chefs, manufacturers, retailers. All grist for her columns, all with valuable information it would be almost impossible to replace.

If Natalie had survived the fire, would she have been able to face picking up the threads of this violently disrupted work? She had apparently been working on a history of English cooking. Darina could imagine the research necessary, the notes painstakingly built up over many years. The most private of writers, Natalie Duke had not been able totally to evade journalistic interest and Darina remembered reading somewhere an interview that had actually taken place in this study. A photograph had accompanied the article and the camera had caught shelves holding what the interviewer referred to as 'an unparalleled collection of English cookery books worth many thousands of pounds'. All now gone. A devastating loss.

Here was where one of England's great cookery writers had died and all hope of salvaging unpublished works from her pen had vanished. Darina felt William put an arm round her shoulders and hold her tight.

'Eeuh!'

They turned and saw an old Frenchman dressed in faded blue trousers and jacket, a hand stiffly held in one pocket, his body ramrod straight from his small, black shod feet to his shoulders, from which his head stuck out at an arthritic angle. His face was as gnarled and brown as a walnut. Bright blue eyes regarded them with suspicious interest.

Once he had their attention, a series of inquiries was fired in salvoes of thickly accented French. Darina was quickly lost, the man's habit of swallowing half his words was too much for her precarious command of the language. But not for William. He held out his hand, introduced them both and explained they were investigating the death of Madame Quantrell.

More strangled French, from which Darina picked out the words 'les Deux Anglaises', and that he was appalled at the death of Madame but happy to see them, to give them the benefit of his knowledge. There was much arm-waving towards the ruined studio.

Darina tired of trying to follow the conversation and wandered round the courtyard. The studio had been linked to the main house by a series of open outbuildings filled with gardening impedimenta and odd items of discarded furniture. She looked back to where William and the little man were deep in conversation and admired the sergeant's command of the language. William beckoned her to join them.

'This is Monsieur Bertauld, he's retired, lives just round the corner. He knew the cousins well. He's given me a detailed account of the fire and seems happy to chat. I thought we'd ask him if there was somewhere we could all have a drink and hear more. What do you think?'

In no time they were sitting at a small table outside a bar-café not far from the manoir, Henri Bertauld clutching a pastis, her and William drinking an amazingly good Muscadet *sur lie*.

By concentrating hard, Darina found her ears attuned themselves to Henri's accent and the rhythms of his speech and she could understand more. From time to time other Frenchmen drifted along for midday drinking or eating and were drawn into the conversation by Henri. Some stayed, some contributed a few phrases then went off to other tables.

Gradually they built up a picture of the life the two English ladies had led in this small French hamlet. In the main their lives had been private. Once a year they had given a party to which all the locals were invited. They had few visitors. Natasha did most of the shopping locally but every now and then their old Renault motor car would be driven to a larger centre. In the spring they would go to the south of France and always came back deploring the state of the coast.

The postman joined the group. Like everyone else he was distressed to hear of Natasha's death. 'La pauvre Anglaise,' he said. No, he had never had much post to deliver to the manoir but they had always been most generous at Christmas when he had brought their calendar for the coming year. They had all hoped the surviving Anglaise would return after the shock of the great tragedy was past. He brought out a large red and white checked handkerchief and passed it over with suitably solemn tact. 'Quelle désastre,' he ended.

Many of the men had been involved in the fight against the fire in the studio. But it had all been too difficult. By the time smoke had risen above the wall of the manoir and the fire was discovered, it was too late. No one had been near enough to hear the crackle of the flames or the shrieks of poor Madame Quantrell trying to get to her cousin. The state she was in! Her hair singed off, her face blackened with the smoke. So badly burned, and her poor hands! She had managed to open the door but the smoke and the flames had beaten her back. Even so it had taken three of them to hold her away from trying again. Crying and shouting she had been. Ah no, it was impossible to say what she had been crying, it had been in English, you understand? It was a battle to fight the fire without trying to translate foreign languages.

Of course they all knew it was Madame Duke inside the studio, it always was. Madame Quantrell had once joked it was more than her life was worth to go in there, much as she would love to dust and clean it. It was Madame Quantrell who was the *femme de menage*, you understand? Madame Duke was always writing, writing, writing. Quite famous they heard. Her books were even in French but they hadn't read them themselves. Though was it true she had written about French food? That would be something to read, eh? An English woman writing about French food?

They were both good cooks, *bien sur*, their annual party was always an occasion, one to be enjoyed. And now les Deux Anglaises were both gone, they had attended the last of the parties.

Oh, yes, there was one other thing, Henri said as they ate the Breton galettes they had ordered for lunch. The other locals had drifted tactfully away leaving Henri proudly in possession of his English friends.

It was a small detail but since they seemed so interested in that dreadful day perhaps they would like to know that Madame Duke had driven out that morning. Perhaps if she had stayed at home, she would have been more careful, no?

Where had she been? Eh, they didn't expect him to be a mind-reader? All he knew was that he had seen her driving back home mid-morning, some time before the alarm was given. Perhaps she had gone to the studio, lit the stove, an east wind had been blowing that morning, it had not helped control the fire, and it had exploded, no?

How had he known it was Madame Duke? Well, he could tell one cousin from the other, they all could. They were alike but not that alike. Madame Duke's hair was always long, worn up behind, the old man sketched a French pleat with his hands. Madame Quantrell wore hers short.

'We made his day for him,' said William as they walked back to the manoir after several cups of coffee to offset the wine they had drunk.

'And he was very informative,' said Darina.

She averted her gaze from the burned-out studio as they let themselves into the courtyard with Natasha's keys. The descriptions of the fire had been too graphic. Almost she could see the charred figure lying dead amongst the beams and wreckage. Almost hear the cries of the frantic woman trying to rescue her cousin.

She turned determinedly to the house.

No ghosts hung in the air as she stood with William in the hall. No vibrations stirred the dust on the long refectory table that stood against a wall hung with an old tapestry of a hunting scene studded with enchanting wild flowers. It was just an empty house.

They walked through the door to their right and found themselves in a salon furnished with Breton pieces and some comfortable-looking chairs and a sofa. Then they explored the rest of the house.

It was smaller than it looked from the outside. Only three bedrooms, the salon and large hall plus a small kitchen, well-organised but no candidate for featuring in a glossy magazine. No wonder Natalie had found it necessary to create the studio across the courtyard.

One of the bedrooms was obviously for the guests they hardly ever had, its bare furniture arranged simply. One bathroom with adequate but old-fashioned plumbing did duty for all three bedrooms.

The other two looked over the lake and countryside beyond. Large rooms with sloping ceilings and beams, they were furnished in a more personal style than the rest of the house.

'No difficulty in deciding which was which cousin's,' said Darina after looking in each.

'And?'

She opened the door of the first and pointed to a small shelf of books on food. 'These must be Natalie's, they seem to be anecdotal, perhaps of more personal interest than those in her studio. But more revealing is this jar on the dressing-table full of hairpins. Remember what Henri said about her hairstyle?'

'Right, Sherlock, your Watson takes note.'

She went into the other bedroom. 'Here's a sketch of the Bailey. And the old boy in this photograph must be Natasha's grandfather. Here's one of the two of them together.' She picked up a snapshot of a girl in her late twenties with the man in the other photograph. He was very erect. A white moustache hid his mouth but he looked as though he might be smiling. Natasha certainly was. She wore a flowered cotton dress, her legs were bare and dark curls tumbled round her face. The nose and bone structure bore a strong resemblance both to the photo of Natalie Darina had seen in the Bailey and to Verity but the eyes were merrier, the mouth fuller and the face somehow looked softer. It was hard to equate the face in the photo with the scarred countenance Darina had met in Somerset.

'Pretty girl,' said William, looking at it over her shoulder. Then he added, 'If it wasn't for the hairpins, I'd say you'd been a bit premature in your identification of the rooms' owners.' He pointed to a small pile of books on a table on the other side of the bed. Darina examined them. They were all recently published cookery or food books.

'Natasha said she did a lot of the recipe testing,' she commented.

They opened the armoires in both rooms. Natalie's still held a collection of clothes, either simple casual skirts and shirts or classic styles with good labels that looked as though they had done several years' service. On one of the shelves was a collection of wide-brimmed hats. Natasha's armoire only contained some winter clothes in a softer style than her cousin's.

They checked the chests of drawers in both rooms and in one of Natalie's found a large folding leather frame. It held a montage of different shots. Darina sat on the bed and studied them.

There was one of Natasha at about twenty, taken on a beach somewhere in a swimsuit. There was one of a couple that must have been Natalie's parents, the woman very like her daughter, the man with a keenly intelligent face. An older snapshot of Natalie's mother with her twin, they really had been identical. A group of the twins with their husbands. For a crazy moment Darina remembered the old joke about the man married to one half of a pair of beautiful twins. Did he always know which was his wife, he was asked. Did it matter? he replied. There were snaps of other people with no clue as to their identity. Many taken against foreign locations, a Mediterranean beach, a cathedral, a European square. Intelligent-looking young men and women, almost always smiling.

Then Darina stopped and looked at the shot of one young man more closely. There was something familiar about the face though she couldn't put a name to him. The photographer had caught a hasty snapshot, the photo was slightly out of focus and the young man was looking back over his shoulder, laughing at the camera. Long fair hair drifted down over T-shirt clad shoulders and eyes squinted against the sun.

Darina passed the frame to William and pointed out the young man. 'Does he remind you of anyone?'

He studied the snapshot. 'Can't say he does. No, wait a minute.' He looked again, tilting the frame to get a different angle. 'Yes, it's Verity.'

'Verity?'

Darina tried to snatch the frame from him but he held firmly on to it and fished out the snapshot from under the transparent plastic. 'It's the eyes and the mouth. When she first came over at the restaurant that night, she was laughing just like that.' He turned the photo over to see if there was anything written on the back. It was blank and he looked again at the background, revealed for the first time. 'That's the Sheldonian,' he said. 'Oxford undergrad or a tourist?'

Darina gently removed the snapshot from his grasp and studied it again.

It was true, the resemblance was quite unmistakable. Darina tried to find some other clue to Verity's father. But there was nothing. One young man posed for a quick snapshot in Oxford. And that was it. No clues as to who he was, when it was taken, what they were doing there together, even whether he was English. Those fair good looks could just as easily have been German or American, could have taken him to Hollywood. But something about him suggested England.

'I wonder what happened, why Natalie never married him.'

'Perhaps he'd vanished from her life by then. People do, you know. One moment you're in the throes of a mad, passionate affair, the next . . . ' he made a small chopping motion with his hand. Darina gave her companion a quick glance but there was nothing in his face to suggest he had been speaking from personal experience.

'Or perhaps it was slightly more complicated than that? But he doesn't look old enough to have been married, which is the most usual obstacle. Perhaps Natalie found he had other ties?'

'Ah, *cherchez l'autre femme*, you think? Well, anything is possible. I think we will take this with us.' William inserted the photo back into the frame and then tried to slip it into his pocket. 'Have you room for this in your bag? It's too wide to go in my jacket. Right, now let's see if we can find an address book or something with local numbers that includes a dentist. It's such a pity Natasha didn't take it with her to England.' An exhaustive search through her papers at the Bailey had not revealed any details of her life in France. If they failed now they had a tedious time ahead of them ringing round local tooth surgeons.

They finally found what they were seeking in the kitchen, a piece of paper sellotaped to the inside of the telephone directory with numbers for doctor, dentist, fire station and other local suppliers of sundry services.

William rang but there was no reply. He looked at his watch. 'He may have left already. We'll go and try the hospital Natasha was taken to after the fire.'

They locked the house and the gate behind them.

The sister at the local hospital, a modern building with an air of orderly bustle, spoke much clearer French than Henri and Darina managed to understand that Natasha Quantrell had been brought in unconscious and had remained in a coma for a number of days, only slowly recovering. That she had suffered a certain loss of memory and confusion when she first came round, which was only natural in such a case, but that had gradually cleared. However, she had refused to see anyone while she was at the hospital and insisted on returning to the manoir as soon as possible, attending as an out-patient until her burns were healed. Plastic surgery had been suggested as a possibility after a longer convalescence.

From the dates the sister produced, it seemed Natasha had been discharged as an out-patient only very shortly before returning to England.

It was early evening by the time they had finished at the hospital and they called a day to their investigations. The dentist would have to wait until tomorrow.

They ate out that evening at an excellent local restaurant the Quatre Vents in Bain de Bretagne, which had been recommended to William by his friend.

As William said, the menu prices were enough to make Simon Chapman blanch they were so modest. 'And talking of your friendly chef, what do you think the chances are for his and Pru's marriage?'

'Fifty-fifty?'

'No more than that?'

'I don't suppose he will ever lose his roving eye, it's something Pru will have to come to terms with. The whole venture will depend on her. I think she's something of a mystery girl to Simon. The sleeping beauty he managed to kiss awake, that sort of thing. And he's got a real respect for her ability to run the farm. She could give him the security I think he needs, if she's prepared to put up with the demands of a chef's life. But Pru doesn't seem much of a social girl and if he organises things properly, doesn't open for lunch, they should see something of each other. And he will see a great deal more of the boys while they are growing up than many fathers.'

'Hmm, a lot of good will being called for on both sides.'

'Isn't that what most marriages require?'

There was a brief silence then William courteously asked Darina her opinion of their findings at the manoir.

'It's all proved, as far as I'm concerned,' said Darina. 'I reckon you hardly need the dentist's evidence. But I suppose it's necessary for the court.'

'Evidence is always necessary,' said William drily.

'Now that we're sure what Daniel had over Natasha, the theory of the mistaken slice of pâté becomes quite plausible.'

'Plausible, yes. But there is nothing we've found that proves anything yet.'

'Well, I really don't see Daniel Quantrell as a murderer.'

'Oh, why?'

'I suppose it's a basic lack of backbone. Trying to pass off chickens as being better than they should be, cheating the nutrition regulations, that sort of thing I can see would be right down his street. But surely actually killing someone takes more fibre, more character?'

'Crippen was considered very harmless, even spineless, quite ruled by his domineering wife.'

'Worm turning and all that? Maybe.' Darina thought about Daniel Quantrell. 'He must have been very attractive, I suppose, in his youth. All that fair hair could have been devastating and he can have quite a twinkle in his eye if he fancies you.'

'Fancied you, did he?'

'I was thinking of the way he looked at Verity at Constance Fry's funeral, actually,' said Darina with great dignity. 'And remember what Mrs Boult said, how he and Natasha used to get on so well? I can't see her being great chums, even thinking about marriage, with someone as hopeless as he appears these days.'

'Erica Strangeways seems an intelligent woman and she appears to consider him worthy of her attention.'

'Yes, I've been trying to decide if it's the man or what he offers that she's interested in. She's certainly intelligent, she saw the implications of that pâté being poisoned very quickly but never opened her mouth.'

'Noticed you had recognised the implications as well and decided to cover her tracks?'

'Could be, and she could well have been certain it would prove entirely innocent. I just can't find sufficient motive for her to knock off Natasha.'

'It would be very neat,' said William after a pause, 'if we could prove it to be a case of biter bit, poisoner poisoned with her own weapon.'

'What are the odds we can produce evidence?'

'Circumstantial at best, I think.'

Back at the house it was a velvet-smooth night. The sun had shone stronger and stronger during the day, melting away the remains of clouds and bathing the country in golden light. They opened the windows and let the soft night air flood in, refreshing the atmosphere.

William found a bottle of Armagnac to drink with the coffee they'd passed up in the restaurant. He filled a couple of glasses, Darina poured the coffee, then they settled back and looked at each other.

'What happened to Elaine?' Darina asked finally.

'Ah, Elaine.'

'No need to tell me anything if you don't want to.'

'Oh, but I do.' There was silence.

William set down his empty coffee cup and looked at the dregs. 'I think I told you I found her rather attractive and we were seeing quite a lot of each other?'

Darina wanted to say that if William's letter was to be believed, Elaine was the thinking man's bimbo but thought better of it.

'Did I tell you she was a lawyer? Mind like a whip. She'd had a spell in the District Prosecutor's office and now is a partner in a top law firm. Does what crime work they have as well as other litigation.'

'So you had a lot in common,' suggested Darina helpfully.

'We got on very well. First it was just good friends, you know, then we got closer.' He paused.

'William,' said Darina gently, 'you don't have to tell me any of this. We decided when you went to New York we were each free to do whatever we wanted. I had no right to ask.'

'I need to tell you,' he said, looking at her for the first time.

'For a couple of weeks everything was wonderful. Then my investigation started hotting up. I had to cancel a couple of weekends and reschedule some dates we'd planned. The crunch came when she had to attend some high-swanking legal dinner. I was to be her partner. She'd apparently told everyone she was bringing this aristocratic, hot-shot Scotland Yard detective. (I honestly don't think she'd listened to a word I told her about who I was or what I was doing there. The only things she'd really cottoned on to were the CID connection and that my uncle was Lord Doubleday.) Well, at the last minute I couldn't go. I was on a stake-out in Upper Manhattan, sitting in a car, drinking innumerable cartons of weak coffee, swapping experiences with my opposite New York number and waiting for the sale of a batch of stolen credit cards to take place. I had to get someone to call her and say I couldn't make the dinner. She decided I'd just got bored with the whole idea and we had a stand-up row the following night. Finally she accused me of not being able to take a red-blooded career girl, that all I wanted was one of my English "yes" girls, someone who would clean up behind me and think I was marvellous no matter what I did. I'd have to learn, she said, that girls who were any use demanded a lot more from their men.'

Darina thought Elaine sounded terrifying. Terrifying but astute. 'What did you say to that?'

There was a long pause. Then William said, 'I told her she didn't understand anything about give and take, she just took. That I was very sorry because I'd thought she had more to her than that. And she said I was doomed to be thrown over by any girl worth her salt if I wasn't prepared to learn what compromise was all about.'

'She gave you a tough time.' Darina poured him some more coffee and refilled his Armagnac glass.

'At the time I was furious. I'd told her about you, you see, and she'd been all on your side, said I had to learn how to give, let a girl have space, room to do her own thing. And now she seemed unable to let me have the same space.' He drank some of the liqueur. 'Then after a few days I began to think again. And I decided that maybe she'd had the odd point. That I had rather assumed my job had to come before hers, that all I had to do was ring up, hot-shot detective that I was, say, sorry, not tonight Josephine, without really considering how it was going to affect her plans.'

Darina said nothing.

'So I got in touch and apologised and she said she'd over-reacted and we got together again. But it wasn't the same. I hadn't been entirely wrong. She *was* basically very selfish. But she taught me a lot. There's only one thing I really regret.'

'And that is?' Darina asked steadily, watching his hands twist the glass of Armagnac around and around.

The hands were suddenly still. He looked at her again. 'That I couldn't have learned all that from you. That it took a spoilt New York bitch to teach me.' He looked down at the empty glass. 'When I got your letter telling me all about the amusing chef you'd met down here, I was so jealous, I nearly abandoned my job and came home immediately.'

'But I only just mentioned Simon.'

'Ah, it was the way you only just mentioned him.'

Darina remembered when she had written that letter. It had been shortly after the first dinner she had had at Chapman's. Yes, she had been rather smitten with Simon and, yes, it had been intended as a counter to Elaine. She had forgotten she could be so petty.

'One of the reasons I was so keen to bring you to France, even before this investigation, was because I thought if we got away from England, we might be able to start again, on a different basis.'

They sat looking at each other, either side of a long coffee-table. The sound of crickets punctured the night and the scent of roses mingled with the remnants of wood smoke. I shall remember this moment for the rest of my life, Darina told herself.

William continued, 'You've never looked more gorgeous. And I'm having difficulty staying my side of this table. You see, I know we've always brushed our differences under the bedclothes before and I don't want to fall back on that this time. This time I want you to realise that I do understand your need to follow your own career. And that I want, more than anything else, to share the rest of my life with you, for you and me to get married.'

It was such a tiny point but it finally convinced Darina he meant what he said. Before he had always asked her to marry him, now he was suggesting they enter marriage together.

'I'd like that,' she said.

For a moment he didn't seem to take it in. Then the strain melted out of his face and she caught her breath at the look in his eyes.

# Chapter Twenty-four

To be in love and newly engaged should be a hindrance not a help to a murder investigation. It was true that Darina and William felt strongly reluctant to leave the seductive comfort of the bed where they had consummated their new relationship. Once up, however, the lure of the investigation called strongly. The resolution of their personal conflict had left them free to focus on the mystery of Natasha Quantrell's death without distractions.

A renewed attempt at ringing the number of the dentist they had found in the manoir diverted the call to another number. The clinic proved to be in Rennes and M Desrivières on holiday but a M Demurrier was taking his patients. He was sympathetic but explained the service was for emergencies only, scrutiny of dental records was not part of the arrangement.

Darina and William drove into Rennes and visited the gendarmerie. There were more telephone calls. Finally success. 'This afternoon, late, M Demurrier will take you to the clinic of M Desrivières and look up the record you want. But he cannot before. This is all right?' William said he was most grateful for the help.

Outside, he and Darina found their way into the eighteenth-century part of Rennes, with its straight streets and attractive squares. They found a small restaurant and ate more galettes for lunch. And talked about weddings and where they would live.

Walking around the pleasant city afterwards, they found a jeweller with a particularly attractive window display. William insisted on going in and inspecting every suitable ring on offer. The jeweller expressed himself enchanted to assist such a charming English couple and brought out tray after tray, exclaiming over some of the stones, refusing to put others in front of them as not worthy, scouring his stock-room in case there was some gem not yet on display.

When he produced a diamond ring in an antique rose setting, Darina stopped all further searches. It was beautiful, she said, she had given her heart to it. 'Just like monsieur here with his so beautiful fiancée,' the jeweller declared.

While William produced his gold credit card and the various paper work was being completed, Darina sat thinking about Natalie.

How had she felt, pregnant and unmarried, determined not to have an abortion but equally sure she didn't want to raise a child? Just why had she decided her lover was not even to know he was a father? The handsome face in the photograph frame came back to her. Why had Natalie rejected him? Did someone else have a prior claim to his affections? Or had he abandoned her? Had their affair, in fact, ended by the time she found she was expecting Verity?

Darina shivered at the bleakness of Natalie's situation. How strange she had not shared all the difficulties of her position with Natasha, the cousin who was closer than most sisters. Unless, she suddenly thought, unless the father was someone Natasha already knew? Why else hint he was much older than she and already married?

'Right,' said William, 'allow me to slip this on your finger.'

The jeweller watched their faces in approval.

Then they found their way to M Demurrier's clinic.

The dentist, a small, dapper man with soft, prematurely white hair and a thin face, was excited by the drama of detective work. He greeted them warmly, took out a set of keys from his receptionist's desk and walked them over to his colleague's surgery, a matter of a couple of streets away, chatting happily. Details poured out on how long he had known M Desrivières, what friends they were. 'We do this for each other for the holidays, you understand? We keep the keys but usually do not need to enter each other's establishments.'

He opened the door and ushered them into another smartly appointed reception room, opened a filing cabinet and started sorting through sets of cards. 'Quantrell, Quantrell, not a usual name, eh? Ah, here we are.' He drew out a card with a flourish. 'Now, monsieur, if you would be so good as to give me your record we can compare the two.'

William handed over the card prepared by the police dentist and the Frenchman looked at it carefully. His face fell, he sucked his teeth noisily, shook his head, put both cards on top of the filing cabinet and studied them closely, rocking backwards and forwards on his heels. Then he picked up the card he had taken from the filing cabinet, turned it over, checked the name on the top, compared it with the name on the top of the one given him by William and searched in the cabinet drawer again.

Finally he looked at them and said. 'These are most assuredly not the records of the same woman.'

'Are there,' asked William casually, 'are there in that cabinet records for a Madame Natalie Duke?'

The dentist searched again. After a short time he uttered a triumphant little shout and brought out another record card. As he compared this with the one William had handed over, his eyebrows shot up.

'But this is the explanation, monsieur, you gave me the wrong name. This,' he waggled the English card, 'is assuredly the record of Madame Duke, not Madame Quantrell. They match but exactly.'

'And, forgive me, M Demurrier, but you understand I have to be sure, there is no chance the cards in that cabinet could have been mixed up?'

A stare of total non-comprehension for a moment, then a stream of Gallic protestation from which Darina gathered that that possibility was so remote as to be non-existent.

William apologised again then said, 'You have been most kind, monsieur. Can I ask you now, will you please give me a short statement to the effect that the record card I have shown you is the record of Miss Natalie Duke's teeth not Miss Quantrell's, and make available to us both these cards or copies of them?'

Some explanation was necessary, then they had to return to M Demurrier's clinic where he had a photocopy machine, but eventually the dentist was shaking them both by the hand and William had safely put the envelope containing the statement he had signed together with the dental records into Darina's large handbag.

'Well, that's it,' he said as they were walking back to the car park. 'Case neatly wrapped. If it had been a little earlier I would have suggested we tried for the evening boat but I see no point in that now. In fact, on second thoughts, I don't think I'd have suggested we try for that boat even if we had finished earlier. I think we deserve another good French meal, don't you?'

It was not until Cherbourg the following afternoon that the case was exhaustively discussed. There had been no room on the five o'clock boat, even though they'd arrived early, and many hours had to be spent waiting for the evening one.

They shopped at the supermarket outside the town, buying cheese, Normandy butter, wine and Crême de Peche, then sat in a café drinking coffee.

William looked at Darina as they finished their Croques Monsieurs. 'You've gone very quiet, having second thoughts about anything?'

'Only about the investigation,' she smiled at him. The sky could fall down before she regretted agreeing to marry him.

'What about it? Haven't we now got evidence to suggest your theory was right?'

'Yes,' Darina acknowledged, 'except . . . '

'Except what?' he asked as she trailed to a stop.

'I'm not sure.'

'Why don't we go through it all? That is, you outline the facts for me, you know just as much, if not more, than I because you know the people involved.'

If there had been nothing else, this invitation would have told Darina how much he had changed. The William who had gone to New York would never have made such a suggestion. That William would have agreed reluctantly to discuss the investigation as a great concession, maybe used it as a vehicle to get something off his chest, but he would never have acknowledged that she could know more than he did.

All at once she saw this whole French trip as a marvellous gift. He'd arranged it not to get her away from England, though that may have been his first intention, but so she could be part of the investigation. It was the most sensitive, lovely thing he could have done. Producing ad hoc suppers and ironing his own shirts had been touching but how long would such solicitude for her needs last? This was a far more impressive change of attitude. And now he was wrapping the gift in a beautiful ribbon. If she had had any doubts remaining, this would have removed the last of them.

'OK.' She leant her arms on the table and looked at him. 'Here's how I think it must have happened. Natalie goes out for the morning. Natasha sees her chance to clean her cousin's studio, it sounds as though one didn't come along often. Somehow she upsets the gas stove, perhaps just as has been suggested. Or perhaps she gets startled by an unexpectedly early return of Natalie. Whatever, the studio bursts into flames and then the stove explodes. When Natalie realises this, she tries desperately to rescue Natasha but fails and is finally taken off to hospital unconscious.

'When she comes round, it is to find everyone thinks she is Natasha. Her long hair has been burnt off during her struggle to rescue her cousin and no one even suspects it wasn't Natalie in her studio. Perhaps she tries to tell them she isn't Natasha. But her whole head is wrapped in bandages, she can hardly talk, she is being fed intravenously and is heavily sedated as well. And is undoubtedly confused herself. No one would have paid any attention to what she said.

'Then as she gradually begins to recover she starts to think. Her life's work is destroyed. All her reference books, her notes, her work in progress. And she's lost her sense of taste. Her career as a cookery writer is finished. Her history of English cooking she might have been able to continue but the thought of starting from scratch again and without her library must have been too daunting. She has also lost her cousin, her companion for nearly quarter of a century. Not only that, but the house they have been planning to go back to live in, that they both apparently loved so much, now goes to Daniel Quantrell. The choice she is faced with is either to stay on in the manoir with all its painful memories, or to move lock, stock and barrel to somewhere else and where else is there? She has no relations left, Natasha's old home is the only place she has any ties to at all.

'Against this bleak prospect she puts the fact that people apparently believe her to be her cousin. Why not become that cousin? She probably knows by now that her face is so scarred it is unlikely anyone will be able to challenge her appearance. Even plastic surgery is not going to give her back the face she once had. And the fact that her handwriting and her signature have changed, as testified by that lawyer you spoke to, can be explained by the scarring on her hands. As Natasha she could go back and live in the Bailey, a place of happy memories, a place where she would be welcomed and have some hope of building a new life. As long as she abandons any idea of writing. Which has been made more or less impossible for her anyway. The cousins had left everything to each other in their wills, she thinks she knows everything about Natasha's life. It must have seemed too easy.

'So she comes back to the Bailey. And at first everything goes well. Then two things occur she has not taken into account. First, she meets her daughter, the girl Constance has never allowed her to forget, and finds an immediate rapport with her, a companionship and affection that take her by surprise. The relationship grows rapidly and deeply till she can't bear to stand the possibility of being deprived of it. And, secondly, Daniel Quantrell suspects the truth. It seems he had a closer relationship with Natasha than Natalie had realised. Her cousin had not told her everything.

'He is blackmailing her, threatening her with exposure unless she hands over the Bailey. And if she is forced to leave there, where will she go? She is back again with the desolation that faced her in hospital.

'At the Frys' she sees the oleander. She's spent enough time in hot countries to be aware of its poisonous qualities. And there is all that talk of a pâté competition. A competition Daniel has instigated. He has been on the other side of the bush with just as much opportunity to pick a small branch as her. He has access to plant knowledge, knowledge far greater than hers. He has produced a vituperative outburst. If she's clever, she can make it look as though he was trying to kill her, after all, he has a very strong motive. She knew Erica was a vegetarian and never touched meat, there would be no danger of her eating the poisonous slice. And perhaps she knew that Erica would be out all that day and wouldn't know whether Daniel had cooked pâté or not. No doubt if the plan had gone right, we would have been told of a slice left for her with another of those Fry's Farm labels. Perhaps she would have smuggled the tin of pâté from her larder into his. The rest of the poisonous pâté she places on the compost heap, hoping the lethal piece has been completely removed. Or maybe she is not even worried about that aspect, after all, it's Daniel's heap. She might have thought she had a good chance of getting away with it if only she hadn't muddled the slices.'

They sat in silence for a while, mulling over the story.

'So what worries you about it?' asked William.

'There are an awful lot of "ifs",' said Darina. 'It really doesn't seem the most clear-headed of plans.' Now that she'd outlined it, it sounded like something dreamed up for a detective story.

'I doubt if she was at all clear-headed. She can't have been ever since that fire. Grant seems happy enough at the moment. We have evidence that the woman who died of poison was Natalie Duke not Natasha Quantrell. Daniel Quantrell had no real reason to kill her, all he had to do was voice his suspicions and the subsequent check would have meant he could move into the Bailey without a murder charge hanging over his head. He swears he never even suggested she give up the Bailey to him.'

'He would, wouldn't he? What did he say about his relationship to Natalie Duke?'

'Says they were friends, nothing more. That it was Natasha he wanted to marry but, though they had an affair, she turned him down. He still sounds bitter about that.'

'I wonder,' said Darina slowly.

'Wonder what?' William smiled at her; he was being remarkably patient, she thought, how long would it last?

'I wonder if there was something else. Something Natalie knew about Daniel.'

'You mean something she was blackmailing him with? You keep quiet about me being Natalie and I'll be quiet about, what?'

'I can't imagine. I'm just convinced we haven't got to the bottom of the story; there's something else, I'm sure of it. There are too many odd ends hanging around. There's Constance Fry's death, for a start.'

'But I thought you'd decided she knew Natasha was Natalie because she called her "Nat" at the end of that telephone call you overheard? We know from Mrs Boult that the cousins called each other Nat and Tash, so it was probable that if Constance Fry shortened their names it would be in the same way. And because of that, Natalie would have known that her secret was out. She knew when Constance would be coming down that road, she could have thought all she had to do was drive towards her and run her over.' The words were confident but William's tone of voice betrayed doubt.

'You've never been happy with that bit of my theory, have you?'

'No,' he acknowledged, 'not on the medical evidence. If someone had wanted to kill her, they would have needed to run her over properly, not trust to luck and a chance rock. And that there would be no other cars around at the time. I think we've got a genuine hit-and-run accident here that's nothing to do with the other death.'

'Maybe. But suppose someone thought she was Natasha or Natalie? She was wearing her hat, and riding a bicycle similar to hers?'

'Daniel, you mean?'

'It's a possibility, isn't it? Except he wasn't in the kitchen when Constance spoke to Natalie on the phone. After all, no one else knew she was going to be riding along that road at that time.'

'You don't know that for certain,' pointed out William.

'You mean she could have told someone else, called them before she actually set out?'

'Or there could have been someone else in the room with Natalie when she rang.'

William had shaken the kaleidoscope Darina was holding and the pieces shifted into a new pattern. She sat thinking hard.

'Let's have a walk through the town while you tell me more about the Frys and the Quantrells,' suggested William.

They walked in the late afternoon sun and Darina raided her memory for every tiny detail she'd heard about the two families. She relished the way her companion's quick mind picked up the details she gave him and turned them this way and that, presenting new implications for her consideration.

But it wasn't until they were undressing in their cabin that night, feeling the slight sway of the ship beneath their feet, that Darina's kaleidoscope of pieces shook itself once again into a new pattern without any aid from either of them. During dinner, eaten at a small restaurant near the port, they had put the investigation on one side and talked of other things. But though Darina listened to tales of New York police with every appearance of deep concentration, a part of her mind continued to consider a number of odd little tassels on the fringe of the investigation that still teased at her. Then the brightly coloured pieces suddenly assembled themselves in a totally new design and she knew, with an awful certainty, exactly why Natalie Duke had died.

# Chapter Twenty-five

'You do see, don't you?' Darina said again to William as they sat in his car, waiting to disembark from the boat at Portsmouth the next morning.

'I do. And I agree, I think it explains everything. But there's no proof. One fact can be checked, thank heavens for modern science, but what follows from that is all circumstantial and would never stand up in court.'

'Can evidence be found?'

'We'll discuss that with Grant.'

They drove straight to the police station. There William insisted Darina be allowed to lay out the facts and theories of the case as she had put them together.

Grant was very quiet when she finished. 'Hmm,' he said at last. They were all sitting in his spare little office: the inspector, William, Darina and Pat James.

'I think it makes sense,' said the policewoman and gave a slight smile in response to Darina's grateful glance.

'I don't like it,' Grant shook his head. 'I don't like it at all. But I have to agree, we've got to look into it.'

There followed days of investigation. Gradually fragments of evidence were assembled and the picture slowly built up.

At last Grant announced he thought they had a case.

William arranged for Darina to sit in on the meeting where the decision was reached. There was considerable discussion on how the approach should be handled. Darina put forward a suggestion, at first tentatively then with increasing force. 'It must be the best way to handle it,' she pleaded.

There was another lengthy discussion, various angles were thrashed out but finally it was agreed and she made the necessary telephone call.

The next day, as arranged, she was in her Chelsea house. Ten thirty came and went. Darina began to feel anxious, was the plan about to go wrong? But at ten forty-five the doorbell rang. She went towards it summoning her resources. Despite all her urgings of the merits of this meeting, she was not looking forward to it, had to admit she was dreading it.

Verity looked tired, she had lost weight, there were shadows under the blue eyes and, stripped of its usual lively expression, her face for once failed to give an impression of beauty, its large nose dominating the other features. But when she smiled at Darina some of her charm re-emerged.

'It is such a lovely day,' she said, 'I walked. We're only in Victoria but it took longer than I thought, I'm sorry I'm late. What a lovely house.' She stepped inside looking curiously around her.

The decorators had nearly finished. The hall was still hung with dust-sheets, and ladders and pots of paint stood by the stairs. But the sitting room had returned to normality. Almost.

'I haven't had time to put everything back properly yet,' Darina apologised as she led the way through to the little stone-paved garden outside.

'Oh, I love it. Oliver's place is a penthouse, on top of one of those tall blocks a stone's throw from the station. Wonderful view and terribly convenient but it's very stark and modern. He likes everything pared down, reduced to a minimum. If you have a vase, it has to stand by itself on a particular table chosen specially. Otherwise he says you can't appreciate it properly. It's very restful in a way but then I come somewhere like this and think how wonderful to see so many beautiful things all jumbled together.' Darina winced. 'You can look and look and still find something you haven't noticed before.' She stopped by a table with the collection of calling-card cases and some antique scent bottles. 'Did you collect all these?'

Darina laughed. 'No, I was lucky enough to be left it all by a cousin. His wife was the collector. As I said, I haven't had time to arrange it all properly, it shouldn't look quite such a jumble.' She cut short Verity's apologies and suggested they sat outside. 'I've made some iced coffee, I thought that would be nicest now that we've got the hot weather again.'

She brought out the tray a few minutes later. Verity was lying back, her face held up to the sun. 'Oh, this is wonderful. I've had such a week. Oliver has been abroad, he only got back yesterday and I'd been rushing from one thing to another and hadn't even had the time to cook him anything. We had to go out. I think he'd been looking forward to a home-cooked meal but he was very good about it. Now, tell me all about France.'

Then she caught sight of Darina's hand as she was handed a glass of iced coffee. 'Darina! You're engaged!' Her delighted smile faded a little. 'It's not that tall chap you introduced to us, William somebody?'

'You didn't see him at his best that evening, he was still jet-lagged. We got engaged in France,' she added, deliberately bringing the conversation round to where she wanted it, conscious this was going to be even more difficult than she had thought.

'Oh, tell me all about the manoir, where Natasha and my mother lived. You did see it, you said?'

Darina gave her a description of the house. She filled in the facts of the studio fire with particular care, watching the way Verity's eyes darkened as she listened.

When she had finished, the girl banged her empty coffee glass down on the table between them, got up and walked a few steps, whirled round and said violently, 'It's so frustrating, so tragic. They were planning to come back to England to live in the Bailey. They should have been living there together, I should have been able to meet my real mother.'

There was a pause. Darina said nothing and after a moment Verity continued, 'All the time I was growing up, I felt like a cuckoo in the nest, someone who'd been abandoned, unwanted. I knew Constance loved me but there was something strange about it, as though it was a secret between her and me. Even when I suspected Constance *was* my real mother, it didn't feel right. Why didn't she tell me, if that was the case? Why did she have to deny it?

'When Natasha told me the truth it was as though everything had suddenly come right and I knew who I was. As though I'd been given an identity. Even though Natalie Duke was dead, had never wanted to acknowledge me, it was still like stepping out into the sunlight.'

'And when you realised she wasn't dead?'

Verity looked at Darina for a long while then gave a small sigh.

'I don't know how you know but I guessed a few days before,' she faltered a moment, 'before she died. It was the way she spoke about their life together and especially about Natalie and me as a baby. I just knew she had to be Natalie. I challenged her, at that last lunch we had together. All she did was smile in a secretive way and refuse to say anything. I was quite sure it was true but she wouldn't come right out and say it.' Suddenly Verity's voice was all bitterness, sour as an unripe lime. She pulled at the leaves of a plant.

'I couldn't believe it. Who was this woman? Who'd cast me off as something she couldn't be bothered to cope with. Who had come back into my life pretending to be someone else and now wouldn't acknowledge me all over again!'

'Perhaps she couldn't.'

'I began to wonder if perhaps she hadn't killed Natasha. She loved that damned house, the Bailey, so much. Sometimes I thought she loved it more than the idea of her daughter.'

'The idea?'

'She wasn't interested in a real, living and breathing person.' Verity turned a flushed face to Darina. 'That was too difficult. She wanted a puppet, someone who could be manipulated the way she wanted. Someone she could continue her work through. If I hadn't been interested in cookery, hadn't already started making a name for myself, do you think she would have wanted to tell me who I was? It was all too convenient. She couldn't continue as a cookery writer herself, I'm sure that hadn't been part of her plan when she burned poor Natasha to death, but she could live in her favourite house and pursue her career through me. She didn't want me to marry Oliver because that would have meant she couldn't manage me the way she wanted. She wouldn't have been able to manipulate Oliver. No way!'

'What did she tell you about your father?'

Verity flung herself back in her chair. Frustration seeped out of every pore of her body. 'Almost nothing. She told me that Natalie never spoke about him but hinted that she'd loved him, that there was some reason they couldn't marry. She also said that Natalie wasn't a maternal woman. As though she was telling me something new!

'I also got the impression that Natasha would have been quite happy to bring me up. Apparently when I was first born, it was Natasha who did everything for me but that she hardly knew which end of a baby was up.' Verity's voice softened. 'Apparently Mother took one look at me, squalling with outrage at not having my needs understood, and fell in love. I suppose, considering everything, it was probably the best thing that could have happened to me.'

'So you have no idea who your father was?'

'None.'

'No suspicion at all?'

Verity stared at her. 'What do you mean?' she whispered at last. 'Do you know?'

Darina got up and leant against a small pillar, hands clenched tightly in the pockets of her cotton trousers, and looked down at Verity. This was the most difficult thing she had ever had to do. 'I have to confess something. I haven't been quite straight with you about William and our trip to France. He is a detective sergeant in the Avon and Somerset CID and we went there to confirm that Natasha really was Natalie.'

Verity continued to stare at her, her face white and her hand shaking as it plucked unconsciously at a loose thread in her dress.

'We spoke to a number of the villagers who were involved in fighting the fire and I think we can be quite certain that Natalie did *not* start it and really did everything possible to rescue Natasha. Your mother didn't kill her cousin.'

Verity lay back and closed her eyes. It was impossible to tell what she was thinking.

That was the easy part over. Darina braced herself for the next stage. Then heard the telephone ringing.

When she replaced the receiver after the call, she tried to still her trembling. It was as though her body had been shaken inside a washing machine. She leant her forehead against the cool wall, closed her eyes and tried to make her mind a blank. When that failed, she told herself that it was all for the best. The phrase lacked meaning, offered no comfort.

After a moment the trembling lessened. She went to the cabinet where she kept drink and poured out two glasses of brandy. She took both outside and was amazed to find the sun was still shining and the blackbird who lived in the lilac tree in the corner was pouring out his liquid song; over and over the sweet notes repeated themselves. Fine careless rapture indeed!

She carefully put the glasses on the garden table beside Verity. The girl looked at them and gave a short laugh. 'Do you think I need strengthening after learning my mother may have been a bitch but wasn't a murderess?'

Darina pushed one of the glasses a little closer to her. 'That was William on the phone. He and Inspector Grant have been interviewing Oliver.'

If Verity's face had been white before, an invisible brush now added an extra coat of bleach. 'Oliver?' The word was a croak.

Darina couldn't think which piece of the news she had to tell was the least awful. She took a quick sip of her brandy and then coughed as it caught her throat. She set the glass down again and took hold of Verity's hand, holding it firmly as the girl tried to pull away.

'Verity, darling, you have to be very brave. There is no easy way to say this so I'll get it over as quickly as I can. Oliver confessed that he killed both Constance and Natalie and then, I'm so sorry, Verity, but I'm afraid he jumped out of one of the penthouse windows.'

Verity's head sagged forward. Darina quickly crouched alongside her, lifting the brandy to the girl's lips.

'I'm sorry,' she repeated as Verity took an involuntary gulp and spluttered. 'I couldn't think of any way to make it less of a shock for you.'

She put down the brandy and held Verity against her, wrapping her arms round the girl's back, feeling the solidity of the bones almost implode, as though every breath had been expelled from the slim body.

Then Verity wrenched herself free. Her face was full of anger. 'You say the precious police were there, why couldn't they have stopped him?'

'He wanted to go to the bathroom,' Darina said as steadily as she could, William's shaken voice echoing in her mind like words round an empty room. 'He'd agreed to make a formal statement, had rung his lawyer. He seemed completely collected, gave no clue that he was thinking of anything like that. They even checked the bathroom would be safe. I don't know how he actually managed it.'

Desolation fought with deep anger in Verity's face. 'How could he?' she said at last. 'How could he leave me here to face this thing alone?' Then she caught her breath, her expression altered, her eyes widening into deep pools in which horror gathered.

'Mother,' she wailed. And it was impossible to tell which one she meant or if the cry included both, the birth mother and the mother who'd reared her.

Finally she looked full at Darina. 'Why?' she whispered. 'Why did he kill them?'

The moment that Darina had dreaded had come. She looked at the girl, at the agony in her eyes. Was there some way she could avoid having to explain the furious fates that had howled at Oliver's heels, the classical tragedy that had woven itself around him? She could think of nothing to say that wouldn't cause greater grief in the end. If Verity was to have a chance of understanding Oliver's terrible conflict, she had to know the truth.

She drew the girl gently down beside her again. 'Verity, darling, he was your father.'

# Chapter Twenty-six

Much later Darina listened to William's account of the Oliver Knatchbull interview.

'It was almost as though he had expected us,' the policeman said, stretching out long legs in Darina's sitting-room. 'He was most courteous, asked us to come in and showed no surprise at finding I was a member of the CID. Then we all sat down as though a business meeting was about to commence. I expected a secretary to come in any minute and offer us coffee.'

Darina poured a glass of white wine and placed it next to his elbow. 'How did you start?'

'Grant produced the photograph from that leather frame we found in France together with a copy of one of Oliver at Oxford that we'd managed to track down. There was no doubt of the identification or that he didn't remember when the first one had been taken. He looked at them both, smiled at us and said, "So, many years ago I knew Natalie Duke. Has that suddenly become a crime?" Then Grant told him how we'd discovered he'd sold his Volvo, identified the number through a plan in his company's garage and used the Vehicle Licensing Office to find the company that had bought it, arriving just as it was about to have a respray job because of a long scratch on the offside panel, and that forensic examination of the scratch had found minute fragments of paint from Constance Fry's bicycle.

'At that point he looked us full in the face and said something about wretched boys pushing their grandmother's bicycle into innocent visitors' cars.'

'Do you think he'd worked that one out, just in case, or produced it on the spur of the moment?'

'I think he'd worked it out. He'd switched to the Rolls to come down in after Verity had told him of Constance's death but the

Volvo could have got damaged at Verity's party, he'd been driving it that day, apparently he usually only used the Rolls when he wanted chauffeuring. Very cool customer, Oliver Knatchbull. When we told him we'd found a farmer who remembered seeing Constance Fry's old car going towards the Bailey the afternoon before Natasha died, an afternoon neither Pru nor Verity Fry could have been driving it, he gave a dismissive wave of his hand. Then Grant told him of Pru Fry's customer who'd arrived to collect her meat late that morning. How she'd rung the bell at the kitchen door, the way she always did when calling outside the shop hours, then had stepped inside and seen two tins of pâté sitting on the kitchen table, smelling, according to her, quite marvellous. How Oliver had suddenly appeared and hustled her along to the shop and found her her meat. Again, he treated the information as though it was a chimera, something conjured up out of nothing and as easily dispersed into nothing.'

'But he must have realised the way the circumstantial evidence was building up against him?'

'All he said was, "I cannot imagine what you gentlemen think would have been my motive." '

Darina gave a small sigh. 'And?'

'Grant handed over to me at that point. I took him through Natalie Duke's impersonation of her cousin. All the while his superior expression merely got more superior. It gradually eroded the slight sympathy I'd had with his terrible situation. But there he sat, cool as anything, with that tiny smile on his mouth and boredom, would you believe, in his eyes. The man should have gone on the stage.

'So then I told him we believed him to be Verity Fry's father and that Natalie Duke had been threatening to make it public if he didn't break off his engagement.'

'He must have reacted to that?'

'Merely said we would have to prove it. Then I told him that DNA analysis would do that for us.'

'And then?'

'For a long time, nothing. It was one of those situations where you know the first one to speak has lost the contest. Grant and I were prepared to sit it out until Doomsday. Then he lifted his hands, had you noticed what beautiful hands he had? Anyway, he looked at them briefly then laid them flat on the long glass coffee-table in front of where he was sitting. He studied the backs as though they could reveal how to escape the nemesis we'd unleashed then finally looked at us and the quality of his smile had altered. All the bullshit had gone. And . . . and once again I could feel pity for him. He said quite simply, "Well, gentlemen, it seems the game is up." Then he told us everything.'

'And it was as we supposed?'

'As *you* supposed. Verity told Natalie all about her engagement the first time she met her. Natalie said to Oliver it was the most dreadful shock she'd ever had, worse even than finding the studio on fire. Apparently Oliver and Natalie had originally met at his father's Embassy in Rome. He was an undergraduate and she was interviewing his father. It was a freelance assignment for some weekly magazine and she was combining it with a short holiday. Oliver volunteered to show her around. He found her enormously attractive, she responded, despite the ten years' difference in age, and they took off for a few days together in Tuscany.'

'Oliver told you all this?'

'I think it was a relief to be able to talk at last. He said their affair continued in a spasmodic way for three years, the rest of the time he was at Oxford and for some time after he'd started working in the City. He was very much in love and wanted to marry Natalie. She said she was far too old for him and, in any case, wouldn't marry a man who'd expect her to produce dinner every evening at eight.'

'Would Oliver have been so conventional?'

William gave a faint smile. 'I asked him that and he said, at that stage, probably, yes. And apparently he was also very jealous of what he called the bohemian side of her life. He tried to control it, tried not to pressure her to spend more time with him but one day he found she had disappeared.'

'This was when she went to Greece?'

'He said she didn't tell him a thing. Made all her arrangements and just left. He said the last time they'd made love she'd idly, as he thought, asked him what he'd do if she became pregnant.'

'He didn't think she might be pregnant already?'

'No, but he told her he'd be overjoyed because then it would mean she would have to marry him. Remember it's the mid-sixties we're talking about. Forget the permissive society. In the sort of circles Oliver had been brought up, it would have been scandalous not to marry a girl bearing your illegitimate child. A discreet abortion, yes, unmarried motherhood, never. He said Natalie had been quite rude, told him to get that idea out of his mind immediately, she would not allow herself to be trapped into marriage with anyone and certainly not with him. A few weeks later she had gone.

'It took a little time for him to realise she'd disappeared, there'd always been long gaps in their relationship. Then he bumped into a colleague of hers one night and heard how she'd taken a sabbatical to write a cookery book.'

'Did he suspect why?'

'Not at first but when he didn't hear anything from her and couldn't find out where she'd gone, he said the possibility did just occur to him. Then when the cookery book came out and there wasn't the slightest suggestion she might have had a child, he forgot about it. He faced up to the fact that she wanted nothing more from their relationship and after a long search found what he thought was a girl of the right sort and settled down to home and family.'

'Except he was never at home and there wasn't a family.'

'Exactly. I gather after the divorce his wife remarried, underwent some fertility treatment and now has two boys. I think Oliver was pretty bitter she hadn't made greater efforts when they were married.'

'But then he met Verity?'

'But then, as you say, he met Verity and felt that everything else had been merely a necessary prelude to achieving the perfect relationship. Life was idyllic, they became engaged and then, out of the blue, he gets a call from Natalie Duke's cousin, someone he's never met, asking him to come down on a matter of great importance and to tell no one.

'Greatly mystified about the secrecy but thinking she was going to give him some keepsake from Natalie, he went down to the Bailey, driving the Volvo.'

'To be told he'd become engaged to his own daughter?'

'He said he couldn't believe it.'

'Did he recognise Natalie?'

'Not at first. The so-called Natasha claimed Natalie had confided the secret of Verity's paternity not long before she died. Oliver said that was when he smelt a rat. He couldn't understand why Natalie should have kept quiet all those years and suddenly decided to tell all just before being removed from the scene. And then too much about Natasha started to remind him of Natalie. "When you know someone very well," he said, "when you love them, sleep with them and study their every move, certain little habits, certain looks, are burnt into your memory. Even if you were to live a thousand years, if you were to love a hundred other women, they would be stored in the back of your mind somewhere." ' William looked at Darina. 'I told him I knew exactly what he meant.'

She smiled but said nothing.

'She'd had a trick of running her forefinger beside her ear when she was thinking deeply. And when she was irritated, she'd drum the fingers of her left hand on her knee. She and Natasha might have looked alike but there was no way, Oliver said, they could have had identical tricks of gesture.'

'So he refused to break off his engagement and threatened that, if she breathed a word to anyone, he would expose her impersonation of her cousin?'

'Exactly. And then she broke the news that she had already told Constance Fry, who was now on her way to meet him. She wanted Constance to understand exactly what the situation was so she would be able to help Verity when the engagement was broken. Oliver told Natalie he was leaving immediately and she would have to tell Constance it was all a mistake, he wasn't Verity's father after all. She could say he couldn't be because he was sterile and that was why his ex-wife had divorced him. And he would ensure Verity and he did not have children, surely that would take care of the situation? Natalie pleaded with him to be sensible. It was a tragedy but he must see the engagement couldn't continue.'

'And?'

'He said he couldn't think of himself as Verity's father!'

'But he believed Natalie?'

'In the end, yes. He felt it accounted for the very close understanding between him and Verity, how sometimes they knew exactly what the other was thinking. But he had met and fallen in love with an attractive, adult woman, had courted and become engaged to her, just like thousands of other young or not-so-young men. Suddenly to be told she bore his genes, that he'd fathered her, in no way altered his feelings for her.'

'I wonder if Verity would have agreed they should not have children?' William was silent and Darina answered her own question. 'I don't think she's any more maternal than Natalie and she's had such an ambiguous relationship with motherhood, she may well not have minded at all. So, I gather he left before Constance arrived?'

'Right. He said he stormed out of the house, beside himself with anger at Natalie and furious with fate. The sun was shining right in his eyes, he was driving much too fast and never saw Constance coming round the bend on her bicycle until it was too late. Before he knew what had happened, he had hit her a glancing blow. He hadn't recognised who was riding the machine. He got out of the car expecting to find a badly bruised cyclist who might need a quick run into hospital for some quite minor attention.'

'Only to find it was Constance and that she had hit her head on that stone and been killed?'

'Oliver said after he'd got over the initial horror of the situation it seemed like a message from heaven. One of the only two people in the world to know his story was dead, leaving the other in a highly invidious position. Not only that, there were no witnesses to the accident and no reason why he should be connected with it, as long as Natalie kept quiet. And, after all, it had been an accident, he hadn't intended to hit Constance, so why distress his fiancée by telling her he'd been responsible for her mother's death? Much better, he thought, just to drive back to town. Which is what he did as fast as he felt he could without attracting police attention. When he received the call from Verity, he'd nearly reached London. Once there, he set arrangements in train to sell the Volvo and switched to his Rolls. Oh, and he rang Natalie and warned her to keep her mouth shut.'

'Did he tell her about Constance's accident?'

'By that stage she knew and Oliver thinks she was under the impression he had killed her deliberately. He said she sounded terrified.'

'Poor Natalie. She must have been desperate.'

'Oliver told her he had to have time to think about what she was asking him to do, that it wasn't something he could rush into, Verity's happiness was at stake as well as his own. But he was afraid Natalie would not keep quiet for long, that if he didn't break off the engagement quickly, she would come to believe telling the truth was the only way to guarantee he wouldn't kill her as well as Constance. Her cousin's house would be no use if she was dead!

'The rest was exactly as you worked out. Oliver saw his chance the day he was left alone at the farm, went over to Natalie's house in the morning, found a couple of loaf tins and the meat she had bought the previous day and took them all back to Fry's Farm, where he made the pâté – he says Natalie had taught him a lot about cooking. That afternoon he returned with it to the Bailey and left a poisoned slice in the fridge and an unpoisoned slice under the milk cover outside Daniel's cottage, both accompanied by one of Pru's labels.'

'Did he mean to try and incriminate Daniel?'

'He claimed he just thought it would deflect attention from the possibility of the pâté being poisoned, in case Natalie had been able to tell someone what she'd eaten that night. There would be a perfectly innocent tin of the stuff in her larder and there would be Daniel who would have eaten another slice without coming to any harm. He hoped it would then be decided she'd been poisoned by something else.'

'But why put the rest on the compost heap?'

'He thought it would be safe there, buried amongst other debris. He never imagined an animal would eat it, Oliver's a town, not a country boy. He also hoped there wouldn't be any of the poisoned part left, you were quite right about him only lacing the ringed end of the tin with the chopped-up oleander, and he also tied string around it to identify which tin held the poisoned pâté. But he didn't want to give Natalie too big a slice in case she didn't eat it all and some was left for analysis.'

'Did he learn about oleander in Italy?'

'He'd also spent periods in Greece and California and he said he'd been told several times how poisonous every part of the plant is. I don't think he realised quite how devastating its effects are, though. The only time he appeared at all shaken was when he described how Verity and he found Natalie.'

'It must have been quite a shock when she rang and Verity insisted on going round.'

'Oliver thought it would all be up with him then and there. He sat in the car on the way over trying to work out how he was going to deal with the situation, only to find that by the time they arrived

Natalie was in a coma. He looked around her room and the rest of the house to see if she'd managed to scribble a note incriminating him but there was nothing. He took the opportunity while making tea to wash up her supper things, thus removing any possible traces of the poisoned pâté, and to pocket the Fry's Farm card sitting on the kitchen table, after which he reckoned he should manage to get away with it.'

'Until you arrived this morning. It must have been the most bitter blow.'

'At the end of his story he was still very composed. Grant arrested him and even then he had himself under perfect control. He rang his lawyer and then he said he wanted to visit the loo.' Distress cracked the quiet calm of William's voice. 'I looked inside, saw it had no window and the only razor was electric but I never really thought he had anything in mind. And I completely missed the fact that the bathroom had another door, it appeared to be a mirror. I waited outside for him to emerge. But he must have gone straight through the mirrored door into his bedroom and out of the window. There came this horrifying cry, I shall never forget it, it was as if a sigh could scream. The bathroom door was still locked. I ran along the corridor and into his bedroom and there was the window wide open. I didn't need to look down, I knew what I'd see. But of course I had to. There was already a crowd of people gathering.'

'How did Grant take it?'

'Completely dead-pan. At first I thought he was hanging on to the last shreds of his temper, then I realised that for him it was a neat end to the investigation.'

'Neat!'

'It meant we didn't have to expose the weakness of our case to cross-examination by a no doubt brilliant defence lawyer. Confessions to the police hold little water in court these days.'

'But he might have pleaded guilty.'

'I don't think so, not after contemplating the consequences and talking to a good solicitor – and I can't imagine Oliver Knatchbull having anything but a top man. So we can now draw a line under the whole affair. I typed up my report this afternoon.' William stretched his arms wearily. 'Is Verity going to be all right?'

All right? Darina thought that Verity might never be all right again. The scene in her small terrace garden that morning came back vividly. The girl had sat quite still on the gaily-striped lounger after Oliver's identity had been broken to her. Then her hands had risen in the air like those of a votive priestess and she had given a cry that belonged to some primaeval animal, there had been nothing human in its raw pain and incomprehension. She had curled her body into a foetal knot and thrown herself down on the padded canvas, screwing fisted hands into eye sockets, long shudders shaking her frame.

Darina tried to hold the unyielding figure, tried to offer soothing words, but knew nothing she could say could comfort her.

Slowly the shudders began to lessen, the slight body to relax. Darina continued to hold and soothe. Then Verity jerked herself away and looked at the cook, her eyes curiously blank.

'It's not true, you know. Oliver didn't do those,' her voice faltered then gathered strength, 'those things you said. You'll see, he'll tell you he couldn't have done them. We're going to be married. Spend the rest of our lives together.' Her voice fell, her gaze shifted away from Darina's, seemed to study the roses blooming along the garden wall. She stood up, looked about her in a vague way, then moved with a certain air of purpose inside the French windows.

Darina followed quietly. She found Verity carefully rearranging the little collection of card cases and scent bottles, lining them up on the marquetry table first one way then another, destroying patterns as soon as they were made. All her attention was concentrated on her task.

Gradually her movements faltered. She looked up at Darina. 'Oliver would know how they should go,' she said. 'He's got a wonderful eye for this sort of thing. I'll ask him how they should be arranged.' Then something seemed to pierce through the blankness of her face, the features crumpled, the mouth pulled down into an ugly rictus. With a swift movement of her arm, she swept the little cases and bottles off the table, sending them spinning against the wall and floor, then her hand was brought up to cover her features. The slim shoulders shook.

'It's true, oh God, I do know it's true. What am I going to do?' The wail was addressed to Darina's shoulder as she was gathered into the tall girl's arms and Darina gently rocked her, the torrent of weeping shaking her own frame as much as Verity's.

Much later she got the girl into bed, sitting beside her until she fell into an exhausted sleep.

'She told me she would never marry,' Darina said to William now. 'And I don't think she'll change her mind, this isn't the sort of shock you recover from. She desperately needs someone to love who will love her but my instinct says she's going to find it very difficult to build a stable relationship with anyone else. At least she's got a promising career ahead of her.'

'Will it still be promising after all this gets out?'

'Does it have to?'

'Not necessarily, but questions are certainly going to be asked why a highly successful man like Oliver Knatchbull, recently engaged, should throw himself out of a window after being questioned by the police. Most scandals die down after a little though. Let's hope the speculation won't involve Verity too closely.' William reached across and took Darina's left hand in his; he looked at her ring. 'This hasn't put you off our engagement, I trust?'

She shook her head. 'Why should it?'

'I remember you once being worried about the effects of passion.'

'That was in my young and foolish days. The effects of passion do anything but worry me now.'

He leant across and softly kissed her lips. Then drew back to look at her, his fingers on hers, his thumb gently caressing the back of her hand. Darina felt her bones melt like a candle at Christmas.

'Just what was it that made you suspect Oliver Knatchbull?'

It should have been a moment of triumph but William had been so generous throughout his part in the investigation that Darina only wanted to share her moment of inspiration with him.

'It was the photograph. I was sure I recognised it and not because it looked like Verity, even though I could see the resemblance immediately you pointed it out. I had been thinking how odd it was that Oliver had hung around Fry's Farm for so long. It didn't seem in character with him somehow, this high-powered financier content to spend days looking into his mother-in-law-to-be's estate. He could have ground that up for breakfast and still have had room for kidneys and bacon. I could see he'd want to look after Verity but he could easily have hauled her back to London and done that with far less inconvenience to himself. His consideration seemed out of character, after all, he was late to the Savoy the morning Verity won her cookery competition, the great event of her life. If he was at all willing to put himself out for her, surely he would have made sure he got there for the announcements at least? The only other reason for hanging around could be concern to help Pru. Pull the other one, I thought. Oliver Knatchbull struck me as someone who liked things organised to suit him, not other people.

'The more I thought about it, the more I thought there must have been some other motive behind his continued presence in Somerset. Then, probably because I'd been thinking about meeting him at the Savoy, I remembered him laughing. Had you seen enough of him to notice that he hardly ever laughed? A slight smile is usually as much as he would offer. But that morning he really laughed, it quite altered his appearance, made him look much younger, more carefree and relaxed. As I remembered that laughter, I realised he was the man in the photograph.

'Once he'd been identified as Verity's father, everything else fell into place. There was the reason for the antipathy between him and Natasha. That was why he hung around Somerset, he was wondering how to make sure Natasha didn't tell anyone the truth, had probably already made sure Constance didn't. It was all there: passion, incest, blackmail. The perfect recipe for death.'